"Hold on—are we in some sort of danger?"

Looking into Avery's wide eyes, Ryan let a wry chuckle escape his throat. He removed her hands from his lapels and held her wrists. "Right now I can't decide if you're honestly that clueless or if you're the world's best liar."

She jerked away from his grip as if he'd burned her. Another twinge of regret jolted through him. He forced himself to remember it was a good sign, that feeling. It meant he had at least a shred of humanity left in him, which was saying something after all he'd seen and done in his life.

"I don't understand," she said. "I thought you were conducting routine surveillance tonight, nothing dangerous. Otherwise, the whole team would've been here to—"

In time with the pounding bass from the ballroom, a booming shot rang out nearby. A second shot followed before he could react, lodging in the wall behind Avery. She shrieked.

Ryan pushed her ahead of him down the stairs as he retrieved his S&W .45. "Change of plans. How fast can you run?"

Dear Reader,

I love secret-agent movies and books, always have. From the larger-than-life action scenes and exotic locations to the even more spectacular heroes (hello, James Bond). *Secret Agent Secretary* features a Bond-worthy hero in ICE agent Ryan Reitano, who is ICE office secretary Avery Meadows's tall, dark and drool-worthy office crush...and the only man who can keep her alive after she inadvertently plows into the middle of Ryan's covert op to catch an international criminal mastermind.

Like me, Avery Meadows loves all things secret agent, but she takes her devotion a step further. Okay, *several* steps further. It's the reason she became an ICE agency secretary and why her cats are named... well, you'll have to read on to find out what she names her cats. By the end of Avery and Ryan's story, you're going to covet your own gadget watch and maybe even consider building your own secret lair. And you're definitely going to want a smooth operator like Ryan Reitano to blaze into your life and whisk you away for a lifetime of adventure and true love.

Happy reading!

Melissa

SECRET AGENT SECRETARY

—

Melissa Cutler

HARLEQUIN® ROMANTIC SUSPENSE

Recycling programs
for this product may
not exist in your area.

ISBN-13: 978-0-373-27856-5

SECRET AGENT SECRETARY

Copyright © 2014 by Melissa Cutler

Printed in U.S.A.

Books by Melissa Cutler

Harlequin Romantic Suspense

Seduction Under Fire #1730
*Tempted into Danger #1758
%Colton by Blood #1764
*Secret Agent Secretary #1786

*ICE: Black Ops Defenders
%The Coltons of Wyoming

Other titles by this author available
in ebook format.

MELISSA CUTLER

is a flip-flop-wearing Southern California native living
with her husband, two rambunctious kids and two suspicious cats in beautiful San Diego. She divides her
time between her dual passions for writing sexy, small-
town contemporary romances and edge-of-your-seat
romantic suspense. Find out more about Melissa and
her books at www.melissacutler.net, or drop her a line
at cutlermail@yahoo.com.

This book is dedicated to my two favorite secretaries:

Joanie, my inspiration for the story,

and my mom, Loutrisha,

who taught me that if you want to succeed in life,
always be nice to the secretaries.

Chapter 1

The ICE Agency office was decidedly free of gadgets. Avery had known that in advance of accepting the secretarial position six years ago, but in her enthusiasm over the job offer, she'd overlooked the details that didn't sync up with her lifelong dream to work in national security. Besides, no covert ops agency displayed their gadgets in plain sight. Everyone knew gadgets belonged in the basement.

She still adored her job even though she had yet to stumble upon a secret basement, but she could've seriously used a gadget tonight, some sort of mechanical arm or miniature grappling hook or the like. The problem was that she wasn't flexible enough, nor were her fingers long enough, to grasp the zipper of her party dress.

In the office restroom, she spun in a circle, her body torqued at an odd angle, reaching for the zipper that was stuck in the middle of her back. Then it hit her that she was acting more like a dog chasing its tail than a single girl ready to dance her way into the New Year.

After giving up, she marched to her desk and flounced into her chair, chewing the lip gloss off her bottom lip in irritation. She should've taken Kristen up on her offer to primp at her house. Granted, that would've been awkward now that Kristen and Charlie were newlyweds, but at least she would've saved herself from engaging in a wrestling match with the slinky pink dress she'd spent half her paycheck on.

Rendezvousing at Kristen's house also would've saved her from indulging her overactive work ethic. Here it was nearly ten o'clock on New Year's Eve and she'd put in another thirteen-hour day at the office, leaving herself only twenty measly minutes to change clothes and walk four blocks to the downtown San Diego club where she was meeting her six friends.

"Oh, well. I bet Moneypenny works New Year's Eve, too."

Actually, the true reason she'd worked longer than any sane, healthy person would on a holiday night had nothing to do with her work ethic. The project she'd been helping several of the office's agents with was bringing her the closest she'd ever come to assisting in the capture of an international criminal mastermind, which happened to sit at the top of her bucket list.

It didn't hurt that the man in charge was none other than the office's newest tall, dark and droolworthy agent, Ryan Reitano.

With a little smile, she glanced at his desk across the room. He'd transferred from a different branch of the department six months ago, and while the two female agents on staff hadn't shown much interest in him,

Avery sure had. Even if the man barely seemed to notice her presence, much less that she was female—and recently available.

She'd stayed late tonight composing a memo for Agent Lucey while stealing furtive glances at Agent Reitano as he got organized for his surveillance detail at the Mira Hotel in preparation for the big sting operation later that week. She'd just about worked up the courage to give him a genial "Happy New Year's" hug on his way out when she heard his hasty exit as she was in the back hall making copies, off to do his supersecret spy thing while Avery couldn't manage to zip up a stinkin' dress.

She smoothed the creased fabric over her thighs with a frown. Six hundred bucks and the dress wasn't even wrinkle resistant. Between the wrinkles and the obnoxious zipper, the dress was way too high maintenance for her taste.

When she'd seen it hanging in the window of an uptown boutique, she'd thought it a perfect symbol of her New Year's resolution to move on with her life after her disastrous breakup with Zach in October. Plus it was exactly the sort of curve-hugging dress Pepper Potts might wear to a Tony Stark cocktail reception, which made it a must-have in Avery's book.

Well, Pepper Potts would never let a high-maintenance dress get the best of her. She spun the chair toward her desk and grabbed a box of paper clips. She might not be Pepper Potts or have access to secret agent gadgets, but Avery was nothing if not resourceful.

In two minutes flat she'd fashioned a paper clip chain and shimmied out of the dress. Though the office had been crawling with agents all day, Agent Reitano had been the last to leave, so she didn't have to worry about someone catching a glimpse of her Spanx or beige ultra-support bra.

With only a few minutes to spare until she was supposed to meet her friends, she didn't have time to wallow in the irony of lingerie that made a woman look sexy in clothing but did exactly the opposite once her clothes came off. But given how clingy and revealing this particular dress was, a teensy lace thong wasn't going to cut it. Avery's figure required high-performance undergarments.

Once she'd secured the end paper clip to the zipper, she donned the dress once more and raised the chain over her shoulder, pulling up. The zipper began to close.

"Ha! Take that, sucker."

When the dress was half-zipped, her desk phone rang. The shrill, unexpected sound made her jump. Heart thudding madly, she leaned her elbows on the desk to check the caller ID and yanked the dress's zipper the rest of the way closed.

Odd. Agents never called the office landline from their personal cell phones after hours, especially when on surveillance missions. They had partners and ops contacts and all sorts of important people to touch base with—anyone but the office secretary.

Then again, it was after ten. He should've been done with the surveillance detail already and off celebrating the last night of the year. Brows raised in disbelief, she lifted the receiver. "ICE Agency. This is Avery Meadows." Even her usual telephone greeting came out sounding skeptical.

"You're there. Good." Agent Reitano had the kind of deep velvet voice that resonated in Avery's body all the way to her toes, even though coaxing more than a few clipped words from him at a time was no easy feat. The man gave new meaning to the word *laconic*.

"Agent Reitano, is everything okay?"

He chuffed. "That's debatable. Listen, I need you to get on my computer and email me a document labeled LM1204. Would you do that for me?"

LM1204 was a classified piece of evidence from the Chiara case. Why would he need that tonight?

"Our computers are password coded and we're not allowed—"

"I know it's against department policy, but I can change my password tomorrow. This is too important."

A little voice inside her told her to decline. It went against her better judgment not to alert her bosses that one of the ICE agents might be in distress and had asked her to go against the rules regarding the handling of classified intel.

But a bigger voice inside her, the proverbial devil on her shoulder, said, *This is what you've been waiting for, Meadows. They don't call it covert ops for nothing.*

Her gaze caught on the Department of Homeland Security emblem on the wall opposite her desk. An eagle, its wings outstretched and its body guarded by a shield. ICE, the department's Immigration and Customs Enforcement division, was a critical component of that shield guarding her country's freedom.

"Yes, of course I will." She jotted down the password he gave, then decided to indulge her curiosity by asking, "Are you still at the Mira?"

The line went silent, as though he were thinking deeply about her question. "Yes."

She bit her lip against asking for more details. Clearly he wasn't in a talkative mood. As if he ever was. She rolled her eyes and her attention caught on that afternoon's mail. "Oh! One more thing. I forgot. A letter came in for you a few minutes after you left from an express courier service. It's international and it's got *urgent* stamped all over the front and back. From a Mr. Paolo Hawk."

She paused as a crazy idea took shape in her mind. Her only New Year's resolution was to finally start crossing items off her bucket list, and one of those items was to be more daring—at work and in her social life. It might be less than two hours until the stroke of midnight, but this was her first chance to get started.

"Wait, what did you say?"

"A letter from Honduras. And it looks urgent." He started to speak again, but she cut him off, knowing if she didn't get this out now, she might never. "What if… How would you like…" She drew a bracing inhale. *Come on, Meadows. You can do this.* "Would you like to meet for coffee tomorrow? I could bring you the letter then."

He sighed. Not a good sign. She waited in silence, her mortification growing. Just when she thought she couldn't take it anymore, he answered, "Yes. Okay. Take it home with you. That would be best. I'll get it tomorrow."

"Over coffee?" She cringed. She'd sounded a bit too desperate with that question.

"I have to go. Don't forget to email me the file. Oh, and don't tell anyone we talked. Got it?"

"Oh." What the heck was going on?

"Avery, will you do that for me?"

Any other time, she would have thrilled at the sound of her name from his lips, but an uncomfortable tingling had begun in the back of her throat. This wasn't normal, not the request for secrecy or the strain that had leaked into Agent Reitano's usually unemotional voice. "What's happening? Is there someone I need to call? Agent Mickle or—"

"No," he barked before continuing more softly. "Please. Don't tell anyone, especially Mickle. If you want to help me, email me the file, then go home and take that letter with you."

Despite her misgivings, she trusted all the agents in her office. If Agent Reitano needed her to keep a secret as a matter of national security that might aid in Vincenzo Chiara's capture, then she would.

Vincenzo Chiara was one of the world's most wanted men. An Italian black-market mercenary, his crimes included forcing children into slavery and prostitution, the murder of innocent people and orchestrating the sale of drugs, weapons and anything else on demand in the black market.

She glanced again at the department's emblem. It was time to step up and do what she was born to.

Pumped and feeling good about her decision, she sat up straighter and looked at her watch. *Drat.* She was already late. Kristen was going to kill her. Oh, well. National security never took the night off. "I'm on it, Agent Reitano."

"Thank you. And Avery? Call me Ryan."

Oh. What she needed now was a witty comeback, something flirty and fearless. She screwed her mouth up, thinking hard, but before her brain had a chance to kick into gear, the line clicked dead.

She held the receiver away from her face and stared at it for a beat before dropping it into the cradle. So much for witty banter.

Waiting for Agent Reitano's computer to boot up, she fingered a stack of Post-it notes and tested his name aloud. "Ryan. Good morning, Ryan. Have a good weekend, Ryan. Would you like to take me home and have your way with me, Ryan?"

Hmm. Felt weird on her lips. Apparently, a first-name intimacy with Agent Reitano was going to take some getting used to. She turned her attention back to the computer.

"Uh-oh."

The monitor was black save for an error message.

"No, no, no," she muttered as she pressed every function key to no avail. She tried again, this time pushing the function keys and the control button simultaneously. Nothing. Avery knew her way around a computer. She typed a hundred words a minute and could locate *anything* on the internet. Spreadsheets and data fields were her comfort zone. But when it came to the actual technological components that made her beloved machine work, she was as clueless as a monkey.

In desperation, she resorted to the only key combination she knew—Control, Alt, Delete. She depressed all three keys with a silent prayer, but the dang thing had the audacity to beep at her like the survey machine on *Family Feud.*

With an offended scowl, she pushed the power key until it shut down and began to reboot.

The office was loaded with computers, Avery didn't have access through her own computer to the virtual storage cloud the agents used and she couldn't jump onto another agent's computer because each was privately passworded. If she couldn't get Agent Reitano's computer to work, her best bet was to scan the hard copy—if there was a hard copy.

Still barefoot and with the paper clip chain attached to the zipper slapping at her back with every step, she walked to the rows of file cabinets and went straight to the drawer where she'd put the Chiara case file that afternoon. She flipped through the files but found nothing on Vincenzo Chiara.

Baffled, she searched again. It should've been right in the front, but it was gone. She laid her palms flat over the tops of the files and considered her options. Before she got ahead of herself coming up with a plan C, she checked back at Agent Reitano's—*Ryan's*—computer. It had finished rebooting and the same error message from before still glowed on the screen.

She poked the monitor, muttering a mild curse, then jogged into Director Tau's office. A quick scan of his desk for the file's hard copy yielded nothing.

His file cabinets were locked, as she knew his desk would be, so instead of wasting more time, she pivoted and went straight for Agent Mickle's desk, the other agent working the Chiara case.

It was locked.

With another, more stringent curse, she walked back to Agent Reitano's desk. Maybe the hard copy of the case file had been right under her nose and she'd been too focused on the computer error to notice. The desktop was bare except for the bald eagle bobblehead figurine Director Tau had given him when he'd transferred to the department, as was the office tradition. And, as was the office's tradition, Mickle and the other agents had promptly dressed the eagle in a pink Barbie bikini top and coordinating hat.

With her hand on the top drawer handle, she warned the desk, "Don't be locked," then gave a tug.

It opened, sending Bald Eagle Barbie's head bobbling and pens in the drawer rolling. She eyeballed each drawer in turn but didn't see the file. Or anything interesting or personal in nature. Nothing to give her a clue into the life or personality of her stoic office crush.

She had her head in the bottom drawer, riffling through form letters and expense reports, when the "Bootylicious" ringtone on her phone started. That would be Kristen, wondering why Avery wasn't in front of Club Brazil like they'd planned. She hustled to her desk and fished her purse from the floor.

"Hey, Krissy."

"Where are you? We've been standing here for twenty minutes."

That late already? She chewed her lip and glanced at her computer screen to check the time—but all she saw was the same error message as on Agent Reitano's computer. Stifling the curse that was on the tip of her tongue, she smacked the side of the monitor, then sunk into her desk chair. "Sorry I didn't call. Something came up."

"Aw, sweetie, are you still at the office? You've got to snap out of this work rut you've been in lately. You need to get a life."

Avery was about to protest that she had a great life, and was, in fact, on the verge of crossing off the first item on her bucket list. And maybe a second one if Agent Reitano followed through on her coffee offer. But she didn't have time to get into it with Kristen over the merits of working late on a case, not when Agent Reitano was expecting that transcript.

"Yes. I'm still at work. National security never sleeps, ya know."

"You already used the work excuse to weasel out of joining us for dinner tonight, and now this? I know what's really going on."

"You do?" Avery asked.

"You mentioned the other day how lame you felt being the only single person in our group. You don't still feel that way, do you? 'Cause you'd be the only one."

True, it bugged her that she'd be partying with three couples. No one liked being the odd man out, but she'd never use that as an excuse not to go dancing with her friends. Just this once, though, she was going to let Kristen run with the idea.

"It's so awkward, Krissy. Who am I going to kiss at midnight while you, Gina and Megan suck face with your men?"

Kristen groaned. "Oh, come on. Midnight's not for two more hours. Plenty of time for us to find you a hot guy to ring in the New Year with. Have a little faith."

Avery stuffed the letter from Honduras into her tote bag along with her work clothes. "All right, you win. You guys head into the club and scope out the scene. I'm going to have to meet up with you in an hour or so, after I take care of something here at work. If you see a cute guy who's my type, do whatever you have to do to keep the other girls away from him until I get there."

"I hope you've picked a new type because Zach was the last pretentious, tofu-obsessed jerk I ever want to see you with."

Zach was the son of her parents' best friends, and Avery had only stayed with him as long as she did because it'd made her parents happy to see her with someone they approved of, someone with their same lofty ideals and political leanings—or so they'd all thought.

Avery glanced at Agent Reitano's desk. "I think from now on I'm going to go for the strong, silent type. Tall, dark hair and eyes. And lots and lots of muscles."

"I like the way you think, but every girl goes for the strong, silent type. If I find an unattached one, I'll try to save him for you, but you're going to have to do your part and get here fast."

Avery slapped the side of the computer monitor, but the blasted error message shone firm. "I'll do my best."

Once she got Kristen off the phone, Avery took one more look around the room. If there was any place she forgot to check for the Chiara file, it certainly wasn't announcing itself with a neon blinking sign. There was nothing left to do but call Agent Reitano and find out how he wanted to proceed.

She called his number, but it flipped straight to voice mail. She left a message, then wrote him a text message.

Now what did she do? She had no idea why he needed that transcript of a wiretap tonight while he cased the hotel, but, frankly, it was none of her business. She wasn't even supposed to know the LM1204 file was a transcript of a wiretap. Besides, if he said he needed it, then that should be good enough for her.

She had one more option left, but it wasn't a particularly great one. Agent Reitano wouldn't know this because Avery tried not to spread it around, what with all the national secrets she was privy to at the office, but she'd been cursed with a near-perfect photographic memory. She knew the contents of the LM1204 file by heart and could re-create it for him word for word, because the week before, when she'd waited at his desk while he signed off on a stack of evidence transfer paperwork, she'd seen the file open on his computer monitor. All she needed now was a functioning computer to type it out on and she could re-create it in minutes flat.

Her apartment was a half hour away through New Year's Eve traffic. It would be much faster to walk the six blocks to the Mira Hotel and lay out his options for him in person. She could even recite the transcript if he wanted to go that route.

Far from being concerned about blowing his cover, she was confident she'd fit in great with the downtown party crowd, dressed to kill as she was in her slinky pink gown. She couldn't imagine a solid reason why she shouldn't go for it.

She slipped her feet into the pair of four-inch strappy black heels she'd spent two weeks breaking in by wearing every waking minute she spent in her apartment. Though she'd probably walk with a limp for days afterward, she was determined to start the New Year off in the shoes she'd maxed out her Macy's card for.

A dab of gloss to her lips, a toss of her hair to give it some oomph and she was ready to go.

She set the office alarm, turned off the lights and locked the door, tote bag and purse in hand. After a quick stop at her car in the underground parking garage to drop off the tote bag in the trunk, she strode to the street-level exit and into the cool night air. Halfway down the first block, she recalled the paper clip chain swinging behind her. Mortified, she pulled her hair out of the way and tried to remove it. When her efforts failed, she stuffed the chain down the back of her dress and kept moving.

Computers or no, this secretary was seeing her job through to the bitter end tonight. After all, Moneypenny would never allow such trifling matters to stand in the way of her work, and neither, by God, would Avery.

Chapter 2

The ice machine released another round of tumbling ice as Ryan dragged the second unconscious man into the supply closet attached to the ice and vending machine alcove and cuffed him to a plumbing pipe. The first man groaned. It was the only noise he'd made since Ryan had smashed his head against the mirrored vanity in the hotel room.

Reaching around to the small of his back, Ryan withdrew the 9 mm he'd confiscated from the groaner and tapped him on the head with the barrel. "Anybody home?"

After he let out another pitiful sound, the man's head lolled to the side. Out cold again.

With his dress shoe, he toed the sneaker of the second man, a lean, fair-haired Eastern European–looking sort. "What about you? You alive in there?"

Nothing.

Damn it. With so much at stake, he didn't have time for this. He rolled his head back and stared at the ceiling, reining in the maddening frustration. Ten long years he'd been at this, hunting the man who haunted his nightmares. Ten years of near misses and outright failures, of getting so close he could taste the closure that killing Vincenzo Chiara would bring—the freedom it would bring—and yet here he was, in the middle of his last good chance to get the deed done, and he'd spent the past half hour in a hotel supply closet waiting for two unconscious hit men to rouse so he could pump them for information.

He returned the gun to the waistband of his dress pants and shook his head. "Note to self, Rambo—next time two guys jump you, try not to incapacitate them so enthusiastically."

He'd dragged them to the closet because remaining in the hotel room made him an easy target for the next batch of punks dispatched to do him in. Ryan had no doubt this first attempt to silence him wasn't going to be the last before the night was over.

The main question he needed to ask the hit men was not who they worked for. That was as plain as the crude prison tattoos on the one man's arms and face. Nor was the question why they wanted Ryan dead. He was crystal clear about that, too.

What he needed to know was *how.*

How did Chiara know where to find him, down to the exact hotel room he'd secured under a pseudonym two weeks ago? In other words, he was still at square one, puzzling over the same damn question he had been for the past six months—which of the twenty-five San Diego ICE department employees was double-dealing?

He'd narrowed down the answer to four possibilities.

Make that five now. He'd dismissed the office secretary as a suspect months ago, but she was the person who'd processed his paperwork for the hotel room and she hadn't come through with his one request tonight. She hadn't emailed him the file he'd asked for. So Ryan had to wonder, was that because she didn't understand how critical the document was to deciphering Chiara's business and contacts in San Diego...or because she did?

Either way, the longer he stayed on the sixth floor of the Mira Hotel, the greater the risk. Time to leave before Chiara's men got the jump on him again. His window of opportunity to catch the man was shrinking fast, so he refused to contemplate aborting the surveillance mission, but there were any number of positions in surrounding buildings from which he could observe the Mira without getting himself trapped again.

He straightened the blue tie he'd worn with a crisp white dress shirt and suit to blend in with the festive hotel atmosphere, then used the phone he'd confiscated from the groaner—he'd smashed his own on the off chance it'd been bugged—to check one last time for the transcripted conversation on his email account. Nothing.

He pocketed the groaner's phone. Then, leaving his own pistol in his shoulder holster and his service piece at his ankle, he took the confiscated 9 mm in hand again. Gun first, he nosed around the corner to scan the hallway for trouble before heading for the stairs.

He knew from his arrival earlier that the hotel was swarming with guests of the massive New Year's Eve celebration taking place in the main ballroom on the second floor, but judging from the silence in the hall and in the stairwell, the party had already gotten under way.

As expected, the ground level was hopping with New

Year's revelers. He tucked the gun out of sight, rolled his shoulders and did his best to look relaxed and happy as he moved closer to the lobby. Just a regular guy on his way to meet friends for a celebratory drink.

There were no potential hit men in view, or anyone who registered on his radar as connected to the man he'd been hunting for ten years. Hunting with the laser focus of a man poised to lose everything he held dear, a possibility that might be closer than he realized if the letter from Paolo Hawk was the warning he dreaded it was.

His eyes followed a lanky bellhop pushing a loaded luggage cart toward the service elevators. Ryan stepped aside to give him room. He tipped his hat with a "Good evening, sir" before moving on. As the luggage rack moved past him, a gorgeous, shapely backside adorned in a pink dress caused him a moment of distraction before his eyes flickered back to the crowd. No time to enjoy the scenery when he could be ambushed again at any moment.

He allowed himself a last look at the woman standing at the bar, this time taking inventory of her legs. He was just starting to wonder if her face matched the sophisticated sexpot allure of the rest of her body when she accepted a martini from the bartender, then turned to look across the lobby.

Ryan's jaw dropped. He might've made a little sound of disbelief, but it was hard to tell given the volume of music streaming from the ballroom.

This changes everything—she *changes everything*.

Ducking farther into the hall's shadows, he reflexively brought a foot up to tap his service weapon, his backup piece for the night. Double-checking the presence of his guns was rather pointless, but after seventeen years as a soldier, it was one nervous habit he couldn't see fit to break.

Maybe he'd mistaken the woman's identity. San Diego was full of women with long, wavy blond hair and big brown eyes.

Taking care to keep his face in the swath of shadow created by the enormous lobby Christmas tree, he tipped his head around the corner until he had a clear view of the bar.

No two ways about it; the woman in pink was Avery Meadows.

With her lips on the rim of her martini glass, she glanced around anxiously, as though she was waiting for someone. Him, he assumed. What a dangerous move, to waltz into the middle of the undercover op she knew full well was happening here. She looked like a pink bull's-eye, standing in plain sight dressed like she was, as though she had zero concern for her personal safety.

Then again, if she was working with Vincenzo Chiara, maybe safety wasn't a concern. Maybe, instead of looking for Ryan, she was meeting up with Chiara's men to ensure they'd followed through on their job to off him.

But why the dress and the drink—to blend in with the New Year's Eve party crowd? Why would she bother? Nothing made sense.

He strained his brain to remember what she'd been wearing when he'd left the office but couldn't pull it up from his mental files. Maybe a charcoal-gray dress and a sweater…or was it a pantsuit? He'd pretty much been avoiding eye contact with her since arriving at the San Diego office. Mostly because she wouldn't stop looking at him in that sly way women did when they were making plans for a man.

Watching her watch him gave him the willies, as though maybe he'd been right to suspect her of misdeeds. But even if she hadn't been on his short list of corruption suspects, he wasn't in San Diego to get involved in a relationship or even have a bit of no-strings-attached fun. He was there for only one purpose: to bury Chiara along with the secret Ryan had dedicated his life to protecting. He couldn't afford to get distracted—not even by his office's sweet, cute secretary.

She certainly didn't look sweet and cute tonight. More like trouble wrapped in a pink hourglass. And Ryan already had plenty of trouble.

He smoothed a hand over his hair and straightened his tie. Whatever dirt Avery was mixed up in, it was time for her to come clean.

He skirted the room along the wall. She hadn't noticed his presence, so he took advantage of the element of surprise and walked around the far side of the bar to approach her from behind. She looked even sexier the closer he got. His eyes traced the line of her calf to the skin on the back of her knee. And that butt—how had he never noticed it before?

When he was near enough to see the movement of her teardrop pearl earrings as she fished the olive from her drink, he double-checked his body language. *Just a guy meeting his date at the bar.*

He wrapped his hand around her elbow and ducked his lips close to her ear. "You know what they say about people who eat the olive before finishing the drink, don't you?"

Startled, she stiffened and sucked in a sharp breath. The martini sloshed over the rim of the glass. "Agent Reitano, thank goodness. I was starting to think I'd never find you."

She tried to face him, but he maintained his position of power with an unyielding grip on her arm. "Ryan," he corrected. No need to advertise he was an undercover agent. "What are you doing here?"

"I left you a voice mail and texted you that I was coming."

"I tossed my phone."

"What? Why?" She tried to turn again, so he pressed against her back, pinning her between the bar stool and his hips.

"My question first."

She fiddled with the base of her glass. "Okay. The answer is no. I don't know what they say about people who eat the olive first. That we're hungry?"

Huh? "Avery, what are you doing here?"

She angled her head over her shoulder and whispered out of the corner of her mouth, "There was a problem with the document you asked for."

Damn it. Now what was he supposed to think? Avery definitely wasn't giving off a double-agent vibe, but her actions were suspicious as all get-out. Once upon a time, Ryan had valued his intuition first and foremost, but ever since the betrayal that had broken up his black ops crew and turned Ryan into a lone hunter, he knew better than to trust anyone or anything— including his own instincts.

And wasn't that a royally jaded thought? When had he become such a cynic? Actually, he could pinpoint the exact day and time he'd turned into a cynic, not that it made the transformation any less jarring.

He shook off his regret and frustration about the past. There was nothing he could do to change the way things went down with his crew.

"What sort of problem?" He leaned in for a view of her facial expression when she answered.

"The office's computers crashed, so I searched for the hard copy, but the file was missing. I didn't know what else to do but come find you."

Scowling, he shook his head. "You expect me to believe that?"

"Uh, yeah. Why wouldn't you?"

Another loud, beat-heavy song drifted into the lobby from the second-floor ballroom as the New Year's Eve ball went into full swing. Regardless, the ground-floor lobby bar was not an ideal place for an interrogation.

From his research on the hotel, he remembered a row of conference rooms on the third level. Taking the service stairs would be quicker, but with Avery's dress, they'd stand out too glaringly to anyone on the lookout for incongruous movement. Staying with the horde of revelers attending the ball was the best camouflage he could manage under the circumstances.

After dropping a twenty-dollar bill on the bar, he slipped his arm around her waist, working to ignore the heat of her body and the provocative curve of her figure. "Let's walk."

Hip to hip, they strode in pace with the impenetrable crowd lining up at the base of the escalators. Well, Avery didn't so much stride as teeter along in a pair of black stiletto heels that looked downright torturous.

As soon as they shuffled onto the escalator, Ryan turned their backs to the lobby and looked out the wall of windows at the sea of cars and pedestrians on the packed downtown street. Chiara was out there somewhere nearby. Ryan could feel it.

Times like these, constrained by the rules of his job, he didn't feel like the man with the advantage. Especially given that he was locked in a deadly game of cat and mouse with a man of no scruples and no loyalty but to himself.

Avery shifted, reclaiming his attention. She tilted her mouth toward his chin. "Where are we going?"

"Somewhere to talk."

She nodded, the worry lines on her face easing. "Good. Because I think I can help you with the Lassiter transcript."

Her words threw him off-balance again. The LM1204 document was top secret. There would be no way for her to know the names involved in the wiretap unless she'd read the file. Even if she was lying about his computer breaking down, she couldn't have opened the file, because it was individually passworded. Lassiter was a rogue computer hacker and a known associate of the Chiara brothers. His connection to the current investigation into Chiara was highly classified intel that she had no business knowing.

He gave her body a calculated perusal. "I'm curious—why the costume and the drink?"

He'd chosen the word *costume* purposefully and injected some venom into his tone to lob that off-balance feeling right back at her, but he still felt a twinge of regret when she smoothed a hand down her dress in a self-conscious gesture. He touched his shoe to his ankle holster, a reminder of the dangerous mess he was in.

"There are a lot of women here in cocktail dresses holding drinks," she answered. "I think I blend in rather well, thank you very much."

He ran his tongue along the backside of his teeth, fighting the urge to break it to her that her rationale was flawed. Sure, there were a lot of fancy-looking women in the lobby, but a hot blonde in a skintight pink dress standing alone at the bar? He'd bet the contents of his safety-deposit box that every male in the room had taken note of her.

The escalator poured them into a wall of people waiting to gain entrance to the ballroom. With one hand on Avery's elbow and the other on the small of her back, Ryan cut through the crowd, his destination the service stairway entrance on the far side of the second-floor landing near the restrooms. Neither he nor Avery tried to speak, as the effort would've been futile given the earsplitting mash-up of dance music and people talking.

As he bypassed the elevators, then the restrooms, she tugged his jacket sleeve. "Wait a sec. Where exactly are we going?"

"Conference rooms on the third floor."

"What about the hotel room you reserved? Wouldn't that be the safest place?"

It was happening again. His intuition was going bonkers. Was she trying to lure him there thinking he had yet to visit the room where the hit men had been lying in wait? Or was she asking an honest question? At this point, he couldn't see any harm in telling her the truth. "Chiara's men were waiting to ambush me in the room when I got here tonight. So, no, it's not the safest place for us to talk."

He opened the stairwell door and leaned in to make sure the stairs were clear. Avery yanked him back by the jacket and gave him a shake. "Hold on—are we in some sort of danger?"

Looking into her wide eyes, a wry chuckle escaped his throat. He removed her hands from his lapels and held her wrists. "Right now I can't decide if you're honestly that clueless or if you're the world's best liar."

She jerked away from his grip like he'd burned her.

Another twinge of regret jolted through him. He forced himself to remember it was a good sign, that feeling. It meant he had at least a shred of humanity left in him, which was saying something after all he'd seen and done in his life.

"I don't understand," she said. Glancing over her shoulder at the crowd they'd navigated, she rubbed her bare arms. "I thought you were conducting routine surveillance tonight, nothing dangerous. Otherwise, you wouldn't have come alone. The whole team would've been here to—"

In time with the pounding bass from the ballroom, a booming shot rang out nearby and a piece of wood splintered from the doorway above Ryan's head. A second shot followed before he could react, lodging in the wall behind Avery. She shrieked.

Ryan pulled her into the stairwell and jerked the door shut.

He pushed her ahead of him down the stairs as he retrieved his S&W .45. "Change of plans. How fast can you run?"

Chapter 3

Ryan had to hand it to Avery. For a dolled-up chick in high heels and a tight dress, the lady could book it. He paced her at a jog, the soles of his shoes crunching over debris and crumbled stucco on the dingy, dusty staircase.

"Oh, my God. We were shot at, weren't we? Oh. My. God." Maintaining a litany of exclamations and curses, she skidded around the second turn in the staircase and slammed her side into the wall.

Arms flailing for balance, she barely slowed down until, somewhere above them, a stairwell door opened with an echoing boom. Her speed faltered before cranking up another notch, until she was virtually flying around the final corner.

The stairwell bottomed out on a dim, concrete-floored landing with a door leading, Ryan hoped, to the hotel's underground parking garage. He sped past

Avery before she had a chance to dart through the door. He wasn't a big fan of running scared, which meant it was time for him to neutralize the threat.

He snagged her around the ribs and tossed her into the shadowed space beneath the stairs, in front of a second door he hadn't noticed earlier that had the look of a supply closet. Her eyes locked on his gun for the first time and she squeaked, dropping her purse. After flashing his fiercest warning glare, she clammed up. Last thing Ryan needed was her giving away their position. Then again, if she did, he'd have his answer about who her allegiance belonged to.

At least two sets of men's shoes thumped along the stairs in descent.

He pulled back into the shadow, smushing Avery's body into the corner behind him. Assuming a defensive position, he aimed at the turn in the stairs, his finger on the trigger. Avery's shallow, quiet breathing fanned over his neck. From her stomach to her chest, her body quivered against his back, as though she was trying so hard not to move that her muscles spasmed with fatigue.

Too late, it dawned on him that if she was the double agent, she might be armed. He had no idea where she'd stash a weapon in that dress, and her purse was on the ground between their legs, but nevertheless, it was a stupid move to have his back to her.

Torn between protecting her from Chiara's men and protecting himself from her, he decided to go with his gut—however unreliable that'd proved tonight. After all, hesitation, not double-crossing secretaries, was the number one killer of people in his line of work. The debate fled his mind as a man's legs materialized on the steps.

Avery's body quivered more violently.

Three men took the steps two at a time, their eyes on the door to the parking garage. Ryan recognized none of them, which told him Chiara had an even deeper reservoir of attack dogs than he'd been aware of.

Two men, Ryan could've neutralized before they knew what was happening, but the third man changed the odds. He'd have time to react while Ryan felled the first two, putting both Ryan and Avery in serious danger.

Close combat was his only viable option.

As the men descended, their focus on the door, time slowed. The world went silent.

Ryan felt the rush of adrenaline through his veins, a hot, dark burn of power and purpose. His favorite feeling in the world. All his years of experience had taught him to harness its potential, syncing the strength of his body to the strength of his will. He released an exhale in a slow stream through his nose and prepared to attack.

The tallest man put his hand on the door's push bar.

Ryan took a deep breath and lunged, squeezing the trigger as he flew.

Avery watched with crippling fear as Ryan charged their assailants. Every bang of his gun made her heart squeeze and froze her body further, until she couldn't even flinch away from the violence. Cowering against the far wall, the long-forgotten paper clip chain cutting into the skin of her back, she could barely breathe or blink.

One of the three assailants fell to the ground almost instantly, an angry hole gaping in his torn and bloody shirt. She'd never seen a real gunshot wound before. It didn't look anything like in the movies.

Ryan latched onto the back of the nearest man still

standing and foisted him into the taller of the two as he continued to fire. She caught a glimpse of a black-ink tattoo of a cross between the shorter man's shoulder blades before Ryan's right arm hooked around the man's neck. A crack like a bone breaking made Avery blanch.

Ryan dropped the shorter man. Tucking his gun into his jacket, he stepped over the body to seize the wrist of the remaining man's gun hand. He slammed it into the door over and over until the gun clattered to the ground near their feet.

The other man caught him with a punch to the cheek.

His face a cold mask, Ryan threw his fist into the assailant's neck, then his gut. The blows continued from both men, their arms moving so quickly Avery couldn't tell who was winning. The two fell to the ground and rolled toward the stairs.

When they came to a stop, Ryan had the other man's neck balanced against the edge of the bottom stair, his palm against his chin, locking him in place.

The man gasped, his legs kicking beneath Ryan's weight. Before Avery's eyes, Ryan's mask of cool control morphed into a look of fierceness as lethal as his skills had proved. She was so fixated on his face, she didn't notice the other man's knee coming up until it made impact with Ryan's groin.

With a guttural sound of pain, Ryan's grip eased and the other man pounced on the opportunity to counterattack. He flipped on top of Ryan and wedged his head between the stair and the bar of the rail.

Ryan let out a wheezing breath that shook Avery from her fear-frozen state. Anger and irritation bubbled in her throat like acid. How dare those shooters threaten her and her coworker. And on New Year's Eve, no less. She was supposed to be partying with her friends to celebrate the end of a crappy year that included catching her boyfriend in bed with another woman, not running for her life or watching her office crush get the snot beat out of him.

Trembling with rage, she rose to her full height. She couldn't die yet. Not when she hadn't crossed a single thing off her bucket list. And she couldn't let Agent Reitano die either, even if he barely noticed she existed.

She reached back and grabbed hold of the paper clip chain, yanking as hard as she could. It snapped free of her dress, popping the zipper off with it. Whatever. The damn thing wasn't even wrinkle resistant. Rushing forward, she wrapped the chain around her palms and held it taut between her hands.

She hurled herself onto the bad guy's back and dropped the chain around his throat. Tucking her elbows, she pulled the chain with all her strength. Caught unaware, the man let out a strangling noise. Avery rose to a crouch, straddling his legs, and pulled harder, until she felt the paper clips bending and giving way.

Time to give this guy a taste of his own medicine. Maintaining her hold on the paper clips, she jammed the toe of her shoe into his crotch and twisted. He reared back, howling, then keeled sideways onto the stairs. She kicked him onto his back and ground her spiked heel into his crotch. His eyes rolled back in his head.

That's right, buddy. No one messes with Avery Meadows's bucket list.

With a nod of satisfaction, she swung the chain out and grabbed hold of a single paper clip that had pulled straight. Without giving it a second thought, she jammed the paper clip into the assailant's shoulder. She heard his shriek of pain as if from a distance and pushed the metal in deeper as the image popped into her head of Zach in bed with that two-faced pole-dancing instructor.

A hand on her arm shook her out of her trance. She whirled around, wielding the paper clips.

It was Agent Reitano. He eased the chain out of her hand, his eyes huge, as if he couldn't quite believe what he'd witnessed.

"Avery, stop screaming."

Screaming?

He put a finger on her chin and pushed her mouth closed.

Confused, she met Agent Reitano's eyes with a look of challenge. "I wasn't screaming. Don't be ridiculous."

Amusement flashed in his eyes. It was the first time that night he'd looked at her without accusation. "My bad. You were as stealthy as a ninja."

She smoothed her dress. Cold air nipped at her back, where the dress now gaped with a broken zipper, but she couldn't find it in her heart to care. Power and energy like she'd never experienced buzzed through her system, pushed along by her pounding heart.

She chanced a look at the assailant. He'd passed out cold. *Good.* "Any chance that guy was a criminal mastermind?"

"Not quite. More like a hired gun. Anyhow, thank you for coming to my rescue."

Looking over her shoulder, she studied the limp form of the man more closely. Then reality crashed over her. "Oh, my God. I saved you, didn't I? I kicked that bad guy's butt. Wow."

Ryan retrieved Cross Tattoo Man's gun from the floor, popped it open and inspected the inside, then put it back together and stuffed it into his jacket. "More like ground his nuts to a paste, but yeah, you saved my bacon."

"I saved your bacon," she echoed in a whisper of disbelief as a bone-jarring shiver racked her body, bringing with it a hefty dose of nausea. Desperate for a distraction so she didn't give up her butt-kicking status by spewing her martini all over Agent Reitano, she paced to one end of the landing and back, trying to calm down.

He glanced up from where he was sifting through the pockets of the man with the broken neck. "Avery, take some deep breaths."

She stepped over the men's legs, rubbing her jittery arms. "Trying. Not working."

The next moment, his hands clapped onto her shoulders, his thumbs stroking the straps of her dress. "Your adrenaline's crashing. Totally normal. It'll fade soon."

She dropped her forehead onto his shirt and concentrated on the rise and fall of his solid chest to distract her from her queasiness. His hands slipped from her shoulders to her head. He smoothed her hair in slow, easy strokes.

All the years she'd dreamed of gadgets and high-speed chases, clever riddles to solve and fake identities to assume, she'd never once stopped to think what it would actually look like to watch someone die. Nor what it would feel like to listen to a man scream in pain that she was causing.

Her mom would say no human being deserved to be the victim of violence, no matter how repugnant his crime. Avery knew, logically, that her mom was wrong, that some men were evil and had to be stopped by whatever means necessary when there were no other options.

But growing up the child of two grassroots pacifist leaders, she'd come to understand that believing in the occasional necessity of violence and letting go of the guilt about feeling that way were two entirely different issues. She'd wrestled with both for most of her life, but that struggle hadn't prepared her for the way she felt tonight.

Watching Agent Reitano battle the bad guys had certainly frightened and shocked her, but what she'd felt when she joined in the fray was a hundred times more potent. She'd *liked* the way it had felt to wield power. It had given her satisfaction to do harm to another person. The realization scared her to her core.

"Maybe I should stick to being a secretary."

Against her forehead, she felt the rumble of his chuckle.

She pulled back, annoyed. "Are you mocking me?"

His smile fell. "No, I… Absolutely not." He rubbed his neck, his expression turning guarded again. "I'm going to finish searching these guys, and then we'll get out of here. I'm going to let go of you. Don't fall."

"I won't."

He set her away from him, holding her shoulders until she found her legs again.

"Thanks, Agent Reitano."

He frowned down at her. "Just Ryan, okay?"

Nodding, her gaze slid to the fallen men.

Ryan squatted over the man she'd felled and patted down his pockets. Then he rolled him onto his stomach and continued the search.

"Are you looking for ID?" she asked.

Shrugging at her question, he lifted the flap of the man's sports coat and removed the gun hidden there. "Not really. These guys aren't going to tell us anything I don't already know."

He pocketed the gun, then tried the doorknob of the

employee locker room she'd stood in front of during the attack. It was locked. "Here's the plan. We're going to make a break for it through the parking garage, so I'm going to get my gun out and load it with a fresh magazine, okay? Don't freak."

Avery drew herself up, giving him her best indignant glare. "Oh, please. I'm not going to go nuts at the sight of a gun. I see guns every day at the office." Holstered, of course. But still…

He straightened his tie, smoothed a hand over his hair, then removed a big black gun from his jacket and positioned himself against the wall next to the parking garage door.

Despite her words to the contrary, Avery drew a sharp breath and her heart skipped a beat. But her reaction was purely reserved for the man holding the weapon. She followed the line of his shoulder to the bunched muscles of his biceps beneath his pricey-looking, perfectly tailored jacket, then farther, to the large, steady hand holding the gun. With that suit, the gun and his devastatingly handsome face, he looked like the most dashing and sophisticated secret agent the world had ever known.

He looked like James Bond.

A hot flush crept over her cheeks. No doubt about it, Agent Reitano—Ryan—hit every one of her buttons in just the right way.

Without seeming to notice her perusal, he said, "Stand behind me, out of sight."

Avery complied, flattening herself against the wall, her bare arm brushing his sleeve. "You're going to make sure the garage is free of bad guys, right?"

"Definitely." He opened the door a crack and listened. Avery held her breath. He opened the door wider and stuck his head and gun through. Then he closed it again and lowered the gun. "The door's at a bad angle, so I couldn't see much, but it's too quiet in there. No cars moving, no people's voices. Totally silent."

"It's New Year's Eve and the hotel is crawling with people," Avery said. "The parking garage should be packed. Can't we call someone to help us get out of here? Director Tau or Agent Mickle, maybe Agent Lucey?"

"No."

"But—"

"Avery, you're going to have to trust me that we're on our own. I'm hoping the silence is a random coincidence because I'm not crazy about going back upstairs. Let me think for a sec about the exit locations in the parking garage from the hotel blueprints I went over this morning."

That, Avery could handle. She closed her eyes, visualizing the blueprints. "Except for the employee locker room on the other side of that door—" eyes still closed, she gestured her head toward where she'd been standing moments before "—the parking garage takes up the entire underground level beneath the hotel. The only car exit ramp will be on our right, approximately fifty yards away. It exits on Fifth and J Street. There are four emergency exit stairwells in the garage. The nearest one is three rows past the first pillar on the west side. It exits to Fourth along an alley."

She opened her eyes to find Ryan staring at her with an inscrutable expression.

"Did you memorize the blueprints?"

She shrugged noncommittally. "I didn't *try* to memorize them."

Cocking his head, he looked like he was about to

speak when a door opened somewhere in the stairwell above them. Footsteps moving fast, growing louder. Before Avery knew what was happening, Ryan had pulled her into the parking garage.

The door shut behind them with a clatter that garnered the attention of four machine-gun-toting men standing near the valet parking booth. In a flash, all four guns trained on them.

Avery gasped, then clamped her mouth shut and bit her tongue. It hurt like mad, but she couldn't get her jaw to open again to stop the pain.

Ryan's expression was unreadable as he raised his hands.

The men with guns looked to be in their mid-thirties or early forties and were dressed in jeans, sweatshirts and ball caps. And they each had huge, nasty guns that looked capable of firing a million rounds a minute with the slightest depression of the trigger.

They sprinted in Avery and Ryan's direction, with the burliest of them shouting in a heavy Eastern European accent, "Drop the gun! On your knees or we kill the girl."

Avery's arms shot in the air of their own will. She maneuvered to her knees awkwardly, her movement hindered by her dress. Ryan followed suit, placing his gun on the ground a few feet in front of him.

Behind them, the stairwell door opened again, but Avery didn't dare look. Ryan did though. Whoever it was, he kept his arms raised and his expression stony. Guess the police or a random team of navy SEALs hadn't charged in to save them.

One of the men nabbed Ryan's gun and stuck it in his sweatshirt pocket; another went through Ryan's jacket and withdrew two more guns, a cell phone and a knife. A third man circled them, calling something in another language to whoever had come through the stairway door.

Orange cones had been placed across the car entrance ramp, along with a sign that read Lot Closed. The thug at the valet booth, dressed as hotel security, was arguing with an unarmed man in a bellboy uniform.

As subtly as she could, Avery swung her eyes toward the emergency stairways. They were unmanned, but she bet they'd been rigged to stay locked. It looked like whoever these guys were—probably Vincenzo Chiara's men, she'd hazard to guess—they wanted some privacy for whatever nefarious activities they planned to perform tonight. She'd also bet that the crew of valet parkers were either dead or had been strong-armed into taking an extended coffee break all at once, like she'd seen in a movie one time.

Ryan nudged her leg with his shoe. "The locker room," he said under his breath. "Where in the hotel does it come out at?"

A man rushed at Ryan and speared him in the gut with the nose of his rifle. "Shut up!"

Grunting loudly, Ryan crumbled into a fetal position.

Avery held her breath lest she erupt with the scream building inside her. It was unbearable, watching him be hurt again.

"Where?" he whispered without moving.

Avery forced herself to move, though fear had once again nearly paralyzed her. She leaned over him as though to comfort him. "Behind the lobby reception desk," she breathed. The question baffled her. How would they access it if it were locked?

"Back on your feet!" one of the men barked. "Move it!"

It was a whole new round of awkwardness, returning to her feet in the dress, though she wasn't sure why she gave a whit about modesty anymore. She stalled on her knees, wondering how to manage it, when Ryan offered her a hand. His other hand slid against her skin at the gape in her dress where the zipper had popped off.

It was work, keeping the utter shock off her face as his hand, warm and sure, dipped below the broken zipper. His fingertips breached the top of the Spanx. Quite the terrible timing to get fresh with her, even if he clearly knew his way around a woman's body. He helped her up gradually, and as she straightened her back, cold metal replaced the feel of his fingers. Avery nearly choked on her own spit.

The metal was heavy. It felt like…

No.

Did he actually drop a weapon into her Spanx? She wiggled and a metal finger wedged into the cleft of her backside. Yep. That was a gun.

Holy smokes.

She turned to him, her mouth agape. His eyes narrowed in warning; then he looked straight ahead. With her blood pressure skyrocketing, she glanced over her shoulder. A lone woman, dressed in a hotel employee uniform, held a small handgun aimed at Ryan's back while two men dragged the bodies from the stairwell into the garage.

Avery whipped her face forward, her eyes counting the number of guns pointed at them. If she and Ryan made it out of this night without being shot, it was going to be a miracle of epic proportions.

They were shuffled across the garage to an old brown

Chevy Malibu. The woman jogged ahead of them and opened the trunk.

No way. Everybody knew you should never let the bad guys lure you into a trunk. She tugged Ryan's sleeve. "What do we do?"

"Chill. I've got this," he whispered.

"Chill?" she hissed. *Sure thing.* She'd get right on that after she stopped freaking out that they were being bullied into a car trunk by a bunch of angry men with huge guns who knew they'd killed two of their angry friends on the stairs.

When they reached the trunk, the man in the valet uniform hollered something in another language that grabbed everyone's attention. Leaving the woman and an armed man to guard Avery and Ryan, the rest of the men jogged to the top of the entrance ramp, where a black limo idled. The limo driver's window rolled down. The bearded driver and the valet began an animated discussion.

Avery darn near jumped out of her skin in surprise when Ryan's hand settled onto her bare back once more.

The man and woman who'd been left to stand guard were distracted by the presence of the limo. Even Avery knew this was the perfect window of time to act. But she was scared witless about it. All she could do was hope Ryan didn't expect her to pull off any moves like she had in the stairwell. She'd used up all her allotted spy powers for the day.

In one fluid motion, he pulled the gun from her Spanx, shoved her to the ground alongside the car and pivoted toward the man with the machine gun. The man went down with a single shot.

Next Ryan lunged at the woman, who fired in his general direction but missed, obviously flustered by the turn of events. He paid her gunfire no mind as he took hold of her blouse and pulled her into the open trunk.

Avery scrambled to her knees. She couldn't see much but knew there was no way the men talking to the limo driver had failed to hear the gunfire. Sure enough, as Ryan slammed the trunk closed, someone opened fire in a continual staccato of shots.

Ryan dived to the ground near Avery. "Let's jam," he said, cool as a cucumber.

He gestured with his gun toward the rear of the garage. Avery kicked her shoes off and followed after him, threading in a crouched position between car bumpers and the wall.

Bullets flew in all directions, crumbling car windows and the concrete wall and ceiling. Avery ran as quickly as she could. License plates tore chunks of her dress off and slashed at her legs, but she never slowed more than an arm's length from Ryan's back. Every so often, he'd pause and return fire, buying time for them to dart across empty parking spaces.

Finally, he ground to a halt behind the passenger door of the last car. Avery fell to her hands and knees beside him. The dress, now ripped to shreds, no longer impeded her movement.

"What's the plan?" she asked between breaths. Her voice sounded muffled to her ears, damaged as they were by machine-gun fire.

Ryan glanced at the stairwell door, then lifted his pant leg, exposing an ankle holster where an extra magazine rested against the inside of his calf. That must've been where he'd had the gun he stashed in her underwear, she reasoned.

As she caught her breath, he exchanged the empty magazine for the fresh one. "I'm going to cover you while you run for the door." He flashed a set of keys. "I lifted these from that woman. Hopefully one opens the door to the locker room."

She had to play his words over in her mind twice to make sure she'd heard him right. "You want me to run? Out in the open?"

"Yes. Are you ready?"

Avery gauged the distance from their hiding place to the door and estimated it to be at least fifteen feet. "No," she answered honestly.

He blinked at her; then his eyes turned soft and his lips twitched like he was contemplating a smile. He looked playful. Boyish. Like they were back on the employee softball team last November when one of the other agents was razzing him about a missed catch. Like in the next few seconds they weren't going to risk their lives all over again.

"I'm not ready for you to make that run, either. But it's our only option."

He pulled the tail of his shirt free of his pants. Strapped to his waist over his undershirt and above his belted pants was a black canvas belt with lots of pockets and zippers. Reaching near the small of his back, he withdrew two small canisters.

"What're those?"

"A decoy grenade and smoke screen."

She gaped at the objects in his hand. Unreal. Then she looked into his deep brown eyes, intense but for the slightest touch of amusement, and tried her best not to swoon. Sure, the thrill of the battle was starting to course through her system again like a bizarro happy drug she couldn't control, but still, they were cornered in an underground garage while being fired at by machine guns.

Her fingers danced over the decoy grenade as she shot him a sidelong gaze. "You carry gadgets on your belt?"

She couldn't help it. She swooned a little anyway. Mr. Tall, Dark and Droolworthy just got even more intriguing.

Chapter 4

For someone who'd freaked at the sight of his gun, Avery sure did caress the grenade canisters in Ryan's hand like they were her favorite sex toys. And calling them gadgets? Ryan didn't know anybody who referred to grenades as gadgets, but if it gave Avery courage for the life-risking run they needed to make, then she could call them whatever she wanted.

Fighting a smile, he bought Avery a few more seconds to make peace with what she was about to do by squeezing off several rounds that forced Chiara's men to scatter for cover. "Yeah, I've got a few gadgets. Are you ready to move?"

Avery gave a thumbs-up and crouched into a sprint starting position. A pulse of admiration for her bravery nearly had him smiling again as he removed the pin from the first grenade and tossed it. It exploded in a screen of smoke.

The decoy he lobbed at the garage entrance. The hostiles' gunfire stopped, and Ryan could see them running for cover. Spraying gunfire to cover Avery's sprint, he gave her back a nudge. "Move!"

She took off running. Ryan followed, shooting through the smoke screen. Machine-gun fire resumed all around them. Bits of wall and ceiling crumbled over Avery as she threw the door open, but she kept moving like a champ. Ryan slipped in behind her. There was no way to bar the door from opening, but lucky for him, Avery had kept her wits about her and was already working the keys in the locker-room door.

Ryan held his position near the door, ready to neutralize anyone who dared open it.

"Got it," Avery called. She shouldered the door open, kicking her fallen purse in with her.

Ryan sidestepped her way, gun trained on the parking-garage door until he was at the employee entrance. As he closed his hand over that door, the parking garage door opened, followed by another succession of gunfire.

He ducked behind the door, paused to squeeze out a half-dozen rounds, then slammed the door behind him. If Chiara's men had another key, he and Avery had maybe thirty seconds to bolt. If they didn't, their window opened to a minute or two, perhaps more until Chiara's attack dogs either blew the door down or found another way to reach them.

A thunder of noise from beyond the door preceded the appearance of dimples in the metal plated wood. Gunshots. Ryan dived away from the door. "Let's move!"

He scooped up Avery's purse and jogged with her past the kitchenette and dining area, toward the lockers. Behind them, the sound of the doorknob rattling was followed by another long roar of gunfire.

So they didn't have another key. *Excellent.* He tucked Avery's purse in the inside pocket of his jacket. "How do we get out of here?"

"Stairs, straight ahead."

Halfway down the row of lockers stood a solitary young man, shirtless, his eyes and mouth wide-open as he stared at Ryan's gun. The poor schmuck looked harmless but frozen with terror, which was probably why, despite the gunfire in the parking lot, he looked more ready to pee his pants than flee. While Ryan was busy mentally debating whether or not to incapacitate him so he didn't call hotel security on them, Avery rushed the guy, spearing a finger in the air.

"You. Take off your shoes. Now!"

The man gaped at her. Ryan was taken aback, too, but he caught on quick. She'd left her heels in the parking garage and had correctly reasoned that even used, ill-fitting shoes were better than no shoes at all.

He moved beside her, his gun aimed at the poor, half-naked employee. "You heard the lady. Get those shoes off."

His focus riveted on the gun, the man whimpered and sank to his knees. "Don't kill me."

Avery rolled her eyes and swatted at the air between them. "It's a gun. Get over it. Give me your shoes, or I'm going to make you."

His lower lip trembled, but he nodded and complied.

It was an entirely inappropriate time to feel like smiling, but Ryan nearly did. *It's a gun. Get over it?* That was quite the change of tune since she'd first laid eyes on Ryan's S&W in the stairwell.

Once Avery had slipped into the black sneakers,

Ryan gestured his head toward a staircase along the wall that led to the ground level. "Lead the way." Pointing his gun at the employee, he added, "Count to one hundred—then call 911. Got it?"

The man nodded like the bobble-headed eagle on Ryan's desk.

Avery took the stairs two at a time, the heels of the sneakers clunking like flip-flops, clearly too big. He climbed sideways behind her, keeping one eye over his shoulder at the employee to make sure he didn't try anything heroic and the other on her bare back. Boy, had he been wrong to think her a possible double agent. She was like a shot of sunshine with a heart of pure moxie—about as far from the shady underworld Ryan operated in as a person could get.

All those months he'd wasted stewing on his suspicions he could've spent having impure thoughts about her.

Behind them, the door to the stairwell rattled. Muffled shouting came from the other side. At the top of the stairs, Avery paused at the closed door. He came up close behind her, ready to resume his lead position. There was only one problem. "I'm out of ammo," he said under his breath.

She turned, brushing against him. Her hair flouncing over the right side of her face, she fingered his tie. "But you've got more gadgets, right?"

What was it with her and gadgets? He tucked her hair behind her ear and let his gaze drop to her full, heart-shaped lips—the kind that straddled the edge between sweet and wicked. The kind that begged to be scandalized with a hot, wet kiss. Maybe later—after they made it out of the hotel alive.

"I've got more gadgets." Maybe, for once that night,

luck would be on his side and he wouldn't have to use them.

Reaching past her, he cracked the door and took stock of the reception area. Nothing seemed out of the ordinary. "Here's the plan. We're going to walk straight out the Mira's front doors. You think you could pretend we're a couple, out for a night on the town?"

He hoped she was game because that wasn't going to be a problem for him. There wasn't going to be a single ounce of pretending on his part to look like he was totally into the smoking-hot woman at his side.

She inhaled deeply, determinedly. "Okay, but there's one teensy issue."

He cocked his head in question.

"If we're trying to blend in, then this dress and these shoes aren't going to work." She held the tattered edges of her skirt as evidence.

He stared down the length of her body. Most of the skirt had been torn off in the parking garage, dirty smudges covered most of the material and the back hung open due to the broken zipper. *What a shame.* "It was such a nice dress."

"You approve?"

He doffed his jacket and draped it across her shoulders, his jaw growing tight as a fresh zing of approval hit him below the belt. "Something like that."

Given their height difference, the jacket was long enough to cover Avery's body from her neck to an inch or so above her knees. Her clothes were still an obvious wreck, but at least the whole of downtown San Diego wouldn't be treated to a view of her bare skin.

He dropped his empty shoulder holster onto the floor and double-checked to make sure his shirt covered his concealed carry belt. Holding the door open with his shoulder, he wrapped an arm around Avery's waist and pulled her firmly against his side. Damn, she felt good there. If only they weren't fighting for their lives against one of the deadliest men in the world.

Ducking his lips near her earlobe, he whispered, "Showtime."

She shivered at the word, so he searched her face, looking for fear or hesitancy. If she froze up now, he'd have to rethink their getaway. But all he saw in her face was brazen determination. Impossible not to admire her for that kind of courage, given how her life had been flipped upside down that night.

Nothing he could do about it now except protect her the best he could. That was one of his duties tonight, but not his biggest problem. Getting them both out of the hotel wasn't even his biggest problem. Apparently, his biggest problem had come in with an express courier late in the day. The thought made his gut lurch.

He maneuvered them through the maze of managerial offices at a brisk clip, as though they belonged there, then around the back of the busy receptionist desk and into the lobby.

As they moved through the crowd, he whispered, "Where's the letter I asked you to take home?"

"In my car."

Ryan didn't consider himself a cynic, but it was almost too good to be true that something had gone off without a hitch tonight. He'd been afraid it'd gotten dropped somewhere in the hotel. "Where's your car now?"

"In the ICE parking garage."

That was going to be a problem. Chiara's men would know to look for him at the ICE office. For all he knew, they'd been hunting him as surely as he'd been hunting them. True, Ryan could probably still take on an army of Chiara's goons with the various weapons and defensive devices strapped around his body, but without at least one loaded gun at his disposal he felt positively naked. They'd have to regroup and return for the letter once he was fully loaded again.

A bellman opened the front door, but before they'd stepped a foot outside, gunfire sounded all around them. The wall of windows above the lobby shattered.

Ryan's reaction was immediate and visceral. He ducked over Avery to shield her from the raining glass, pushing her through the door. They spilled onto the sidewalk with dozens of screaming, fleeing guests.

While the cover provided by the panicked crowd had its benefits, Ryan fought against getting swept away with them. He and Avery needed to move at twice the speed of the masses and get out of view of the street, out of range of the hostiles' bullets and the law enforcement officials who were guaranteed to swarm the building at any moment. Already, sirens sounded in the distance.

Ryan kept his arm around Avery and pulled her into the first building they came to. A restaurant. Though it was nearing midnight, the place was packed. They ran past the hostess, dodging tables of diners who seemed dumbstruck. Wide-eyed, several of them stood in slow motion, like they were still processing the noises they'd heard from outside and it was finally sinking in that something bad was going down.

Behind them, more gunfire rang out. Ryan turned to see three of the men from the parking garage giving chase. He pushed Avery faster, pulling the pin of another smoke grenade with his teeth. He chucked it at the men as he and Avery pushed through a swinging door into the kitchen. They sprinted past prep tables and stove tops, dodging startled cooks and waitstaff.

Finally they burst out into a dark alley. Not exactly an ideal locale for avoiding shady underworld thugs, so Ryan took Avery by the hand and steered her toward the next block, where a cluster of employees huddled under a light, smoking, just outside an open door. Hoping it was another back entrance to a nightclub or restaurant, Ryan pulled his gun out. Sure, it was out of ammo, but these guys didn't need to know that.

He ground to a stop in front of the smoking workers and took aim at them with his S&W. "Out of our way."

Cursing, they scurried off. Ryan boosted Avery ahead of him, then reached for an offensive grenade. Using it was a huge risk given the close proximity of the other buildings. There was little else in the world that Ryan hated more than collateral damage—innocent civilians getting hurt or killed. It was his one thing.

He'd vowed to his father when he had entered the service to never take collateral damage lightly and to avoid it at all costs. But he and Avery needed to create some distance between themselves and the men trailing them and he was running out of options.

"What are you waiting for?" Avery asked from inside the doorway.

"Just a sec."

As soon as the three thugs shot into the alley from the restaurant, Ryan made sure they got a good look at him. They ran at him, shooting wild. He waited until they were in range, then pulled the pin and lobbed the grenade.

He slipped through the door as an explosion ripped through the alley, a tsunami of shock waves and fire.

He shook off the jolt to his body and slammed the door then locked it with the dead bolt.

Avery took hold of his arm. "Are you all right?"

All right was a relative term at the moment. "Better than dead." It was something he and his black ops crew used to say. Remembering the crew sent a knife of longing through his heart. He missed those times, before it all fell apart. "Let's jam. You lead the way."

He followed Avery through the nightclub employee break room, ignoring the protests of the workers, and into the main area of the club. The music inside was deafening, so loud that no one seemed to have registered the grenade explosion or trouble at the Mira only a few blocks over. This place was dark and crowded, perfect for two people on the run to get lost within.

Halfway across the dance floor, Avery put on the brakes and turned to look over her shoulder, like she wanted to say something. Ryan ducked his ear close to her lips to hear her over the techno music.

"I know this place," she called. "It's a string of connected dance rooms and bars, each linked to the club next door. We might be able to sneak out an exit the bad guys aren't expecting us to."

"Perfect. I'll follow."

"There's a problem."

He cocked a brow at her.

"This is Club Brazil, where I was supposed to meet my friends tonight."

No way. "Seriously?"

"We can't let them see us or they'll want to know what we're up to. We don't have time to explain and we can't take a chance of the bad guys seeing them with us. They don't deserve to be put in danger."

She was right on every level. "You're short. Keep your head down and—"

"Avery!"

Her eyes closed, her face scrunched. "Too late."

Ryan swallowed a curse and plastered a genial expression on his face as three sets of couples gathered around them. The women were young and dolled up much like Avery, with tight dresses and flushed, happy faces. The men were just regular guys, corporate businessman types and sort of puny, the kind that made Ryan feel like an ogre in comparison.

"You made it," one of the women said. She hooked Avery in a one-armed hug that threatened to slosh the drink in her other hand, but her attention was locked on Ryan, as were the other women's. "I see you found someone to ring in the New Year with, and you didn't even need my help." She nudged Avery and whispered something. Ryan wasn't a lipreading expert, but it looked like she said, "He's hot. Nice job."

"Sorry I'm so late, but you can see I had a good reason." Avery took Ryan's hand, like they were an item. Her hand was so tiny and slender; he loved the way it felt in his. He held on tight. "I hate to do this to you, but we're on our way to, uh, have a little private party of our own. We just stopped by so you wouldn't worry about me."

Wow. Bold. Then again, taking off with guys she'd just met must not have been her normal M.O. because her friends' eyes grew wide and they gave Ryan a brand-new head-to-toe inspection. The men seemed more skeptical than pleased at the news compared to their dates' reactions. One of them stepped forward, hand out like he wanted to shake Ryan's and make extra sure their friend was safe in his company.

Avery lurched sideways, waving and pulling Ryan along with her. "Okay, we're out of here."

Ryan offered the group a conciliatory wave and matched Avery's quick stride.

"You didn't even tell us his name," the curly-haired brunette called after them.

"James!" Avery hollered, smiling with too much enthusiasm.

They ducked through a hall between that dance floor and the next. This room was even more crowded with revelers and dancers than the last, so that they were squeezed together as they wormed their way through the throng.

Ryan couldn't muster the desire to let go of Avery's hand, and now that they were pressed back to front, it was easy to get close to her ear to tease her.

"James?" he asked. "Is Ryan not a good enough name?"

Sweeping her chin over her shoulder to regard him from below her thick, long lashes, she smiled. "That was my attempt at subterfuge."

And damn it all if he didn't break out in a chuckle right there on the dance floor of Club Brazil while fleeing with a civilian from a ruthless pack of hit men. He couldn't stop the lightness Avery summoned forth from him.

They were partially across the floor, moving toward the lighted exit on the far end of the room when the music volume lowered. The DJ's voice boomed over the speakers, announcing midnight's imminent arrival. The number twenty appeared on the numerous television screens around the room, counting down to midnight.

Ryan and Avery exchanged glances but kept moving, though their progress was made more difficult because the partiers were all standing still. Champagne was passed around. Everyone's eyes were on the screens.

Ten, nine, eight...

The emergency exit came into view down the restroom hallway behind a mass of people only four deep. In moments, they'd be out on the street. The midnight celebrations would be the perfect cover for them to slip away. But all he could think was, *What the hell. You only live once.*

He ground to a stop, tugging Avery's hand, spinning her to face him.

She bumped up against his chest, looking confused. "Why did we stop?"

Three, two...

As the first second of the New Year turned over, he took her cheek in hand and captured her lips with his. She stiffened, then her mouth went soft. She threw her arm around his neck and kissed him back. Her kiss was as luscious as her body, full of passion and heat and supple softness. It'd been a while since Ryan had really kissed a woman so that it crashed through him, all the way deep down inside. He forgot how profound a feeling that was, how addictive.

He touched the tip of his tongue to her lip, and the moment her tongue found it, flicking against it, a jolt of arousal ripped through him. Oh, yeah, this was the best idea he'd had all night. He could've stayed there until morning dawned, but the city was crawling with hostiles who wanted nothing more than to destroy him— and now Avery, too. He couldn't afford to take his eye off the game, not even to puzzle out the secrets of the charming, beautiful woman in his arms.

He ended the kiss, then looked down at her dazed

eyes and moist, parted lips, and had to hold himself back from sampling her again. "Happy New Year, Avery."

She blinked slowly, as if awakening. "Happy New Year, Ryan."

He smoothed his hand over her bare back under his suit jacket, hungry for the feel of her flesh. "I'm back to being Ryan again?"

"It's a lady's prerogative."

He caressed her lower lip with his thumb, and the grin that had been threatening to break out did exactly that. "How about we get out of here?"

Chapter 5

Hand in hand with Ryan, Avery stepped out into the winter air, which was a blast of refreshing cold compared to the heat of the club. No doubt their lives were still in peril, but for the moment she wished badly that she weren't just pretending she was still the ordinary secretary she'd been a couple of hours earlier, out for a night of fun with one of the hottest men she'd ever had the pleasure of kissing.

And by pleasure, she meant a toe-curling, life-changing, better-than-in-the-movies kind of pleasure. A what-are-you-doing-for-the-rest-of-your-life kind of pleasure. Holy smokes, could that man kiss. It made her wonder what else he was an expert at.

Yet forgetting the dire situation they were in wasn't something she had the luxury to do. Not even close.

Tipping her chin over her shoulder, Avery studied the Mira Hotel, three blocks south and now the site of a chaotic crime scene. Fire engines, police cars and ambulances were piled in the street out front. Barricades were being erected for the block, resulting in a major traffic jam.

She hugged herself, thinking about all the violence she'd seen and participated in that night. Men had died. Even more men had tried to kill her. They'd tried to kill Ryan, too. And that wasn't even the worst of it.

The worst of it was her dawning awareness that a bunch of international, violent offenders with deep pockets and even deeper connections had seen her face. She'd read the files on Vincenzo Chiara. She knew what he was capable of. As desperately as she wished that her biggest problem could continue to be the persistent sting of discovering her boyfriend cheating on her and the loneliness that had come with her subsequent singledom, the gravity of her situation was finally sinking in.

The men who had tried to kill her and Ryan would try again. She huddled closer, working to keep pace with him as he navigated the crowded sidewalk in the opposite direction of the Mira Hotel.

More than anything, even breathtaking kisses from suave secret agents or a change of clothes, she needed some serious, pull-no-punches answers from Ryan about how tonight's seemingly low-risk surveillance had gone sideways and, even more pressing, why he refused to contact the agency for help.

"Where are we going?" she asked.

"Someplace safe. The sooner we're off the street, the less opportunity Chiara's men have to find us."

They ducked west, onto a cross-street that was no less jam-packed with cars and people than the street they'd been on but that pointed them away from the Mira.

"Are we headed to ICE or your apartment?" Avery

knew from Ryan's employee records he lived downtown, only a few blocks from the office.

"No, the trolley."

The only way he could've surprised her more would've been by flagging down a pedicab. The San Diego trolley system threaded through downtown, then shot north, south and east. Tonight it would be swarming with people, especially since the midnight hour had just struck and the early birds who'd stretched their nights out to ring in the New Year were now heading home.

If the idea was to get off the streets and out of view, taking the trolley was a bad plan. "My car's closer. It's in the underground parking at the office."

"I figured, but we're not going near that building until I'm fully armed again and have a better idea of who we're up against."

"What are you talking about? I thought you knew who those bad guys worked for."

He took her elbow, guiding her through groups of revelers. "Tonight's ambush was a setup."

"As in, you think Chiara's men were targeting you specifically, so much so that they might track us to the office next?" That revelation only left her with more questions. ICE wasn't even the lead federal department in the hunt for Chiara. Plus, Ryan was only a newly transferred workaday agent—not a logical target for an international criminal by any stretch of the imagination.

"I do, yes."

"I don't get it. The city's flooded with federal and local agencies who are tracking Chiara on the hunch he'd show up for that jade flower jewel that's being unveiled in a few days. He's one of the most wanted men in the world. Why would he target a single ICE agent?"

As he strode, Ryan twitched his face her way enough that she could see the grim line of his lips and his Adam's apple bob with a swallow. "I wasn't talking about Chiara. The setup at the Mira wasn't an outside job. Someone at ICE is trying to shut me down in a permanent way."

No way. That was just…impossible. "You think someone in the office has it out for you and tipped Chiara off? Like, a double agent?"

He huffed. "I *know* someone in the office is a double agent."

"That's why you didn't call for backup," she murmured, processing. She slowed, the pieces falling into place in her mind. Then it clicked. *Oh, hell, no.*

She ground to a stop, grabbed his sleeve and gaped at him. "That's why you were so suspicious of me at the hotel bar. You thought I double-crossed you."

It stole her breath, how that made her feel. Her thoughts went back to their first minutes together at the Mira. In her mind, she could hear his harsh, accusing words as they'd ridden the escalator—no, as he'd forced her up the escalator, holding her elbow much like he was now. *Right now I can't decide if you're honestly that clueless or if you're the world's best liar.*

She jerked her arm away. "Have you figured it out yet—that I'm not clueless or a liar? And I'm not a double agent, either?" Her throat tightened, and her sinuses tingled. She had to pause and swallow before adding, "Or are you pulling one of those 'keep your enemies closer' moves by taking me with you?"

She'd read about that sort of thing in enough books to know how it worked.

Frowning, he reached for her waist, a move he'd done several times that night, but she was too lost in her outrage to feel the usual thrills and chills his touch evoked. Despite her protests, he drew her into the shadows of a closed café, pressing her between the barred glass window and his body until the rest of the world had been blocked from view by his formidable height and breadth.

Her eyes were thick with angry unshed tears, so instead of meeting his gaze, she tucked her chin, pressed her nose to the collar of his jacket and drank deeply of its masculine scent.

"What did you expect me to think?" His voice was a harsh whisper. It was one of the first hints of genuine emotion his voice had ever betrayed. "You show up at the place I was ambushed, looking like this, knowing details about classified intel. You have the layout of the building memorized, for hell's sake."

"There's a reason for that." Despair washed through her. Of course he'd thought she was the double agent. That's what she got for keeping her photographic memory a secret from everyone she worked with. If only her ability to keep her lips from flapping worked as well as her memory, she'd be set.

"And we're going to talk about what that reason is, believe me," he said. "But not here. We have to keep moving."

The sensation of her mood shifting, plummeting, was palpable, like a dark, dragging force pressing on her. Maybe it was only an effect of her adrenaline crashing again, like it had in the stairwell, but the high she'd gotten by being the kick-butt girl who'd choked a bad guy with a paper clip chain and kissed her dream man at midnight was receding, returning her to the secretary who felt safest behind her desk and preferred her secret agent adventures in her imagination rather than real life.

"I just want to go home."

He screwed his mouth up, frustrated. Whether at her or the situation, she had no idea. "You can't. You can't go to the office or your home because we have no way of knowing yet if Chiara's men or the office's double agent have figured out you're involved. There isn't anywhere safer for you right now than staying close to me until we decide what our next play is."

No. Couldn't be. She'd wanted to help catch an international criminal mastermind, not go on the run from one. Moisture stung her eyes, blurring the city lights. She needed answers. She needed to know how in danger she was and from whom, and as soon as they'd found someplace secure to talk where she could stop worrying every two seconds about someone killing them, she was going to demand the truth.

She drew a fortifying breath and met his harsh, searching gaze. "I'm supposed to take your word for that?"

On an exhale, his posture softened. He stroked her hair. "It's a lot to ask, I know. I might've thought you were a double agent when I first saw you tonight, but I figured out fast that I could trust you. And I think you know, on a gut level, that you can trust me, too. I need you to trust me."

She knew next to nothing about Ryan except that he was a smart and capable ICE agent who was an amazing kisser and who'd kept her alive so far, despite the odds stacked against them. She dropped her forehead to his chest. If only they could just stay here, like this. This she could handle indefinitely.

Wrapping his arms more tightly around her, he rubbed his lips and nose over her hair. "I'm sorry you were dragged into this. I wish to God you hadn't come to the hotel tonight, but there's nothing we can do to change that now. I'm going to do my best to get you out of the line of fire. I promise you that."

She slipped her hands higher, splaying them over his stomach. He felt so strong and solid beneath her palms. Lethal and ready for action. If anyone could keep her safe, it would be him. With the absence of any other brilliant ideas, her best bet was to stick with him until she got the answers she needed to take back control of her life, but she wasn't ready to go so far as to trust him. She nodded. "Okay. Let's go."

She made to move past him, but he took hold of her jaw and coaxed her gaze back to his face. Her pulse sped, thinking he might kiss her again, but he pinned her with a look of penetrating intensity. "Do you trust me?"

If he was going to demand the truth, then she was going to give it to him. "No. I've done the whole blind faith thing and it blew up in my face. Big-time." One might call it boyfriend-cheating-with-a-pole-dancing-instructor syndrome. "But I think sticking with you is my best plan—for now."

She tried to hold his gaze, but he still cradled her face in his hands as though in preparation for a kiss and she couldn't stop the slow slip of her focus to his lips.

Maybe he was feeling the same about her lips because his thumb brushed over them. With dark eyes that studied her intently, he continued to cradle her face in his hands. "You're not clueless. Or a liar. I'm sorry I accused you of that," he said in a soft baritone that made her knees weak.

The tension sizzling between them nearly made her dizzy, it was such an about-face from her previous indignity. She licked her lips, grappling for words. In a last-ditch effort to play it cool, she cleared her throat and shrugged. "I would've thought the same thing if I'd been in your shoes, about me being a double agent." Her voice was breathy, betraying how deeply his nearness affected her, but she couldn't help it. Perhaps some gallows humor would counterbalance the uncontrollable heat of their exchange. "After all, I do have a sinister air about me."

His lips mashed together, giving off the faintest shadow of a smile. "We'll have to agree to disagree about your sinister nature, but that dress..." His gaze raked over her body. "That dress is criminal."

His wolfish appraisal had her fighting the temptation to drag his lips to hers to make good on the promise of a kiss she glimpsed in his eyes. "I'll say. It cost an arm and a leg and it's not even wrinkle resistant."

His body vibrated with a silent chuckle. With his arm around her, he tugged her back onto the sidewalk. "Let's jam. We've got to get that letter from your car as soon as possible and figure out what our next move is, but first I need more guns. A lot more guns."

He led her through the crowded open-air station to the trolley ticket kiosk and made a cash purchase of two all-day passes. At Ryan's insistence that it might be bugged, she tossed her cell phone in the trash with a wistful goodbye as a southbound trolley rattled into the station in a blur of red.

"Perfect timing," he said. "Here we go."

The trolley was too packed with people for them to sit. She doubted Ryan would've wanted to anyway. Sitting lacked fluidity of movement and, therefore, didn't seem very secret agent-ish. Instead, they crowded together in the corner of the car, Ryan with his back against one metal wall next to the exit stairs, Avery against the other. Though their shoulders touched and his hand held hers in a loose, confident grip, Ryan's eyes never stopped scanning their surroundings.

At the last stop downtown before the trolley headed south toward the Mexican border, a boisterous group of young men pushed their way aboard. They were the kind you heard before you saw them. The rowdy, volatile kind that made women clutch their purses tighter and fix their eyes on the windows or the floor. Though Ryan's presence ensured she wouldn't be bothered, Avery kept her focus on the men as they muscled their way to the exit near which Ryan and Avery stood.

Ryan stepped a foot out and turned toward Avery, shielding her from the men's view. Calm and cool, he took hold of the jacket she wore and, with slow, deliberate movement, buttoned it.

She wasn't sure why the move added to her anxiety. It should've given her reassurance that protecting her was in the forefront of his mind. But it felt like he was confirming that there was cause for concern.

Behind him, the group of men started shoving at each other. Not fighting, but more like drunken horseplay. An elbow or shoulder caught Ryan in the back and he pitched forward, bracing his hand on the wall above Avery's shoulder.

She inhaled sharply. "Are you going to do something?" she whispered. Ryan could totally put a stop to those guys' volatile, if unintentional, terrorization of the trolley—neutralize them like an action-movie hero might.

"No. Not unless I have to." At her questioning look, he brushed the backs of his fingers over her neck and added, "Number one rule of being a secret agent—there's a time to kick butt and a time to stay cool.

Recognizing which is which can mean the difference between life and death—or worse."

Visions of torture flitted through her head. "What's worse?"

"For an agent? Discovery."

"But you're not a secret agent. You're an ICE agent."

He lifted a brow, his eyes twinkling.

Her stomach dropped. "You're not actually an ICE agent?"

Ryan was hit hard in the back again, caught by a stray flailing arm. The group of men laughed. Not at Ryan but at the flailer. They didn't seem to realize or care that their buddy was taking his rowdiness to a destructive level.

"Is it time to kick butt yet?"

He offered a subtle shake of his head. "After all we went through tonight, this is nothing. Besides, the next stop is ours."

He hadn't answered her question about being an ICE agent, and she was having a new batch of trouble synthesizing all the information coming at her. Ryan thought someone in the office was out to get him, but he might not even be a real ICE agent. Wouldn't that make him the double agent? What if someone in the office had figured out he wasn't who he said he was and that's why they'd ambushed him tonight?

If that were so, then who were the good guys and who were the bad, especially if Ryan had wormed his way into the agency under false pretenses—or, worse, a fake identity?

It was enough to make her head spin all over again.

She looked out the window as the trolley slowed, taking in the run-down houses and apartment buildings near the trolley stop, the graffitied walls of liquor stores and the barred windows of storefronts advertising cash advances and payday loans.

She pulled up her mental map of the area. One of the few positive things she could say about having a photographic memory was that she'd never get lost—having a built-in GPS was one of the few perks of her curse. There wasn't anything around this particular trolley stop except barrio and industrial warehouses for miles in any direction. That and the dead-end of the San Diego Bay to the west. If the plan was to get off the street and into safety, this wasn't exactly the best neighborhood to disembark.

But disembark they did. There was no need to fight their way past the group of men because they preceded Ryan and Avery through the exit and onto the platform. Suddenly Avery couldn't decide what was the bigger threat: the surrounding barrio or the rowdy drunks. What if they followed Ryan and Avery with a mind to cause more trouble?

Her fears were almost immediately answered by Transit Security, who waylaid the drunks, corralling them to the side of the platform. Avery gave Ryan's hand a squeeze and hustled with him down the stairs to the sidewalk.

"Where are we going?" It felt like she'd asked him the same question a hundred times that night. When he didn't answer, she added, "Tell me you've got some supersafe secret lair nearby. Preferably windowless, with a high-tech security system and a massive arsenal of firepower for you to choose from."

He cast her a sidelong glance, his lips pressed together in what she was learning was his version of a smile. The light in his eyes gave him away. "Great guess. Just a few blocks to go."

"Holy smokes, I was right?"

With a confident spring in her step, she matched Ryan's long stride with two of her own. They walked a block along the sidewalk in silence before turning into a dark alley lined with a cinder block wall on one side and apartment garages and Dumpsters on the other. For three blocks, they zigzagged through identical alleyways before emerging onto a quiet street lined on both sides with chain-link-fence-enclosed businesses of tow yards and welders and the like.

They'd passed only two such businesses before a lowered, royal-blue land whale of a car careened toward them from down the street and jumped the curb in front of Avery and Ryan, blocking their progress.

Avery muttered a curse under her breath. She couldn't help it. This night was never going to end. She wrapped her arms over her stomach, infinitely grateful Ryan had thought to button the jacket. Ryan, as usual, was unfazed. With stoic purpose, he stepped in front of Avery. She watched the flex of his muscles beneath his shirt, the strain of the sleeves to accommodate his muscles as he tensed, ready for action.

Taking a break from chewing on her lower lip, she released a long, slow breath. "Is this one of those butt-kicking times? Please tell me this is a butt-kicking time."

"Not sure yet."

The driver stayed where he was, but a second huge guy with neck tattoos and a bored expression got out of the passenger seat. Both men looked like thugs straight out of a music video or low-budget movie. Clearly they had no idea how cliché they came across.

Passenger Thug pulled a small silver handgun from the waistband of his low-riding jeans. Avery squeaked.

These guys might be straight out of a bad movie, but that wasn't going to stop them from blowing Avery and Ryan to bits.

Ryan made a fist, then flexed his hand. "Okay, yeah. This is one of those butt-kicking times."

"You're not going to need my help, are you? Because I'm fresh out of paper clips and stilettos."

His chin twitched toward his shoulder like he had to stop himself from turning to look at her. She clamped her mouth shut. Probably distracting him by talking wasn't the best idea at the moment. In her nervousness, she felt the urge to keep babbling, and so she clamped her lips together.

While she ran a mental inventory of all the weapons he'd had removed by Chiara's men and wondered what surprises he had on his concealed belt that might be effective against a gun, Ryan unlatched his belt.

Chapter 6

Ryan stalked toward the car. Avery watched him pull his belt through the loops and reach into his pants with a mixture of dread and fascination, not unlike the transfixed way Passenger Thug was looking at him. What in the heck was he doing? Was he going to swing his belt at them? How was that going to be any match for a gun?

The driver rose out of the car, an ugly smile on his face. "You undressing for us, fool? Coming into our neighborhood like some kind of perv?" Standing behind the open driver-side door, he flipped up the side of his flannel shirt, revealing the black grip of a gun. He put his hand on the grip. "Maybe I oughta shove my gun up your—"

The gun never made it out of his pants. With a burst of speed, Ryan rushed forward. From seemingly out of nowhere, a short, stiff rope appeared in his right hand. The belt swung from his left hand with the heavy metal latch on the end. Ryan made a spinning leap, getting far more air than his huge body looked capable of. The rope lashed the driver on the side of his head as Ryan came down on the car hood, kicking out.

Ryan's foot connected with Passenger Thug's gun-waving arm. As the man reeled from the blow, Ryan spun again, whipping him in the side of the face with the rope. The gun clattered to the ground.

Passenger Thug staggered back, clutching his cheek. Avery spared a second to glance at the blood pooling between his fingers before wrenching her focus back to Ryan.

The driver was crouching now, using the door as a shield. All Avery could see of him was greasy dark hair and the metal nose of his gun. Ryan leaped again, his foot forward, shoving at the open door, slamming the driver off his feet.

Avery glanced again at Passenger Thug. He was injured, sure, but it was only a matter of seconds before he regrouped and grabbed his gun again.

Desperate for some way to aid Ryan, she stuffed her hands in the suit jacket for something—anything— that might help. All she came across was a pen. She could poke the passenger in the eye, but that would require her to get way more up close and personal than was safe. All she really needed was something to distract Passenger Thug so he didn't lunge at her while she grabbed his gun.

Something bulky inside the jacket caught her attention. She shoved her hand in the inside left pocket and touched on leather. Her clutch purse. *Excellent.*

Ryan and the driver were now duking it out on the sidewalk, the driver with a long, scary-looking knife and Ryan with that rope, which on closer inspection resembled a short whip. She didn't see the belt, but he certainly didn't seem to miss it so she figured it'd out-lived its usefulness. With one eye on Passenger Thug, who looked awfully close to overcoming the pain from the gash across his face, she pulled the clutch out and yanked it open.

Her eyes went straight to her key ring. Poor Passenger Thug. He wasn't going to like this one bit.

Snatching the key ring, she dropped the purse to the sidewalk to free up her hands and skittered around the side of the car, her finger on the release button of her pepper spray.

When she was in range, she depressed the button. A cloud of toxic mist hit her target full in the face. Shriek-ing, he dropped to his knees. Avery spun on her heel, her eyes scanning the ground for silver metal.

The gun had fallen partially under the car, close to her felled victim's foot. She kicked his calf hard and when his hand left his face to grab toward her, she hit him with a second shot of pepper spray. Jamming the spray in the jacket pocket, she lunged for the gun.

"Don't move," she barked in a commanding tone of voice she barely recognized as her own.

She wouldn't exactly call her grip on the gun steady, but it was good enough to keep Passenger Thug out of the equation while Ryan dealt with the driver. She was reluctant to look in Ryan's direction to see how he was faring. In movies, that was when the seemingly incapac-itated bad guy made one last move to best the hero, and it was one trap Avery was determined not to fall into.

Easier said than done, though, because out of the corner of her eye, she watched Ryan battle the driver in a blur of movement—a martial artist, spinning and kicking, lashing the short whip over his opponent with an elegant lethal grace that took her breath away.

The driver swiped with his knife at Ryan's middle, a move that proved his undoing. Stepping out of range, Ryan snapped the whip over the thug's wrist and yanked, bringing his opponent's face to Ryan's waiting fist and his gut into Ryan's knee.

With the whip still wrapped around the driver's wrist, Ryan shoved the driver to the ground face-first, jerking the bound hand behind him. Her attention roved to Ryan's face. He wore his usual mask of calm assurance with only the slightest glimmer of sweat on his brow to indicate he'd just defeated two men in a grueling physical battle.

The disparity between Ryan's pricey suit and the raw potency of his movements was a wonder to behold. She sucked in a sharp breath of admiration, becoming suddenly aware that the flush to her skin and her pounding heart weren't only the lingering aftereffects of adrenaline, but of lusty awareness of Ryan's physical power.

Shaking off her ill-timed arousal, she refocused on Passenger Thug, who'd risen to his hands and knees and was making low grunting noises of pain with every exhale. Yeah, he didn't look like he was getting up anytime soon.

When she glanced again at Ryan, he'd planted a foot in the middle of the driver's back and was in the process of zip-tying the whimpering man's hands behind his back.

"Guess you didn't need my paper clips and stilettos after all."

He stood, his whip in hand, the glimmer in his eyes the only element of expression on his otherwise deadpan face. "I miss the stilettos, actually."

He delivered the line with such dry wit, she couldn't decide if he was teasing her or if he really had liked her shoes. Without waiting for her reply, he bent into the car.

She couldn't see what he was doing, but the trunk popped open.

"In you go," he muttered to the beaten and bloody driver as he hoisted him inside.

"What's your plan for these guys?"

"I'm sure their friends will be along shortly to rescue them. If not, then we can make an anonymous call to the cops in a few hours. For now, I think they've earned some quiet time to think about what they've done." He nodded toward the far side of the car. "How's our other friend over there?"

"I got him with pepper spray."

"Ouch. You're hard-core—you know that?" He pocketed the driver's discarded gun and knife, then walked to Avery's side, hands on hips, eyeballing Passenger Thug, who'd finally given up the idea of standing and lay curled on his side. "Pathetic, isn't he?"

"Little bit."

She flinched at the feel of Ryan's hand on the small of her back. "I like you holding a gun. You look like a badass. How does it feel?"

The gun or your hand on me? Because she could get real used to him touching her. "Surprisingly good. I've never held a real gun before."

He tucked the whip under his arm, then eased the gun out of her hand. "No? You're a natural."

She shook her hand out, sort of missing the gun. It really had made her feel like a badass. On a whim, she took the whip from under his arm. "Not quite, but thank you for saying that anyway."

He walked to Passenger Thug and nudged him to

his stomach. The man complied with nary a protest as Ryan twisted his arms behind his back, zip-tied him in the same way as the driver using a tie from his back pocket, then dragged him into the trunk.

Avery ran a hand along the thick braided leather length of the whip. It was unlike any she'd ever seen. Well, she'd never actually seen a real whip in person besides the ones she and her friends had used as props during the pole-dancing class. But it didn't look anything like Indiana Jones's whip, that was for sure.

"At least you have a couple loaded guns again."

He inspected each of the guns, opening the slides, then popping the magazines off. "It's a start."

She gave the whip a practice flick. It was harder to wield than she'd expected and all it did in response to her flick was give a limp wave. "Why didn't you, um, whip this out in the hotel stairwell?"

"Funny." With another one of those almost-smiles she was starting to warm to, he cocked his head to the left. "How did I not know about this side of you? Where has the real Avery Meadows been hiding all these months?"

Flustered, she gave the whip another swish. "I've been here all along." *You just didn't notice me.* "You didn't answer my question about the stairwell."

He set a hand on the open driver-side door. "Too narrow a space, too many men. Plus, I still had my gun at that point, and guns always trump whips."

Words to live by, except... "Not these guys' guns."

He shrugged. "These guys were amateurs. I'm not sure they could've hit us even if they'd pulled the trigger."

She painted a *Z* in the air like Zorro might. "Unlike an actual ICE agent, you sound like you've been in enough combat situations to know which methods work best depending on who you're up against."

"Are you fishing for more information about my skills?"

No sense mincing words now. She whapped him lightly on the chest with the whip. "No. About your past and who you really work for."

His brows flickered and he took hold of the business end of the whip, using it to pull her up against his chest. "You are a lesson in contradictions. You know that, right?"

She splayed her hands on his chest. "I'm a woman. We're complicated."

She'd meant to be flippant, but in reality she *was* complicated, now that she thought about it. So much so that she was making her own head spin. She had big plans for herself and her career—plans that went against everything she'd been brought up to believe in. Plans that scared the snot out of her when she stopped to think about them.

Then there was everything that had happened tonight. On the one hand, she liked kicking butt and taking names, but the guilt of enjoying the fight continued to gnaw at her.

She tried to channel her inner Angelina-Jolie-in-a-secret-agent-movie attitude and offered Ryan a sly, smart expression—because it was either that or rock up to her tiptoes and kiss him. "I suggest you let go of my whip."

He tugged a little harder, crushing her chest to his. "Oh, it's yours now?"

She tugged back, and he released it. "I believe so, yes."

"I guess I'd better teach you how to use it before

you hurt yourself. Good thing we only have one more block to go."

They stopped walking in front of the barbwire-topped chain-link fence surrounding a property lit with security floodlights. Bolted to the fence was a keyed, graffitied sign reading Priced-Right Ship Repair. True to the sign, boats of various sizes and quality were up on blocks amid rusty cranes and metal lockers. Beyond the edge of the warehouse to the left of the property she glimpsed a sliver of water. San Diego Bay.

Her internal GPS had short-circuited sometime during Ryan's confrontation with the thugs, so she hadn't realized how close they were to the water. True, she'd noticed the pungent smell of seawater, but the odor of gasoline, dirt and poverty had overwhelmed her senses.

"Why are we here?"

"I have a safe room here that I maintain for exactly this kind of situation." The gate was locked with a chain and padlock. Ryan spun the padlock face, entering the combination. Not exactly high security.

She studied the shipyard more closely. This looked like a place where bad people hung out and shady midnight deals were made and murders were committed in the shadows amongst the rusty, paint-peeling hulls of ships by nefarious crime lords with names like Keyser Söze.

"This is your secret lair?" She hoped he didn't take her skepticism as an insult.

He pushed the gate open a couple of feet and attempted to usher her through. "No, this is a dry dock shipyard."

She stopped halfway through the gate and took hold of his sleeve, frustrated by his lack of forthcomingness.

"I deserve more of an explanation than that. I need to know what's going on here."

His typical stony expression didn't change, but he nodded. "This is my brother-in-law Fernando's business. My secret lair's around back."

What kind of secret lair was it when a bunch of workers were privy to Ryan's comings and goings? "Doesn't the presence of workers make this place less of a secret?"

"Until I moved to San Diego, I only used the place once a year or so. The workers usually don't pay me any mind because they know I rent the apartment and that I'm Fernando's brother-in-law."

It was more information than she'd expected, and she busied herself trying to assimilate it to what she'd already learned. He had family in San Diego. A brother-in-law meant he had a sister.

Ryan followed her in, then closed and locked the gate behind them. Despite the eeriness of the boats and shadows, she felt safer and released the breath she hadn't realized she'd been holding.

"This way," Ryan said. She followed him left to the back side of the hulking two-story building that looked like a factory warehouse. A motion-sensing floodlight flicked on as soon as they rounded the corner.

Ryan stopped at a nondescript door she assumed was an office. He flipped open a plastic lid to what looked like an electrical outlet on the wall adjacent to the door, then pressed his thumb to the black rectangle inside. A fingerprint scanner. *Fascinating.*

The click of a lock opening broke the silence, and a second metal panel popped open high in the wall, at level with Ryan's face. He lifted the lid and peered inside. The red glow of a laser beam shone onto his face.

His secret lair was locked with fingerprint and retina scanners? Okay, now she felt better. This was the kind of high-tech security system she would've expected from a secret agent.

After a chime, a click told of another lock releasing. This time, it was for the door. Ryan pulled it open. He hooked his upper torso around the corner and pressed his index finger to something on the inside wall. Probably entering an alarm code, if she had to hazard a guess.

"The light switch is on the far side. Hold the door, would you? But wait 'til I give you the go-ahead to come in."

She complied and watched him disappear into the absolute darkness within. After a few seconds, a lamp turned on.

Her shoulders slumped. This was not the secret lair she'd been expecting.

This was a cramped apartment with blank white walls, linoleum floors and not much furniture. And by furniture, she meant the kind of furniture that college students had no problem abandoning when they moved out of their first, roach-infested apartment. Avery was no snob when it came to material possessions, not by a long shot, but even she was leery of putting her butt on the faded red futon that sat against a wall in the living room and faced a small, old television sitting on a milk crate.

Ryan stood with his finger on the light switch, his eyes darting around, first to a feather on the floor, then to a wire strung across the floor like a booby trap that he would've had to high step over to get where he was. This must be a system for checking that no one had broken in, she decided. Despite her disappointment in

Ryan's interior decorating, she approved of his security measures.

Once he seemed to be satisfied that they were safely alone and that no one had disturbed the space, he met her gaze. "Coast is clear. Come on in."

She closed the door behind her and stood there awkwardly, holding her whip, taking it all in while Ryan removed the wire. The air was musty with neglect. Dust coated the table for two that sat on the edge of a kitchenette. Again, *kitchenette* was a loose term to describe the minifridge with a hot plate sitting on it.

Avery scooted another few steps in and, tipping her weight to her left leg, peered through the first door to her right. A bathroom with a roll of paper towels sitting on the sink. She shuffled a few more feet and looked through the second door. A double bed sat in the center of the room, topped by an unmade beige and navy blue sheet set. The only other piece of furniture in the bedroom looked like one of those black leather massage chairs you could buy through SkyMall. She couldn't tell if she was right, though, because it was draped haphazardly with clothes.

A sexy secret agent lair this was not.

"This place looks lived in." She struggled to keep her internal cringe from seeping into her words. "But your address on file at ICE is downtown." *And in a really classy condo building, too. With sweeping views of the bay. And a doorman.*

He tore off a paper towel from a roll sitting behind the hot plate and wet it using a water bottle he'd pulled from the minifridge, then wiped down the table.

"Not what you expected?" His voice held a note of amusement in it. For the life of her, Avery couldn't figure out why. This grimy bachelor pad was in no way amusing.

She looked him full in the face, not surprised to see warmth in his expression. Even those full, skilled lips looked on the verge of smiling as he turned his attention back to his task of wiping down the seats of the chairs.

"I didn't know what to expect." Oh, she'd had some fantasies, all right. Fantasies involving a high-rise condo with walls of windows with sweeping views and a modern leather, glass and stainless steel interior—the decorating equivalent of a perfectly tailored tuxedo. A lair where Ryan could press a button and bookshelves gave way to a hidden weapons stash.

Maybe he hadn't had time to trick out his secret lair. He'd only been in San Diego for six months. She eyed the futon again. "Looks like a bachelor pad, which makes sense because—" she waved the whip at him "—you are a bachelor."

Wasn't he? Of course he was. She knew next to nothing about him, now that she was thinking about it, but he wouldn't have kissed her if he were attached, right?

"That's the idea."

The next instant, he was in her space again. He took the whip from her hands and set it on the table. Then his fingers dipped to the buttons of the jacket, slipping each one through its buttonhole.

"The movies all get it wrong. So do spy books." His rich, deep voice poured over her like liquid heat. "In my line of work, flashiness gets you killed. I worked hard to get this place to look like a bachelor pad, but rest assured, it has plenty of secrets."

At the moment, she didn't care so much about the secrets in the room as she did the secrets of this man. "When do I get to learn about these secrets?"

His lips did that almost-smile again as he pulled the jacket away from her body and gazed down the length of her. Avery wasn't sure why he couldn't let her just keep it, seeing as how all she had underneath was a torn and tattered dress with the broken zipper and beige high-performance undergarments exposed for all the world to see—or at least one very sexy ICE agent. But she couldn't find the voice to protest, not with him looking at her so intensely.

He dropped his hands and tipped his head toward the table. "Have a seat."

Chapter 7

Though Ryan fully grasped the gravity of the situation that had unfolded at the Mira, he was also a hot-blooded Latino man and, therefore, understood that when given the opportunity to spend time with a great-looking woman wearing a skintight dress, allowing her to stay covered up by a voluminous jacket would be the crime of the century.

Seemingly unaware of his eyes on her, Avery settled into a chair at the table, took off the sneakers she'd hijacked and wiggled her toes. Ryan's gaze dropped to her feet. He hadn't been paying her lip service when he'd said he missed the stilettos. She'd looked damn fine in them, even though they'd proved to be a dangerous weapon to a man's family jewels.

He tossed the jacket onto the back of a chair, then loosened his tie and popped the two top buttons of his dress shirt at the collar. Though he enjoyed getting classed up in monkey suits, being comfortable and giving himself some eye candy would go a long way toward bringing him down off the night's adrenaline high and temper his dread at the prospect that Chiara might be slipping through his fingers again.

He cleared his throat, wondering what topic he and Avery should tackle first.

She beat him to it. "Do you live here or downtown?" Her attention flitted through the bedroom door to the bed, then roved to the crate elevating the television.

For the most part, Avery's obvious disappointment in the safe house didn't bother him. There was nothing he could do about the low caliber of the neighborhood or the space's Spartan decor, not when their safety was his only legitimate concern.

He did wish he'd made the bed.

It was a stupid, vain thought because the bed was a decoy. When he'd left the navy at age twenty-three, he'd had to fight the hardwiring in his brain to make up beds so tight and clean a person could bounce a quarter off them. Lovers and hotel maids looked at you strangely if you made beds. They noticed, which was a problem in his line of work.

Ryan's survival hinged on two principles: stay lethal and stay invisible. So he'd forced himself to stop making beds and being overtly fastidious. Over time and with much effort, he'd sloughed off the straight-spined, squared-shoulder walk of a navy SEAL. Despite his height and the physique he painstakingly maintained, he'd perfected the art of fading into backgrounds and living his life like water in a river—translucent, yet always moving, bending around obstacles and over falls, going with the flow.

In the eleven years since he'd commandeered the

spare room in his brother-in-law's shipyard for use as a safe house, he'd rarely spent time there and even more seldom slept there, but he'd learned not to take security for granted. Costuming the place like a messy bachelor pad added an extra layer of ordinariness should someone break through his security and get in. He couldn't afford having an ego about his housekeeping habits, even if the first person he'd ever brought to the place had his libido rattling against the bars of its cage.

"I live downtown. This place is strictly for emergencies." He grabbed a couple of waters from the minifridge, settled in the chair opposite her and handed her a bottle.

She rolled her bottle on its edge along the table. "I was right about what I said on the trolley, wasn't I? You're not really an ICE agent, are you?"

It was a great guess. "What makes you think that?"

She offered him a suspicious, sidelong look. "Are you kidding? You carry gadgets, you're new to the local office, and it's putting it mildly to say that your history in the department is vague. If you really worked at ICE headquarters in Washington, D.C., for twelve years, then why weren't you promoted more? Why are you still a midlevel agent? Especially given your considerable skills."

It caught him by surprise that she knew so much about his faked ICE personnel file. Come to think about it, why had she taken the time to analyze it for weak spots? She was a secretary, for Pete's sake.

Before he could dwell on that, Avery continued, "Plus, you can't deny that it's not regular practice for ICE agents to have secret lairs. I mean, I know your job has an element of danger, but not enough to warrant a safe house. Or am I wrong about that?"

She wasn't wrong about the element of danger for regular ICE agents, but she was wrong about him. Ryan's life was never *not* in imminent mortal peril, and because of that, he had safe houses and backup identities scattered all over the world. But his life wasn't nearly as glamorous as all her talk about gadgets and secret lairs made it sound. As if he were a hero straight out of one of his dad's old Ian Fleming spy books.

"I'm an actual ICE agent." He shoved his hand in his back pocket for his badge and held it out for her to scrutinize. "It's just that my job at ICE is more complicated than most agents."

"More complicated how?"

Of course she'd ask that question. Annoyed that he'd left himself wide-open for that one, he shook his head. "I can't talk about that. But I can tell you that I've worked for ICE for thirteen years. Before that, I was a navy SEAL."

She blinked back. "You were not."

"Uh, why not?"

"Because SEALs don't quit so they can work for ICE."

Not unless they're tapped to join an elite black ops crew, as Ryan had been. "I did."

She narrowed her eyes. He could practically see her internal B.S. meter shooting off the chart. "You want me to trust you, but you're making it really hard."

He knew he was, and he hated that it had to be that way.

Holding his gaze, she leaned forward and set her palm down on the table near him. "I'm going to ask you one more time—am I safe with you?"

It was a reasonable question. Everything she'd asked had been reasonable, intelligent questions. He wished he could've rewarded her with reasonable, intelligent answers. "Yes."

She shifted in her seat, her focus dropping to her water bottle. She cracked the lid and drank deeply. When she set the bottle down on the table again, her expression had gone blank, revealing nothing.

For the first time that night, he couldn't read her emotions through her expression. It was alarming, to say the least. A tendril of desperation snaked through him, to quell her nerves and allay her concerns. To get her to trust him, finally. "I'm sorry I can't say more, but I need you to believe me. Vincenzo Chiara and his network are converging in San Diego right now, and someone in our office is in bed with him. I know you're skeptical, but even if you can't trust me, then at least think about this logically. Please."

He barely recognized his voice for the pleading tone in it. It was hard to remember the last time he had been moved to persuade a person to trust him on faith alone. Had to have been ten years ago, with his sister and brother-in-law.

It was ironic how the universe worked sometimes. That conversation with his sister and brother-in-law was a decade ago, yet the events of that night were directly linked with the trouble Avery had inadvertently landed herself in tonight. And at the heart of all the strife and lethal danger, past and present, was Vincenzo—*Enzo*—Chiara.

He thought about the letter that had come to the office tonight from Paolo Hawk, and dread hit his gut like a lead balloon. It couldn't mean what he thought it did. It just couldn't.

Avery used her hands to push up from the table. She paced to the far wall and flipped up the tacky,

Southwest-patterned sheet he'd hung like a curtain. She barely blinked at the discovery that it, in fact, wasn't covering a window, but a window frame filled in by bricks and mortar and topped by a thick sheet of metal. She kept her back to him, her lingerie showing through the gaping zipper of her tattered dress, her fingers rubbing over the sheet.

A long time ago he'd given up having an opinion on those beige bodysuits women wore under their clothes because they all had them. Plus, by the time he got up close and personal with a woman enough to see the bodysuit underwear, it inevitably meant he was going to get laid, so what man in his right mind would care at that point what a woman was wearing? Not him, that was for sure.

She leaned her back against the wall next to the curtain and faced him. It was his turn to be surprised when she pinned him with a look of steely determination. "We're getting ahead of ourselves," she said in an even, strong voice. "Let's go back to the beginning."

No anger, no fear, just icy coolness. It didn't suit her well. Where was the real Avery? The one who'd squeaked at the first sight of his gun and kept up an ear-splitting shriek the whole time she was issuing a smackdown on Chiara's thug in the stairwell. The paper clip and stiletto-wielding badass secretary. He'd liked that Avery Meadows. More than liked, really.

"Okay. How far back do you want to start?" he asked.

She resumed her seat at the table. "What's in the letter from Paolo Hawk?"

Well, jeez, if she was going to go straight for his jugular, this was going to be one royally frustrating conversation for both of them. "We can't go that far back. Let's start with why you were at the Mira tonight."

"I already told you. I couldn't get my computer to work and I couldn't find the hard copy of the transcript you asked me to email you."

From her tone and body language, it was clear she was either telling the truth or was an exceptionally gifted liar. He seriously doubted the latter. "How do you know file LM1204 is a transcript?"

She worried an edge of the water bottle label. "Because I just do."

Not a good enough answer, but he'd circle back to it after they tackled some of his other questions. "Okay, then, what do you mean you couldn't find the hard copy? Was it not in the file or was the whole file missing from the office?"

"The whole Chiara case file was gone from the cabinet where I put it earlier today. It wasn't in Director Tau's office, as far as I could tell given that his desk was locked, and Agent Mickle's desk was locked, too."

It didn't surprise Ryan the file had been lifted, except there hadn't been all that many people in the office that day, being that it was a holiday.

"The file being missing…you think the double agent stole it, don't you?"

She'd put that together fast. "That would be my best guess, yes."

She nodded. "None of the people who were at the office after I filed the Chiara paperwork are people I'd pick out as a double agent. I've worked with them for a lot of years and they're all patriots through and through."

Funny how easy it was to be blind to a coworker's faults. Ryan's thoughts drifted to his own defunct black ops team. Yeah, he'd trusted every one of those soldiers with his life, trusted their patriotism and service records implicitly—and look where it got them all. "I know it's hard to imagine any of your coworkers like that, but think back. Did an agent at the office leak the details in the transcript to you? Is that how you knew Lassiter's name?"

She fiddled with the hem of her dress. "I'd rather not say how I got the information."

"Avery, please. I need to know who it was."

She rolled her eyes. "Oh, God, no. Nothing like that."

Good to know she wasn't being used as a pawn by whoever the office rat was. That would only put her life in more danger. He had a second hunch. "Does it have anything to do with why you'd memorized the hotel layout?"

She bit her bottom lip and pulled it into her mouth, which got him wishing he didn't know how sweet and soft that mouth felt. He forced his focus back to her eyes. Clearly, she didn't want to say how she knew so much. She probably didn't want to get in trouble with anyone at the office.

He walked to the minifridge and took out two of the chocolate bars he kept there. Chocolate was his favorite food indulgence and as American as his S&W .45. Sure, he knew about Swiss chocolate and French truffles and all that gourmet stuff, but to him, chocolate was all about plain old Hershey bars. He set one in front of Avery and had his own opened before he'd hit his seat.

"You keep chocolate here?"

He shrugged. "I told you this place is for emergencies, right? Sometimes you need emergency chocolate."

She opened her bar and broke off a square, then hummed when it hit her tongue. Ryan liked that hum. He wondered what else he could do to make her hum like that.

She nodded. "You were right. Emergency chocolate should be a critical component of any secret lair."

As soon as her shoulders relaxed a hair, he asked, "How did you get the information about the hotel blueprints and the transcript? This is just between you and me, okay? I won't tell anyone, but I have to know."

She absentmindedly picked at one of the innumerable smudges on her dress near the low plunge of its scoop neckline, unaware of how thoroughly the move commanded his attention. "I have a photographic memory."

His gaze shot back up to her face. That wasn't at all what he'd been expecting her to say. Given her predilection for spy gadgets and secret lairs, he'd thought perhaps she'd been trying to crack the Chiara case herself. He'd always thought photographic memories were the stuff of movies and books. Yet the more he considered the possibility, the more it made sense. "That's how you knew the escape routes in the parking garage?"

"Exactly."

"That's why you know so much about my personnel file and various classified documents?"

"Yes."

Hooyah. Life just got real interesting. He began to piece together the implications of such a gift. They were staggering. "Help me understand this. Does that mean you have a perfect memory of everything that happens to you and everything you see?"

"No. Thank goodness. I've met people with that problem and they never get any rest. If you remembered every detail of every day of your life, that would be horrible."

Ryan couldn't have agreed more with that sentiment. There were too many moments in his life that would've driven him insane if he couldn't have forgotten them, or at least if the stark, vile details hadn't blurred with time. He'd killed too many men, seen too many horrific crimes to hold on to every image and stay sane.

Learning how to let go, how to forget, had been as paramount to his survival as learning how to fire a gun. "You're right about that. Tell me more about your gift."

"You mean my curse? Well, photographic memories vary. The thing with me is that I remember anything I've seen on paper. Words I remember exactly and images in good detail, for the most part. Numbers, I'm not as strong with. And I don't have a perfect memory for people's faces or places I see. There's something about reading it that locks it into my memory. I think of my brain like a computer scanner."

That was a hell of thing. "You think of it as a curse? Because if I could do that, I'd be made in the shade. Do the other ICE agents in the department know? Director Tau?"

"No. No one. Think about it. I'm exposed to matters of national security every day. Look at how freaked out you were when you realized I'd put two and two together about the wiretapped conversation with Louie Lassiter and an unknown man in the LM1204 transcript after seeing it on your computer screen last week. I remember every map I see, every letter I write for the agents, every document I glance over before filing. Tell me that's not a curse. My head is so full of information, sometimes it feels like it might explode."

It all clicked together in his mind. "So you could recreate any document from the office you've seen—right here, right now? The transcript?"

She threw up her hands. "That's why I came to the hotel. Over the phone, you made it sound like the information on the transcript was really important, and I couldn't think of another, faster way to get it to you except to recite it for you in person. And then I got there and you wouldn't stop accusing me of double-crossing you long enough for me to tell you that."

He scooted forward in his chair. Time for a demonstration of her skills. "The part of the wiretap I'm most interested in is near the beginning. Can you tell me that part? Word for word, beginning when Lassiter first mentions the Jade Rose?"

"Sure." Avery closed her eyes and took a deep breath. "Lassiter said, 'The Jade Rose will be ready to transport. Everything's been arranged.' Then the unknown man said, 'Benito?' Lassiter answered, 'Taken care of.' 'And where does Chiara want the trade to take place?' Lassiter said, '337 India.'"

She opened her eyes. "If I'm seeing it correctly in my mind, 337 India Street is an Italian restaurant in Little Italy. Is that where Chiara and this unknown man are going to make a black-market trade of the Jade Rose?"

That photographic brain of hers was incredible. "You're spot-on. We think Chiara must be out of funds, with his two brothers put away for life. The general thinking was that he was going to make one last black-market trade to fund his disappearance."

"And you think the unknown man is the ICE double agent?"

"I do."

"Why? It could be anyone."

"This phone tap was orchestrated by the NSA. It was traced to a four-block radius that included the San Diego ICE office. Add to that some other inconsistencies out of the office that raised a red flag."

"Who's Benito?"

"Benito Giocometti is Chiara's third cousin by marriage. He works at the Mira." It had seemed like such a slam dunk, trapping Chiara here. He should've known catching up with his greatest enemy wouldn't be so easy.

"Do you need me to recite more?"

"That'll do. I don't care what you say—that memory of yours is a gift."

She shrugged one shoulder. "I guess it came in handy tonight."

"It did, but you really put yourself in danger coming to the hotel. That was a huge risk."

She released a frustrated huff. "I know that now, but you weren't supposed to be in any danger because the Jade Rose operation isn't for three days. I understand that you can't tell me the real reason you were at the Mira tonight or what's really going on with this operation, but I think I've earned the right to know something."

Ryan hung a finger on his loosened tie. She was right. But where to begin?

Actually, he knew where the conversation needed to start. Like everything else in Ryan's world, it always went back to Enzo Chiara.

"My job with ICE isn't what it seems."

"I got that part."

He rubbed his neck, wondering how huge a security breach it was to concede his secrets to Avery. He settled on the least personal one. "I'm at the San Diego ICE location because I'm working undercover."

"A lot of the agents in the department work undercover. How is that not straightforward? Ryan, just...out with it, please. Tell me what's going on."

Damn, he hated talking. Maybe because he hadn't learned English until kindergarten and it'd taken him years to master. Even besides that, though, he'd been born without the drive to say too much. He just wasn't wired that way. Sometimes he had to remind himself to contribute to conversations, particularly in social situations because small talk stressed him out. Thank goodness he didn't find himself in many of those.

But he had the feeling that if he didn't convince Avery that she couldn't breathe a word of tonight's setup or the presence of a double agent in the office, she'd go to one of the other agents or Tau the first chance she got—and that was one risk he had to stop her from taking. "Director Tau isn't my boss, not really. I work for Internal Affairs."

Her shock was written plainly on her face, which was a relief because he hadn't liked it when she'd blanked her expression and he hadn't been able to get a read on what she was thinking. "So you didn't transfer to the San Diego office from D.C. for the weather is what you're saying."

"No." He did love the weather in San Diego, and his sister and her family lived there, but the only reason Ryan had picked Internal Affairs was because, after the Lassiter phone tap, IA needed someone in San Diego. Ryan was already headed that way to follow Chiara, so he'd figured IA was a good cover and would grant him all kinds of access he wouldn't otherwise have if he struck out on his own.

His black ops handler, Thomas Dreyer, agreed to the move because he recognized that Ryan was probably the leading authority on Chiara in the world. And more than likely he also knew that Ryan would've chased Chiara to San Diego with or without his permission.

Avery squinted at him. "Let me get this straight. You quit your job as a navy SEAL to work ICE Internal Affairs? That doesn't make sense. Nobody in their right mind would do that. Unless you were kicked out of the navy instead of quitting."

Damn, she was sharp. Nobody would quit being a SEAL to work a thankless job like Internal Affairs, including Ryan. But what he'd done during the twelve years between when he'd transferred out of the navy and when Internal Affairs hired him less than a year earlier was a job he wasn't at liberty to reveal. They didn't call it black ops for nothing.

He'd have to make do with partial truths. "The lifestyle was starting to wear on me. I was ready to settle down."

Avery let out a skeptical scoff. But what he'd said was true, in its own way. Not regarding the SEAL lifestyle, but black ops. Thirty-six wasn't old, not by a long shot, but he'd had enough with living out of backpacks, with his life continuously in danger. In his seventeen years of service, he'd never once had the opportunity to cultivate a sustainable relationship outside of his black ops teammates.

That was the one thing he wished he'd been able to have in his life. A woman. Ryan loved women. He loved everything about them, from their skin to their hair and clothes, to the way they talked and talked and talked—and rarely seemed to care if he said two words in response.

He'd known going into the navy that relationships would be tough to have, but with black ops they'd been downright impossible. Soon he'd be free to pick a place in the United States and look toward settling down. Maybe he'd become an office-anchored ICE agent for real, instead of merely posing as one. Then he'd get serious about finding someone to spend his life with. After he killed Chiara.

Avery was still eyeing him. She chewed her lower lip, looking irritated.

"What?" he asked.

"You're not going to tell me who you really are or why you're in San Diego, are you?"

"I just did."

She rolled her eyes to the ceiling.

Her disappointment in him was unbearable. It wasn't because she was the first person he'd had to dance around the truth with, either. He'd been doing that with his family and his lovers for a long, long time. But for whatever reason, he hated that he couldn't spill his guts to Avery. Probably because she was so clearly a worthy partner. If she set her sights on it, she could have a long and illustrious career as an agent for any of the federal agencies, including the CIA—her aversion to guns notwithstanding.

The realization of how poorly she was utilizing her God-gifted skills frustrated him all over again.

"Believe me or not," he said, "I need your word that you won't tell anyone my suspicions on the double agent or tonight's setup. Both our lives might depend on it."

"I still find it hard to believe that someone I've been working with for the past six years is a double agent."

There was no good response for that. He didn't have the authority to lay out the evidence to her, and even if he did, he wouldn't, the information was so top secret. So he fell back on his old standard response. He shrugged.

"I'll promise you that I'll keep my mouth shut, but the truth is I won't need to tell anyone about the setup. Every law enforcement agency in the country probably knows what happened at the Mira tonight. There were explosions and gunfire in a heavily populated building. They'll find bodies."

"Maybe, maybe not. Chiara has cleanup men who probably got to the bodies before the cops could."

He was banking on that, in fact. "How much do you know about Enzo Chiara?"

"Everything I've read in briefings." At his prompting, she continued, "The three Chiara brothers are Italian black-market mercenaries. The San Diego ICE office hadn't been directly involved with the Chiaras until last year when we were the U.S. contact point for the capture of Nico and Leo in Panama. You were a part of that operation."

Ryan squelched a flinch at the realization she knew of his involvement. Her photographic memory was going to take some getting used to. He ought to stop guessing what she didn't know and instead sit back and let her fill him in. She seemed to have far more intel on the investigation than even some of the agents Ryan worked with.

"That was a highly classified capture. Are you saying paperwork that included a list of the ICE agents that had been involved came through the San Diego ICE office?"

"No. That part was a lucky guess."

He laughed. Calling her a lesson in contradictions had been putting it mildly. Avery Meadows hadn't stopped surprising him since the moment he'd laid eyes on her at the Mira bar. For a jaded operative like him, that was saying something.

Avery was one smart cookie. She wasn't going to be pacified by pat answers and half-truths. She took in all the information he told her and assimilated it with the millions of bits of intel already stored in her huge filing cabinet of a brain—seamlessly, effortlessly. What she didn't know, her intuition filled in.

It was a dangerous and brilliant combination. Despite her bubbly, joyful disposition, he'd do well not to underestimate her again. It sucked that such a fascinating woman had come into his life at the worst possible time. He was on the verge of something huge. His life's only true goal. There was no time for romance. No time to explore the person who'd captivated him in every way. No time for him to indulge in selfish desires.

He looked at his watch. "It's two o'clock now. I'd like to be back on the road to the office by five to get that letter out of your car. That would give you three hours to sleep if you thought you could."

She snorted, amused by the suggestion. "Absolutely not. You?"

"No. Which is a good thing because I need to figure out how much the office and local law enforcement know about what went down at the Mira or if anything was captured on security cameras."

"How are you going to do that? Do you have a secret satellite system and police scanner in this place?" She looked around, her expression telling him that she couldn't fathom any high-tech equipment in such a dumpy bachelor pad.

He felt a smile tugging at his lips. "I do. Since you can't sleep, perhaps it's time for a little show-and-tell."

The truth was he'd been looking forward to this ever since she'd spied that unmade bed. No, that wasn't accurate. He'd actually been looking forward to this moment since she'd first uttered the words *secret lair*. That combined with the heated gaze she'd given his decoy grenade, the way she'd stroked it and…oh, man. He'd never been jealous of an explosive device before.

He realized he was probably giving her the wrong impression to mention show-and-tell, then walk to the bed, but she'd get the right idea soon enough. He scooted the bed away from the wall a good three feet, easy enough with its cheap metal frame, until there was enough room to flip the area rug off the trapdoor below it.

He'd fitted this door with the same fingerprint recognition lock as the door to the hideout and so pressed his thumb to it. Avery's shadow darkened the closed trapdoor as the lock clicked open.

"You have a secret basement?"

Man alive, he loved the hushed reverence in her voice. It made him feel about ten feet tall.

"I do."

After straddling the lid, he raised the looped handles and pulled, lifting it completely off the basement entrance. He set it on the bed and got down to the business of enjoying Avery's reaction.

Eyes wide, she edged toward the hole and peered into the darkness.

He slid close to her, close enough to study the curve of her spine. Without thinking, he touched the broken zipper of her dress and let his fingertips bump over the row of teeth. This was a bad move, being this near to her, taking her to see his arsenal. He should command her to get some rest or give him some space so he could think with a clear mind. But he didn't want space. Right now what he wanted—almost as badly as he wanted Enzo Chiara dead—was to see that blazing look in Avery's eyes and the flush of her cheeks that she'd had when she'd touched the decoy grenade.

She twisted to look at him over her shoulder, her expression wary but intrigued. "What do you keep down there?"

"Like I said, a police scanner, satellite communications equipment, guns, other weapons…gadgets."

Her brows flickered. "Are you mocking me again?"

Jeez, she really didn't trust him. She'd asked that before and he could tell it was a pet peeve of hers, this unsubstantiated notion that he was patronizing her. He could see how she might think that, but the reality was he found everything he'd learned about her tonight, including her fascination with gadgets, intoxicating. Addictive.

He tipped his head toward the basement door. "Come on down and see for yourself."

Chapter 8

Like Avery could handle this night getting any more surreal. Sure, she'd been a tad disappointed that Ryan's hideout didn't sync with the image in her overactive imagination, but she'd settled into the idea that maybe the night's surprises were over so she could catch her breath and regroup.

Yet there she was, descending a ladder into a hole in the floor of Ryan's bachelor-pad secret lair to see who knew what. Police scanners and satellite communications equipment? Guns and gadgets? She still couldn't decide if he was serious or teasing her.

A light flicked on. When she reached the last rung on the ladder, she hopped to the ground and turned. Ryan was perched against a metal table in the center of the room, a proud gleam in his eyes. "Is this a bit more like what you expected my secret lair to look like?"

Her eyes swept from one wall to the other, taking it all in. "Maybe."

Totally.

Racks of gleaming weapons lined the walls, artfully illuminated by recessed lighting. Not only guns of all shapes and sizes, but swords and knives, throwing stars and whips.

"You didn't squeak."

She wrenched her gaze away from the sword she was staring at to look at him. "What?"

"Squeak. When you saw all the guns, like you did in the stairwell."

True, she hadn't, but her heart pounded high and fast in her chest at the realization she was surrounded by dozens of lethal weapons. She was light-headed, flushed and couldn't decide if the firepower was more frightening or arousing—which didn't exactly make her a model of calm collectedness. Despite the tornado of emotions inside her, she figured *fake it till you make it* and pressed her hand to the wall, leaning into it, nice and casual. "Maybe I'm getting used to being surrounded by all your big guns."

Nice one, Avery. Real smooth.

Ryan poked his tongue into his cheek, making it look like hard work to keep from smiling. "Doubtful."

From a lower cabinet, he pulled a large black plastic container. "My police scanner doesn't get reception down here, so I'm going to go upstairs and listen in. You're welcome to stay and, uh, browse, if you want."

"Are you going to check your voice mail, too?"

"Not yet. I'm sure there's a way for Agent Tau and the other ICE bigwigs in town to check if I've listened to my messages. I'm not ready for them to know that I'm aware that something bad went down tonight."

"They knew you were at the Mira, even though you were technically supposed to be done with your surveillance by the time the gunfire started. Were you supposed to check in with Tau when your operation was over?"

"Yes, it's protocol to leave a voice mail check-in with the kind of routine ops like tonight was supposed to be, but I'm prepared to face the consequences by not calling in a timely fashion, because there's no way I'm saying anything to anybody until I have a better handle on what we're dealing with, not even to my bosses at Internal Affairs."

"Makes sense to me. I've never been called in for middle-of-the-night emergencies at the office, so it might look suspicious if I check my messages."

"Good plan." He hoisted the black box through the basement opening and slid it onto the ground-level floor. "I'll be back," he added, climbing the ladder.

She watched his firm, perfect backside and waited until he'd disappeared before releasing a whistle of admiration under her breath.

Damn, that man was fine. And now she was alone with his massive arsenal. She spun in a slow circle, taking it all in. She wanted to touch everything in this room, explore every drawer and cabinet. It made her pulse race and a coil of heat settle between her thighs just thinking of doing that.

What was it about weapons that called to her in such a visceral way? Why did she see so much eroticism, so much raw sexual maleness, in the stainless steel and carbine? It had to be because of her upbringing. There was nothing more taboo in her house growing up than these objects of destruction—objects of power. For that reason, they became an integral part of her rebellion and endlessly fascinating.

Wasn't that what desire was all about? Power. Fascination. Wanting what was forbidden.

She skimmed her palm over the nearest rack of guns, all pistols and revolvers. A sleek silver pistol caught her eye. Yes, if this were her collection, this would be the gun she'd choose to carry. Perhaps in an ankle holster. She liked the idea of the gun strapped to her, rather than in a purse or a pocket.

With a glance at the basement trapdoor, she lifted the pistol from the rack. It was lighter than it looked and fit perfectly in her hand. She pulled the slide back like she'd seen Ryan do, then pushed it closed. She repeated the process several more times, getting faster and smoother with each. Maybe she would get that gun. When this was all over, she'd consider it.

She'd never purchased one, fearing that it would feel dangerous to sleep under the same roof as a gun, but now the idea of learning how to shoot, how to protect herself, was taking on a whole new allure. Making a mental note to ask Ryan the make and model of her new favorite gun, she replaced it on the rack.

Her focus strayed to a row of drawers. She pulled open the top one to reveal canisters that looked like decoy grenades and smoke bombs, each cylinder nestled in thick gray foam.

The middle drawer contained all sorts of bindings—handcuffs, zip ties and coils of rope. She lifted a pair of handcuffs and squeezed, contracting the ring with a *zing* that pierced the silence. She raised her gaze to check the trapdoor and found Ryan staring at her, his gaze intense. Hungry.

Her breath caught. "Hi."

"Find anything you like?"

"Yes, actually."

His attention lowered to the handcuffs she held. Feeling her cheeks heat, she replaced the cuffs in the drawer and closed it. "What did you find out from the scanner?"

"They didn't find any dead bodies in the hotel, which wasn't a surprise, and it doesn't look like any of Chiara's men were taken into custody either, which is disappointing. The local news is reporting that at least ten civilians were injured from shrapnel and falling glass when Chiara's men blew out the Mira's windows. I hate that. Collateral damage."

He shook his head and, for a moment, seemed lost in thought. "At least it sounds like the grenade I threw didn't hurt anyone. There was some structural damage, but that's about all, which is a relief."

It said a lot about the kind of man he was that he cared so deeply about civilian injuries. Yet another aspect of his spirit that drew her in and left her wanting to get even closer to him. "Yes, it is. I'm so glad no bystanders were killed."

"That makes two of us. With all that happened at the Mira and the possible connection to Chiara, I bet the ICE office is all hands on deck. Just to see if anyone picked up, I called the office main line and Tau's office line using an untraceable cell phone. No one answered. I tried Mickle's direct office line, too. Nothing."

"Maybe they're all on scene at the Mira investigation."

"Possibly. So what do you think of my secret basement?"

"Your guns are beautiful." Mental smack. He was going to think she was a head case, calling his manly collection something effeminate. "I mean, so macho." Smiling her repentance at her poor word choice, she turned toward the wall and smoothed her palm over the long, thick barrel of the nearest rifle.

Ryan's heat enveloped her as he came up close behind her and brushed his body against her backside. His hand splayed over the curve of her hip. "You like this one?"

"Yes."

He captured her wrist, pinning it to the rifle. "This is a Remington XM2010 sniper rifle. If you want to talk about things of beauty, I think it's one of the most beautiful weapon systems in the world. I was lucky enough to receive this prototype as a gift."

He had some major connections to be given a Remington prototype. And not just any prototype—a sniper rifle. A gun with only one purpose. A shiver rippled through her. How could something so deadly be so arousing? Was she sick in the head to find its power seductive?

Moved to explore this side of her in the safety of Ryan's basement, she leaned back into Ryan's solid body. "Tell me more about this rifle."

He covered her hand with his and guided it along the length of black metal. "This stock is an aluminum high-performance chassis system—precise, sophisticated, sleek. This part of the stock is called the rail."

"I thought it was called a barrel."

He moved her hand farther out and wrapped her fingers around the thinner tube nearer to the tip of the rifle, then drew her grip back toward them along the smooth, cold metal—a stroke that was unmistakably wicked. "This is the barrel. It's free-floating in the stock. Twenty-two inches with a one in ten twist rate."

Avery had no idea what a one in ten twist rate was, but if he kept crooning the rifle's stats to her in that low rumble of a voice as they fondled the weapon together, she was going to turn into a puddle of lust at his feet.

He was so near to her that he had to notice she was breathing hard; he had to feel the need pouring off her. She felt him, that was for sure—his body heat, his breath on her neck, his arousal pressing into her backside. Her inner sex kitten purred to life.

He shifted their joined hands to the underside of the stock and bumped along the skeletonized metal. Hands together, they cupped the metal box sitting to the right of the trigger.

"This is the magazine, right?" Avery couldn't believe how throaty her voice was, how thoroughly it betrayed her desire.

He hummed, the vibrations tickling her ear. "Correct, but not just any magazine. This is a five-round detachable magazine that takes three-hundred-caliber Winchester Magnums, or what we call three-hundred Win Mags."

Magnums. Even the ammo sounded sexy and masculine.

An unwanted wave of guilt rippled through her. Had this rifle been used to kill someone? Had Ryan killed with it? How could she want a part of a lifestyle that involved death and violence? But there was something inside her whispering that she was meant to do this, meant to live in a world of shadows, danger and covert operations in the name of national security.

That's why she'd taken the job at ICE. That's why the number one thing on her bucket list was to assist in the capture of an international criminal mastermind. Not because she actually wanted to live in a movie or some kind of James Bond fantasy world, though it was fun to imagine, but because she recognized the poetry in the power, the necessity of the existence of a group of highly skilled secret operatives moving about the world, doing what needed to be done to protect innocent people from those who would destroy them.

She didn't know why, but she knew she was supposed to be a part of it.

She moved her hand over the trigger and curled her finger around it. She'd never touched the trigger of a gun before, and the sensation made her shiver again.

Ryan rubbed her hip. "Are you okay?"

"What I dream for myself, it scares me."

"Everything worth going after in life should scare you a little, don't you think? Otherwise, what's the point?"

She agreed with that sentiment and had reminded herself of it many times since taking the job at ICE. Still… "Sometimes it scares me a lot."

"Then why do you want it?"

She moved her hand lower and wrapped her fingers around the thick, corrugated metal grip. "*Want* isn't the right word. The danger, the chase, the secrets, being one of the good guys taking down the world's evil forces—it's what I crave. What I've always craved."

"Why?"

"It's a long story."

He dropped their joined hands and threaded their fingers together, holding tight. "Tell me anyway. I want to know you."

Said in that velvety voice, his words conjured all kinds of illicit fantasies about all the parts of her body she wanted him to know. She let the words curl through her like a tendril of smoke, inviting her confidences. "When I was in sixth grade, my parents let me walk to the library by myself for the first time. Someone had left a spy book on the table, so I picked it up and started reading. Whoever set it there had no idea that they changed a little girl's life."

His hand continued to rub her hip in slow, mesmerizing circles. "What book was it?"

"The Hunt for Red October."

"Ah. That's one of my father's favorites."

"It's a great story. After that, I consumed every book I could find about espionage and secret agents. I couldn't get enough of the stories of dashing heroes and brave heroines saving the world. My parents didn't believe in going to the movies, but in high school, I ditched school and snuck into one. I had to because it was based on one of my favorite books. Want to take a guess?"

"A James Bond movie?"

"Good guess, but no. *The Bourne Identity.*"

He huffed. "That was the first movie you ever saw? What religion were you raised in that you weren't allowed to go to the movies?"

"Not so much a religion, but a spiritual philosophy. My parents are activists, leaders of a pacifist movement. My brothers and sisters and I weren't allowed exposure to violence of any kind. Not even water guns."

"You're kidding. Like hippies?"

"Yes. Buddhists and pacifists, really, but they jokingly call themselves hippies all the time. I don't want you to think my parents or their beliefs are simple or naive. They're not. In a lot of ways, how they choose to live is a lot more complicated than the average person. Their world is as black-and-white as yours, but opposite."

"They must hate your job."

They didn't know about her job, and that was exactly why. Because she knew they'd be outraged and deeply, personally offended by her choice. She waved off his comment. "Anyway, after all I'd read, when I watched that movie, I was hooked."

"Then I'm sure you saw the second Bourne movie."

"What about it?"

"Espionage and law enforcement aren't all fun and games. Bourne's love interest dies in the second movie."

"You're trying to remind me of the danger? Because I already know. I get it, even more so after tonight. But I need this for myself anyway. I don't fully understand why, except that it's human nature to want what's forbidden."

That last word hung in the air between them like an electric charge, loaded with implication. She wanted this man. She had no idea who he truly was or why he was in San Diego, and the details he had revealed to her didn't add up, but she wanted him nonetheless. In a bad, bad way.

"Ryan…"

His lips brushed over her hair. His hands caressed her hip. "I know I told you to call me Ryan, but I kinda wish you'd go back to calling me Agent Reitano. Just temporarily. It'd really play into this fantasy I'm working on right now."

So she wasn't the only one grappling with explicit fantasies at the moment. The realization gave her a heady thrill. "In this fantasy, I'm guessing you're the agent and I'm the criminal. And you're going to give me a long, hard interrogation."

He rewarded her remark with a wicked chuckle that vibrated through his chest into her back and made her wish she was facing the opposite direction so she could see what he looked like when he laughed. "I was thinking more like I was the seasoned, experienced agent and you were the ingenue."

The light touch of his lips on her hair became kisses on the skin above her earlobe. She reached up and back to slide fingers along his stubbled cheek and into his hair.

"I want to show you something else."

Grinning, she shifted her hips, letting him know she felt his other big gun back there and was totally on board with him showing her something—as long as that something involved him. With a lot fewer clothes on than he presently wore. That would certainly help them pass the time until dawn.

Tugging on her hand, he guided her away from the wall.

With her eyes taking inventory of the way his muscles played beneath his clothes, she let him lead her to the row of drawers she'd been caught rummaging through. Not what she expected, but no problem. "Are you getting some handcuffs so you can properly arrest me, Agent Reitano?"

Though he smiled, his eyes were dark and serious. "You know what I want?"

"Tell me."

"I want you to trust me."

The charge in the room fizzled. She took back her hand. "We're back to that?"

His dark eyes glowed with heat. "I had you pinned to the wall. My mouth on you. I could've taken you right then and there. And you would've let me."

So much for the fizzle; her pulse-pounding arousal was back in full force. He was right. She would've let him. She would let him still. The truth shocked her.

"So I know you trust me." He fingered the strap of

her dress, then pushed the strap and her bra strap over her shoulder and brushed the backs of his fingers over her bared skin. "You're too savvy to let me this close to you if you didn't."

With a shiver, she closed her eyes but snapped them right back open. *Focus, Meadows.* It was impossible to think clearly with him so near, so she stepped sideways and slipped away from the table, pulling the dress's strap up as she walked to the far edge of the room. She ran her hand along the ridged side of a sand-colored rifle. "Then you have your answer. What else do you want from me?"

"So many things, Avery." The rasp in his voice spoke of endless wicked promises. "But first, I want you to admit that you trust me. I want you to say it out loud."

She whirled around to face him. "Funny. I want to know why you really quit the SEALs to do this. And why an Internal Affairs investigator for ICE has a secret underground lair filled with military-grade weapons. I don't seem to be getting those answers, either."

Except for a slight flare of his nostrils, his face was a mask as he stared at her. Then, with a sharp inhale that seemed to break him from his statuelike state, he opened the nearest drawer and withdrew a bulky watch.

"You and I have something in common. We both grew up loving spy books and movies. My father immigrated to the U.S. when he was twenty and was obsessed with watching *I Spy* and *Mission: Impossible*—all those spy TV shows of the nineteen sixties—and Ian Fleming's James Bond books were some of the few Spanish-language books our local library carried. Needless to say, spies and secret agents were a big deal in my house."

"Where did your father immigrate from?"

"Argentina. Both my parents did."

As he spoke of his family, the hint of a Spanish accent crept into his voice. *So that's where he got those dark good looks from. His Argentinian heritage.* She desperately wanted to ask him to say a few lines in Spanish, but something held her back. Probably the knowledge that if he went all Latin sex god on her, she'd lose her perspective on trust.

Instead, she said, "My parents immigrated from Portland, Oregon."

He took the bait. A hint of a smile graced his lips. "Why did they move to San Diego? It seems like Oregon would be the perfect scene for them."

"Being grassroots activists for peace in Oregon is like preaching to the choir. They wanted a challenge, so they picked a military town."

"I know I'm repeating myself here, but you're kidding, right?"

If only. "Nope."

"I kinda want to meet your parents now."

That'd be the most awkward introduction in the history of daughters bringing guys home to meet the folks. Even if he kept his guns and badge at home, everything about him radiated lethal prowess. "They would hate you."

"We'd have to lie about my job, like you lie to them about yours."

Dang, he figured that out fast and with no help from her. "That's a lie of necessity."

"What do they think you do?"

She debated the efficacy of coming clean, but then she figured what the heck. It wasn't like there was any harm in this particular truth. "They think I'm the personal assistant to a celebrity philanthropist."

A chuckle burst out of him. At her reproving glare, he cleared his throat. "Sorry. I guess we could say you're an undercover secretary."

"I guess I am."

"Which celebrity?"

She knew he was going to ask that, but she wasn't up for more laughs at her expense. "I made a name up, and I'm not going to say what it is."

"Okay, next question. Why the philanthropist part?"

"It was the only way to keep my parents from lecturing me on the evils of celebrity and Hollywood."

"Your parents are extreme. What are we going to tell them I do?"

"Their hearts are in the right place." She gestured to the watch. "What's that for?"

He cocked a brow. "A redirect? But not a very smooth one."

"Yes, well, I'm new to this whole secret agent spy business."

He gathered a lock of her hair and twisted it around his finger. "But you're a fast learner." She shifted her gaze from his hand to his eyes, letting him see the heat she was feeling. Telling him without words that there were some things she was already good at and she was more than happy to show him.

Clearing his throat, he released her hair and held up the watch. "My father gave me this watch when I graduated from high school. He and I weren't the best communicators, but we watched tapes of his spy shows together and traded paperback spy novels. It was our language. And after I graduated, during the two weeks before I went to boot camp, he pulled me aside from the huge party he and my mom threw me. He gave me this."

She hummed, wishing he'd keep talking so she could

listen longer to that slight Spanish accent his voice took on when talking about his parents. The watch wasn't much to look at. A boxy black Quartz with a face block and leather band. Yet, it clearly meant a lot to Ryan, so she studied it intently, trying to look impressed. "That's a wonderful story, and a really special gift."

He snorted through his nose. "I know what you're thinking. It's just an ordinary watch. And not a remotely good-looking or expensive one. But get a load of this." He pressed a button on the watch face and the right edge of the face popped off with a click. He gripped the loosened plastic and metal between his fingers and pulled, revealing a thick wire cable.

Avery felt her eyes widening, her lips smiling. "Your dad gave you a gadget watch."

"It was the first real spy gadget I'd ever seen. My dad was so proud that he'd found it. There are times I wish I were wearing it, like in the stairwell at the Mira, but it's the most valuable possession I own, so I would never use it in combat unless I was out of options."

She reached out to touch the watch, and he handed it over willingly. Under the guise of studying it, she considered whether she believed him or if he was manipulating her with fake intimacy. Zach had done that. Yet her gut was telling her to trust Ryan. Really, she already did, didn't she? He'd been right about her letting him get close to her, about allowing herself to go off the grid with him and giving herself permission to sleep with him.

She made to hand the watch back, but he held up a palm. "I'd like you to hold on to it for me. As a promise that we're a team in this. A token of my trust. You'll keep my secrets. I'll keep yours. And we'll help each other get through our current situation."

If he was telling her the truth about the watch's sentimentality, then that was a heck of a demonstration of trust. She pressed the button, then pulled the cable. "How are we going to go about getting through our current situation? And don't say *very carefully*."

"If Chiara figures out who you are—and I think it's only a matter of time until he does, if he hasn't already—then you won't be safe until he's off the street. Since that's my objective, too, that's what we have to accomplish. Very carefully, of course."

"How are we going to do that? What's our next move, besides getting the letter from my car?"

"We need to figure out what Chiara's next move is toward stealing the Jade Rose and who in ICE is trying to silence me. And I think the clues might already be in your head, though you might not realize it."

There it was—the catch. He wanted to use her for her photographic memory. That's what this watch trust was all about. Then a terrible possibility came to her, one she should've considered before she let her backside get all cozy with his front side. She set the watch on the counter and took a step back. "Were you coming on to me so I'll help you with the missing files?"

He blinked, like he hadn't expected her to call him out on his deception. "No. I came on to you because you're hot, smart and funny." He picked up the watch and held it out to her. "But I'm asking you to hold on to my watch because I want you to help me."

He thought she was smart and hot? She felt more like a hot mess tonight, but she'd take it. Still… "Funny?"

"Don't underestimate the importance of funny. There's not nearly enough funny in the world."

He said it in his typical deadpan style, except that she didn't miss the hint of world-weariness behind his words. Whatever his history was, whoever he worked for, she knew with absolute certainty that he was someone who'd done and seen too much not to be changed by it.

Did she really want a life like that for herself—a life that would change her, harden her? She looked at the watch, then past it. To Ryan, then the walls of guns and weapons that surrounded them. She took a long look at the sleek silver handgun she'd decided to buy.

The night's events were changing her. Ryan and this room were changing her, peeling her layers off, reaching inside her spirit to the most elemental part of her— the part that longed for adventure and subterfuge, the fierce, ambitious woman she felt like on the inside but had been too scared to embrace.

Her bucket list wasn't just some flight of fancy. It wasn't simply a game she might play with her friends over margaritas, like dreaming up a list of celebrities they'd like to be stranded on a deserted island with. There were things she wanted to accomplish in her life. Places she wanted to see. Goals she wanted to meet so someday she wouldn't look back on her life and have regrets.

She was starting to wonder if she was shortchanging herself by not pursuing a career in law enforcement or at a federal agency. Not that being a secretary was undesirable in any way. She loved being a secretary. But the thrill of danger and rush of adrenaline she'd experienced tonight were energizing.

If she could let go of the guilt and shame for wanting this element in her life, then she'd consider looking into a career change. Perhaps she'd become a private investigator, or perhaps she'd apply for a job with the CIA. Surely they'd be interested in someone with a photographic memory. It would mean coming clean to her family about what she really wanted out of life, but just as she was learning to embrace her fascination with weaponry, she was feeling bolder about standing proud as her true self.

She took the watch in hand once more. She couldn't deny this was what she'd always wanted. Already, she'd crossed one thing off on her bucket list, thanks to Ryan—getting her very own piece of spy equipment. Okay, so the watch wasn't hers to keep forever, but it was hers right now, if she accepted his bargain.

There was another item on the list that she just might get the chance to cross off. Maybe. If she was lucky. Even the slight possibility of it made her dizzy with anticipation. She wanted to drive a powerful, dangerous man crazy with desire for her. She'd decided in college, after a tepid fling with an immature classmate had left her thoroughly disappointed in the male gender, that every woman deserved to be lusted after by a real man. A man of substance and power and chivalry. Wouldn't that be the day.

Her attention drifted over Ryan's body as he filled a handgun's magazine with ammo. This particular dangerous man found her smart, hot and funny. He loved her dress and he'd approved of her shoes. The universe was clearly trying to tell her that this was the opportunity she'd been waiting for to do some serious damage to her bucket list—and perhaps change her life forever.

She strapped the watch to her wrist. "You have yourself a deal."

He braced his broad, large hands against the counter and perused the watch for a long, silent moment.

She let her gaze rove over those huge hands, then up his thick, tan forearms roped with muscles to the rolled sleeves of his dress shirt, which strained against bulging triceps, across bulky shoulders to his neck. That disheveled businessman look he had going on with the white dress shirt and tie really rang her bell, but now that she was looking at the sheer size of him up close, she thought it a wonder that he found a dress shirt able to button at the neck, with sleeves wide enough to fit his arms.

Maybe there was some kind of men's clothing store for suave and impossibly ripped secret agents.

"We're a team from here on out," he said.

She snapped her gaze to his eyes. His expression was dark and intense, like she imagined he'd looked when he stood behind her at the gun rack, giving her a tour of his sniper rifle with his hand.

"Are you on board with that?"

She pushed the release button for the cable and it popped out with a snap. Pulling it out, she felt another layer of artifice peel off her, revealing a brand-new Avery who was saucy, strong and ready to kick criminal mastermind butt. Ready to trust Ryan. She looked into the eyes of her new tall, dark and droolworthy partner. Who thought she was hot.

"Absolutely."

Chapter 9

Despite housing an arsenal that would defend against a zombie apocalypse, Ryan's secret lair lacked a surprising number of basic covert ops necessities—like spare clothes or a mode of transportation. Hence the safety pins now holding her dress together and the two of them skulking down the sidewalk carrying license plates and a screwdriver.

"This is a bad idea. Are you sure you don't have some kind of secret agent car stashed in the shipyard? Or maybe a Ducati?"

Ryan glanced at her over his shoulder, his eyes smiling with an *oh please* amusement. "Negative. And I don't know what you're talking about. This is a great idea. I've always wanted to drive a pimpmobile."

Where had he been hiding this dry sense of humor all these months? Before last night, she had no idea he even knew how to crack a smile. Maybe having his life threatened brought out the best in him. Smiling to herself, she hastened her step to keep up, letting her eyes drift over his clothes, which—besides being impossibly-ripped-secret-agent size—looked normal and businessman-like. But beneath his dress shirt he wore a shoulder holster carrying a pistol and a knife. His whip was back in place against his hip, his pockets held another gun and extra magazines and yet another gun was strapped to his ankle.

She'd tried to convince him to let her carry her favorite silver pistol in a thigh holster, but though he'd wolfishly admired her legs when she had suggested it, he'd refused her request. Something about her being more likely to shoot one of the two of them accidentally than doing any good in a clinch situation.

He had a point. So they'd compromised, which was why she was loaded down with a variety of gadgets in the suit jacket, in her underwear and in the concealed belt she'd strapped around her ribs.

True, the word *concealed* wasn't all that accurate since the decoy grenade, flashlight pen and belt were clearly visible beneath the thin, clingy fabric of her dress, and, yes, she'd have to practically put on a striptease to access the gadgets, but she was planning to ask him to swing by her apartment before heading to the office, and while there she could pick a better covert ops outfit and shoes that actually fit.

The so-dubbed pimpmobile was sitting exactly where the thugs had stopped it. Ryan slowed his pace, his gaze sweeping the area. She didn't see it happen, but the next time her attention passed over him, he had a gun in his hand, aimed at the ground.

When they were a few car lengths away, he raised his left hand, two fingers up. "Stay here."

With a crouching sidestep, he approached the back of the car, then peered through the rear window. After he'd walked a complete three-sixty around it, he gestured her over. He holstered his gun and handed her the screwdriver. "You get busy with these and I'll get our friends out of the way."

She set the spare license plates on the ground and unscrewed the original front plate while Ryan unlocked the car and popped the trunk.

From the rear of the car, she heard Ryan sigh. "I thought for sure your friends would be along to help you. It's kind of embarrassing for you to still be in here like this."

She kept loosening the screws, but now she was smiling as she did it. That dry wit of his was her favorite discovery tonight, even more so than his martial-arts combat moves or secret basement.

The men shouted obscenities at the top of their lungs until two loud, low thunks—flesh hitting flesh, if she were to guess—shut them up like a mute button. That wiped the smile from her face.

She kept forgetting this violent side of Ryan. He was so witty and suave that it was easy to ignore that she'd watched him break a man's neck with his bare hands. He didn't scare her, so she didn't understand why her hands were now shaking as she worked the screwdriver. It was almost as though being so close to all that potent lethal power was overwhelming. Not from fear or even arousal—like the sniper rifle had been—but because it was all too much to process.

That was it. If she stopped to think about what Ryan was truly capable of, what she was figuring out that she was capable of, it was too much to deal with for one night.

In her periphery, she saw Ryan drag the men onto the sidewalk. Then his legs appeared next to her before he lowered into a squat by her side. "I'll take it from here. Go on and get in the car."

She was grateful to hand the screwdriver over. *Don't look for them,* she told herself as she walked to the passenger side, fearing that he'd snapped their necks or killed them, too. But she looked anyway. The men were crumpled together in a heap hidden by a scraggly bush between the sidewalk and the cinder-block building behind it. They didn't look dead, just unconscious, but then she had to wonder if she could really tell the difference.

She stood in the open passenger-side door with one leg in. "Did you kill them?"

Ryan stood, two license plates and the screwdriver in his hands. "No."

Nodding, and confused about why she was so relieved at his answer, Avery lowered herself into the car and watched Ryan go around back to repeat the switch of the rear license plate.

In minutes they were on the road. The car was obnoxiously loud, tricked out with one of those altered mufflers designed to set off the alarms of every car it drove past. Ryan left the hip-hop music on but lowered the volume.

"You wanted to get to the ICE office by five, but it's only four-fifteen."

"Sounds like you're going to ask me something."

She was that obvious? "Yes. I was wondering if we could swing by my apartment."

"Come again?"

"There's something we need to do. Something important."

He kept his eyes on the road, his expression flat. "That's going to have to wait because I plan on taking my time."

Oh, my.

He let her stare at him for several seconds before flashing her a sidelong glance. Time for her to come up with a cheeky rejoinder befitting a smart, hot and funny femme fatale. She opened her mouth. Yeah. She had nothing.

Out with the truth, then. "I have to feed my cats." And cue the embarrassed cringe. That particular gem sounded way worse aloud than it had in her head.

It took him a little time to process what she was saying. Then he punched the radio off. "Cats?" he spat.

Clearly, he was not into this idea. "Yes, cats."

She felt ridiculous asking, but she hadn't fed them since yesterday morning before she'd left for the office, and she had no idea when they'd again get the chance. She'd waited until they were in the car because she figured he'd have less time to change his mind about it.

"Can't you get one of your neighbors to do it? It might not be safe for us to go there if Chiara somehow figured out your identity."

"That's all the more reason why we should be the ones to do it. I'd never put one of my neighbors or friends in a potentially dangerous situation. What if they went to feed my cats and the bad guys thought they were me? Besides, while we're there, I can change clothes. I don't care how big a fan you are of the dress, I can't go around looking like this for the indefinite future."

He released a labored breath and she knew she had him.

"Cats?" he repeated.

"Are you allergic or something?" She was filled with a brief, all-consuming panic at the idea. She needed a man who could be around her cats. It was her one deal breaker. She couldn't give up her babies, even for the hottest guy she'd ever kissed. Then she gave herself a hearty mental smack. She and Ryan were not an item. Temporary crime-fighting partners, yes, and hopefully another more intimate kind of partners, too, when the time was right, but when had she started to think about him romantically in a long-term sense of the word?

"I don't think I'm allergic to anything, but I don't know. It's not like I'm around cats all that much. More like never."

"I can't just abandon them when the going gets tough. They're my babies." She cringed again. "That makes me sound like a crazy cat lady, doesn't it?"

She smiled outwardly while inside she girded herself for him to deny her request because it was too dangerous. Her cats had dry food and plenty of water so they'd be fine for another day, but she hated the idea of leaving them neglected for too long.

They pulled up to a stoplight. He shifted in his seat to give her a good, long look.

Please don't think I'm a crazy cat lady....

In the glow of the streetlights, Avery's blond hair cascaded around her face and shoulders, framing her pleading eyes, full lips and fantastic rack. Damn, she was hot. She was much more than that, though.

Ryan drank her in, searching his brain for the right word to describe Avery Meadows.

Vivacious. That's what she was. Every single thing about her world was loud with life and light, despite the violence and crime presently swirling around her and the dangerous turn her future had taken. More than her super memory, that was her real gift.

The kicker was that she hadn't asked for any of this. Last night, when he'd called her at the office, she'd given up her New Year's Eve plans because she'd wanted to help him with a case, yet she'd walked smack into the middle of a deadly international battle ten years in the making.

What he planned to do was put her under a guard watch until the danger had passed. He still needed the help of her photographic memory to get the clues to find and kill Chiara, especially if the files at the office really had been stolen or destroyed, but Avery could help him with that from a safe distance. After he'd checked the police scanners, he'd reached out to the only two operatives he trusted implicitly. They were on their way, but wouldn't be arriving until that evening.

Until she went off the grid with his friends, out of harm's way, Avery's safety was Ryan's responsibility. So if she needed to feed her cats to be on board with her new on-the-run-from-danger reality, then Ryan was going to have to figure out a way to make that happen.

"All right. Here's the plan. We're not going to feed your cats." She opened her mouth, looking like she wanted to protest, so he raised his finger to silence her. "Instead, we're going to grab them and go. We can take them to one of your friends' houses. That way you won't have to worry about them. Got it?"

It was probably a tell that the idea of caring for pets was foreign to him. Moments like this made him more starkly aware of how far outside normalcy his world was. He hadn't lived a normal, civilian lifestyle for almost eighteen years and it showed in everything he did and thought.

While he didn't have anything against pets, the idea of putting their lives in danger over animals was outrageous. His black ops crew would die laughing if they found out he'd agreed to walk into a lethally threatening situation to care for cats.

"Got it. Thank you. Jump on the freeway here. My apartment's only a few miles away."

On the green light, he continued through the intersection, then up the on-ramp, planning for a high-stakes cat extraction.

He'd been involved with dozens of high-stakes extractions. Of witnesses, kidnapping victims, undesirables being taken into custody—all kinds of grab-and-go missions as a black ops agent. So, really, this was no different. It'd probably be easier because they could grab the cats, shove them into a bag or whatever people did with them and scram. No explanation needed, no soothing scared, innocent people. It ought to be as easy as pie.

Chapter 10

Ryan circled the block in which Avery's modest, tropically landscaped apartment complex sat, on the lookout for any red flags that signaled danger. He wasn't taking any chances that Avery's identity had been made, though he doubted it.

Even Chiara couldn't move that fast. Criminals' ability to identify unknown individuals in a matter of hours while on the run from authorities only happened in movies. Even if Chiara had an ICE agent under his thumb who would recognize Avery or some sort of super hacker with advanced facial recognition software under his employ, they'd still need a clear image or video of Avery to make the ID.

And since Chiara had taken pains to clean up the bodies of his employees that Ryan had left in the stairwell, then there was a good chance he'd made sure the hotel surveillance cameras weren't functional.

After three loops around the streets surrounding Avery's complex, he followed her instructions and parked in one of the empty, unmarked spots near the stairs leading up to her apartment. They sat, watching and listening, for another few minutes. The complex was quiet, with nearly every curtain or blind within view drawn tight. No surprise for predawn on New Year's Day.

In the spirit of not being caught without a firearm again, Ryan was armed to the teeth. With his hand on the S&W in his pants pocket and his head on a swivel, he followed Avery over a palm-tree-lined walkway between two buildings, then up a set of stairs and into the second level hallway.

They moved in brisk silence, and Ryan was impressed once more by Avery's aptitude for reading the tone of a situation and adapting accordingly. Ryan estimated they'd be back to the car in less than five minutes.

The moment Avery's key touched the lock of the third door on the left, the crying and calling began on the other side of the door. Cats. Sounded like a good six or seven them. That's when he realized he'd forgotten to ask her how many she owned. *Damn.*

The kind of cats Ryan was most familiar with were feral cats, those that prowled the darkened streets of third world countries, moaning in heat or wailing with battle cries. The kind that flocked like pigeons to discarded food and carried all manner of diseases. Avery's cats sounded so similar to feral cats, he half expected to see a pack of mangy, flea-bitten mongrels waiting for a handout.

"So much for stealthy," Ryan muttered as Avery turned the key in the lock.

She offered him an apologetic smile and shouldered the heavy door open.

The pair of cats that greeted them was about as far from feral as a china plate was from paper—identical, sleek, thin Siamese with humongous blue eyes. They didn't startle and scatter at the sight of Ryan but remained wholly focused on Avery.

He couldn't blame them. He wished he could remain wholly focused on her, too. When she made to enter first, he stopped her with a hand on her arm. Removing the .45 from his pocket, he high-stepped over the cats, his eyes sweeping the room.

To her credit, Avery didn't squeak at the sight of his gun. She didn't show any outward reaction at all. Maybe that sniper rifle therapy they'd engaged in had helped her acclimate to Ryan's weapon of choice.

Rather than leave Avery vulnerable in the hallway, as soon as he'd determined the girlie living room done up in pinks, greens and whites posed no immediate threat, he motioned her in. She eased the door closed behind her, and he could tell she was working hard to do so quietly, as if the incessant mewling of her cats weren't enough to alert any would-be assailant of their return.

He stared down at the two cats, who'd moved on from adoring Avery to wind around his legs. He thought the deal with cats was that they were aloof and untrusting of strangers. Maybe he'd been misinformed. And maybe he'd already spent way too much time thinking about cats instead of his mission. With a little shake to clear his head, he scooted past them, toward the kitchen.

"You stay here," he said to Avery.

Gun at the ready, he moved through her apartment. Both cats tried to follow, so Avery tackled them and held them under her arms like baguettes, which neither seemed to mind.

After a methodical sweep behind every door and piece of furniture, he returned to the living room, holstering his gun, satisfied that her apartment was free of both assailants and explosives. Sighing and looking relieved, Avery set the cats down and they immediately rushed to Ryan again, ready to resume their exuberant greeting.

"Trusting, aren't they?"

With a flirtatious toss of her hair, she shed the suit jacket and dropped it over the back of the sofa.

Ryan nearly growled his approval at the sight of her body in that dress again. He loved women with her body type—curvy and strong, like he didn't need to make them a protein shake so they wouldn't float away.

Perhaps she sensed his bold appraisal because color spots appeared on her cheeks. "Ryan, meet my boys, Aston and Martin."

Amusement tugged at his lips. She really had it bad for spy stuff. What he couldn't figure out was how in the hell, for six long months, he'd overlooked the smoking-hot secretary with the wicked sense of humor and a love of all things spy-related who was sitting right across the office from him. He'd be lucky if he didn't get his man card revoked for that boneheaded oversight.

It was too late for them to embark on any kind of short-term affair now. The flirtation was fun, and if she was game, he'd love for the two of them to do something about the sexual charge that permeated their every moment together, but by this time next week, he'd be in the wind. No matter how fond he was growing of her.

"Of course your cats are named Aston and Martin. It

was either that or Shaken and Stirred, right?" he asked, pointing to each cat in turn.

She flashed him a look of mock indignity. "Shaking and stirring are only for my cocktails, thank you very much."

She'd certainly shaken him up and got his blood stirring, but it wouldn't do to mention that at the moment. The clock was ticking.

He was about to say as much and urge her to get a move on when another lightbulb went off. "That's why you told your friends my name was James."

There were worse compliments than being compared to James Bond, even though to Ryan, the world's best fictional secret agent character would always be John Steed from *The Avengers,* his dad's favorite TV show.

"I don't know what you're talking about," Avery demurred.

"Of course you don't. Let's get these cats packed up and get out of here."

Her focus darted to the microwave as though checking the time. Using her teeth, she drew her lower lip into her mouth to chew on.

Clearly, she had something on her mind. "What?"

"Any chance I have time for a fast shower?"

It was Ryan's turn to check the time. Why he didn't say no was a mystery. Honestly, it blew his mind that he was considering her request. Until eight months ago, he was a Spartan. A warrior with nothing in his mind or in his heart except the will to fight for justice and hunt down Chiara. And a Spartan was what he still needed to be—until the threat Chiara posed to Ryan had been neutralized permanently.

He was so close to completing his mission. So damn close. Sometime in the next three days, Enzo Chiara was going to make a mistake. Ryan had to be there to pounce. After ten years of failed attempts, this was his last good chance to kill his enemy. It had to work. The alternative turned his stomach.

With so much on the line, what was he doing rescuing cats and lingering in an apartment that was a potential bull's-eye for trouble? Why was Avery Meadows so hard to say no to? He sucked in a lungful of air and let it out slow and steady. Daylight was in thirty minutes.

Something soft brushed his leg. He looked down at the cat, then up at Avery, who was all elbows, twisting and turning, trying to undo the safety pins holding her dress together. Her brows were scrunched, her lips puckered as she strained. Simply, utterly vivacious.

"How fast a shower can you take?"

Fifteen minutes—and the fastest shower Avery might have ever taken—later, she felt a hundred times better.

She'd changed into black, formfitting yoga pants and a long-sleeved baby-blue T-shirt under a short-sleeved black T-shirt, the better to hide her concealed carry belt and other gadgets. The lack of pockets left her with nowhere to stash one of the flash-bang grenades, so she made a home for it in her bra, right between her boobs.

Socks and sneakers completed the outfit. Wearing comfortable clothes didn't seem to be something that Moneypenny or Pepper Potts ever considered, but Avery didn't want to fight crime in a pencil skirt and heels. She'd tried that, and while the result had been effective, it didn't seem like a viable long-term plan.

Ryan was waiting at the door, frowning down at the cat carrier, probably because Aston and Martin were making a racket for the record books, protesting with loud, moaning cries the indignity of being trapped.

Avery handed Ryan a tote bag full of toiletries and some changes of clothes.

He slung it over his shoulder, eyeing her outfit. "Are we going to the gym?"

"This is my crime-fighting wear." She faked a karate kick. "The better to kick bad guys' butts with. Also, it'll make me more incognito."

"That outfit is about as incognito as your dress was."

"Exactly. That was incognito for a night on the town. I fit in with the New Year's Eve crowd. Today's the day everyone hits the gym because of their New Year's resolutions. I'll fit right in."

"Nope. Not even close."

What was that supposed to mean? "Well, I'm fresh out of camouflage, so this will have to do."

"Fair enough." He picked up the cat carrier and led the way out to the hall while Avery locked up behind him.

The courtyard her apartment looked down into was quiet. So were the other residences. Being that it was before dawn on New Year's Day, there was no reason for the average apartment dweller to be up at this time unless they were only just stumbling home. Given the ratio of elderly in her complex, Avery seriously doubted they'd run into any all-night partiers.

Ryan wasn't letting his guard down, though, and she was wise enough to follow his lead. With him doing his secret-spy shifty eyes and gripping the gun stashed in his pants pocket, they retraced their steps to the parking lot.

She supposed Ryan would've wanted them to be sneaky, but Aston and Martin weren't keyed in to the whole mortal danger factor of their rescue mission and kept up their earsplitting cries all the way from Avery's apartment, through the hall, down the stairs and along the walkway.

Only a few steps from the turn into the parking lot, a man rounded the corner.

Avery's heart sank at the first glimpse of the male form, and she nearly ran into Ryan's back.

"Mickle. What are you doing here?" Ryan's body was beyond tense. Out of the corner of her eye, she saw him tap his shoe to his ankle, where she knew he'd strapped a gun before they'd left his lair.

Avery peeked around Ryan's side. Lawrence Mickle stood in the center of the walkway, his legs in a wide stance and arms crossed. Not for the first time, it struck Avery that he looked every one of his forty-five years. The wide, slanted angle of his eyes set atop huge bags of puffy skin and cheeks that sagged, pulling down the corners of his mouth into an unintentional frown gave the illusion that he was always disappointed. Or maybe it wasn't an illusion. She could see how working in Homeland Security would wear a person down.

"The surprise is all mine, Reitano," Agent Mickle said. "I was coming to check on Avery."

She had no earthly idea why he'd be at her apartment complex—unless he was the double-crossing agent and Chiara's men had tipped him off about her involvement in what had gone down at the Mira. For the first time since Ryan had confessed to her his double-agent theory, Avery seriously considered the possibility that he might be right.

Agent Mickle had been with the San Diego office for twenty years and was an excellent ICE agent—the top dog in the office, who always got his man. Avery liked working for him. He was polite, organized and never made unreasonable demands. He'd been assigned as

Ryan's partner, and as far as she could tell, their styles complemented each other well.

Yet Ryan was unwilling to share his true purpose in San Diego—or last night's trouble—with Agent Mickle. Suddenly, she wished she'd pressed Ryan more for the details of who his list of suspects included.

She was still debating what to say next when Ryan spoke first. "Why would you do that?" His tone had gone icy.

Agent Mickle raised his hands, palms out in a gesture of surrender. "No need to get testy. She'd told us she was going dancing downtown last night and with all the violence within blocks of where she said she was going to be, everyone was worried. She didn't answer her cell or home phone when Director Tau called, and her car was still in the parking lot this morning. I think a better question is, what are you doing here with her?"

Avery's stomach twisted. Without overthinking it, she grabbed Ryan's hand.

It took some coaxing for it to soften and mold to hers, but she made it happen because there was only one possible explanation she could think of giving Agent Mickle for her and Ryan walking out of her apartment together in the wee hours of the morning.

Wariness clouded Mickle's features as he zeroed in on their joined hands. "When did this start?"

"None of your business," Ryan said. She darted a glance at him. His body was statuelike, his eyes narrow. If looks could kill, Agent Mickle would've fallen to the ground and his spirit would've left his body.

Instead, though, Agent Mickle gave a hard laugh. For partners, Agent Mickle and Ryan sure weren't acting partnerly. Avery scrambled to smooth things over. She let go of Ryan's hand and slid her arm around his waist, then toyed with a button on his shirt, draping herself on him like she was the cover model girlfriend to his pro-football player and they were posing for paparazzi.

"We try to keep our personal life personal. You know how it is," she said.

"Why were you at the office this morning?" Ryan asked Agent Mickle. "We're closed today."

"That's rich, Reitano. You're a real wise guy, acting as though you're not aware of the code-red situation we're in, like you weren't at the Mira last night. You never called the office to let us know what was happening. We got notified of the situation by the local police, for Christ's sake. For all we knew, Chiara took you hostage. What the hell is wrong with you, leaving us high and dry like that?"

"My surveillance detail ended at ten, just like it was supposed to."

"What code red situation?" Avery asked for the sole purpose of hearing Agent Mickle's take on it.

"Gunfire, as well as several secondary explosions and outbreaks of gunfire. Nine civilians and a security guard were injured."

"Oh, my God," Avery faked. "Has the Department of Homeland Security ruled out terrorist involvement?"

"Not yet, but with it happening at the same location that we suspected Chiara would be attacking in three days' time, the thinking is that it's the ghost himself at work."

"The ghost?" Avery asked.

"Enzo Chiara," Mickle provided. "The one Chiara brother no one can catch."

She felt the liquid fire in Ryan's veins, in the stiffness of his body—the frustration that he, too, had been unable to apprehend Chiara.

Into the yawning silence, she asked, "Any fatalities?"

"No, thank goodness."

It still shocked Avery that Enzo Chiara had the manpower on hand in San Diego to chase Ryan and Avery all the way to Club Brazil, yet hold enough men back to dispose of the evidence and bodies at the Mira. She should've expected nothing less from one of the most wanted men in the world.

"Did they catch anything on security videos?" Ryan asked.

That was another great question, one he and Avery hadn't been able to answer on their own via the police scanner or local news.

Mickle wiped his palm across his chin. "No dice. This was a premeditated act all the way around. The cameras in the hotel and parking garage were destroyed. All the first responders found on the stairwell were bloodstains splashed with bleach and two men, alive but woozy, zip-tied to a drainpipe down the hall from the hotel room you and I reserved for Saturday. What a coincidence, right? And get this—one of the two men was a deep-cover FBI agent."

"You're kidding," Ryan said. The emotionless way he said it, Avery knew those were the men who'd jumped him in the hotel room and whom he'd neutralized—but not killed, thank goodness. The presence of an undercover agent brought up a whole mess of questions Avery planned to ask Ryan as soon as they were alone again.

"Wish I was kidding. The police have bystander cellphone film footage and photographs coming out of their ears, and they're sifting through it as fast as they can. I'm confident that we'll find the clues we need to put together what happened." He ran his tongue along the inside of his lower lip and leveled a steely look at Ryan. "Unless you want to fill me in."

Avery's stomach took a dive. Mickle knew they were there. He was baiting Ryan. Another thought occurred to Avery. It was within the realm of possibility that Ryan was the person who'd destroyed the surveillance cameras at the Mira ahead of time. If he was working outside the purview of his job, then that would make sense. He wouldn't want ICE monitoring his movement. She added it to the list of issues to ask him about.

What she and Ryan were doing now, lying straight to Mickle's face instead of coming clean about their presence at the hotel, meant that if footage of them was found, they wouldn't have any wiggle room to get out from under a cloud of suspicion.

Then again, they had more immediate problems than being spotted on video. Her thoughts curved back around to wondering what Agent Mickle was doing at her apartment, really. Would altruistic concern really prompt an agent in the middle of a code-red event to visit the office secretary's apartment to check on her? Avery seriously doubted it.

All this covert ops stuff was making Avery's head spin again. None of it made any sense, unless, of course, Mickle was the double agent.

"So, the office is open right now?" she said.

"With a situation like this, you're damn right it's open." He nodded to Ryan. "We haven't been able to reach you. What happened to your phone?"

Ryan didn't skip a beat. "The battery's dead. I forgot to charge it before we went out last night."

"Mmm-hmm." Mickle didn't sound convinced. He flipped the tail of his jacket open, revealing a handgun in a belt holster, and fingered the grip of his gun. "I just want to make sure Ms. Meadows here isn't taken advantage of or put in danger. Would you like to drive with me to the office right now, Ms. Meadows?"

So she was Ms. Meadows now? That was awfully formal. He was definitely suspicious of Ryan, accusing him of being a danger to Avery. Perhaps that was why Agent Mickle's suggestion creeped her out and raised chill bumps on her arms.

She stretched her lips into a plastic smile. "That's sweet of you to worry. But Ryan's doing a great job keeping me safe." She patted his chest for emphasis.

"Ryan," Agent Mickle muttered in echo.

Ryan muscled past Agent Mickle, thumping him with Avery's tote bag as he passed. "We have a stop to make, then we'll report in at the office. Let Director Tau know, would you?"

Avery attempted to follow Ryan into the parking lot, but Agent Mickle clamped a hand around her upper arm. Tight. She sucked in a sharp breath.

"I think you should come with me. There're things going on here that you don't know about, and I'd hate to see you get hurt," he said in a whisper. The concern in his voice was believable, reminding her that secret agents didn't earn the title by being bad liars.

"Get your hand off her," Ryan growled in a tone more menacing than she'd ever heard it.

The cat carrier and tote bag he'd been holding were on the ground, and Ryan had assumed a slight crouch that Avery knew was his fighter pose. Agent Mickle must've recognized it for what it was, too, because he released his grip.

He stepped around Avery and got right up in Ryan's face, his right hand continuing to caress the grip of his holstered gun. "You're a jealous prick, you know that, Reitano?"

Ryan loomed over Mickle by a good half a foot, fury in his eyes, every solid, powerful inch of him an alpha soldier who could snap men's necks with his bare hands. "Then don't give me anything to get jealous about."

Avery wasn't sure what warning the two men were giving each other, but she was certain both knew jealousy had nothing to do with the tension crackling between them. Agent Mickle thought she should be afraid of Ryan. Truthfully, looking at Ryan now, she wasn't sure why she wasn't. Except that she knew with her whole heart that he'd never focus that lethal, violent side of himself on her.

She only hoped that he remembered the advice he'd given her. *There's a time to kick butt and a time to stay cool.* This was definitely a time to hang back. Actually, it was a time to get moving. She was ready to be away from Mickle's judging, disappointed eyes.

She walked behind Ryan. "Time to go," she said in a quiet voice, smoothing a hand over his back.

Though his attention didn't stray from Agent Mickle as she passed, he made a stiff gesture toward the parking lot. "Ladies first."

Mickle followed them to the car and watched Ryan set the cat carrier in the backseat.

"That's your car, Reitano? Jeez, I knew you were a cholo punk at heart, but a pimpmobile? That's real classy of you." He let out a hard laugh. "No wonder you never drive it to the office."

She could feel the waves of aggression rolling off Ryan as he swung the passenger door open for Avery with stiff movements, as though the effort to keep from pummeling Mickle took everything he had. She wouldn't have blamed him if he did. Heck, she wanted to pummel Mickle for playing the race card, goading Ryan into snapping with a cheap shot below the belt.

Agent Mickle crouched to look at Avery through the passenger door before Ryan had a chance to close it. "You call me if you get in a jam, okay? Call me if anything at all comes up."

Ryan slammed her door in Agent Mickle's face.

"There's something not right about you, Reitano," Agent Mickle said in a loud voice. "And I'm going to figure it out. I know you had something to do with what happened at the Mira. Consider yourself warned."

Then Ryan was behind the wheel, revving the engine. He threw the gearshift in Reverse and shot back quickly enough that Agent Mickle had to jump out of the way.

Chapter 11

Aston and Martin were not fans of being in the car. Ninety-nine times out of a hundred, car rides meant vet appointments, so they made sure Avery and Ryan knew how displeased they were at the proposition with a constant stream of meows at the top of their lungs.

Probably not the most stress-reducing sound for Ryan to listen to while he got his emotions in check after the confrontation with Mickle, but there was nothing she could do about it.

She watched her apartment complex grow smaller in the side mirror, wondering when it would be safe enough for her to return, if ever.

"What are you thinking, Avery?"

His tone and the question threw her off. His voice was soothing, speculative, not that of a man who'd been on the verge of exchanging blows with his coworker. "Agent Mickle's onto you."

"Not even close. He'll never figure out who I really am or why I'm in San Diego."

Neither will I. "Are we really going to the office today?"

"I don't see any way around it. I need that letter."

"Why is the letter so important?" She knew he wouldn't tell her, but she had to ask. She had to remind him that, for a partner, he was doing a lousy job keeping her in the loop.

He swabbed a hand across his forehead. "I can't get into that. How about you tell me where we're going to drop off these cats so I can hear myself think again."

Ten minutes later, Ryan watched from the side of the car while Avery pounded on Kristen's bedroom window after her several doorbell rings had gone unanswered. "Krissy? It's Avery. Wake up."

Finally, a groggy, wild-haired Kristen with raccoon-eye makeup answered the door. Behind her stood Charlie. They both looked like they'd had the time of their life the night before and had the hangovers to prove it. When Charlie realized who was at the door, he muttered, "It's just you" before he plodded away, presumably back to bed.

"Hey," Kristen croaked. She looked down at the cat carrier. Aston and Martin hadn't shut up since the moment they'd seen Avery that morning and now was no exception. They cried and whined at Kristen and poked their noses through the airholes. "You brought me cats. Why? Everything okay?"

"Everything's fine. So sorry to wake you up, but I have a huge favor to ask."

Kristen rubbed her eyes, smearing her mascara farther down her cheeks; then she blinked past Avery. "Oh, my God." She straightened, perking up fast. "It's that guy you were with last night. James."

It took Avery a second to remember the pseudonym she'd called Ryan by at Club Brazil. "James. Yes."

Kristen squinted at him. "What kind of car is that? It looks like something Snoop Dogg would drive."

"I'm pretty sure Snoop Dogg doesn't drive himself around. I bet he's got an entourage for that. And I know James's car is strange, but he's hot, so we're going with it."

Kristen gave a thumbs-up. "Totally."

"So…here's the favor. James and I are going away on an impromptu trip together, like a minivacation." It was a line she'd worked out on the way over and she prayed that Kristen didn't ask too many questions. Avery pointed to the cat carrier. "Can you watch my boys? Pretty please?"

Kristen probably would have thrown more of a diva fit about Avery waking her up at five in the morning on New Year's Day to watch her noisy, high-maintenance cats, but Avery could tell by Kristen's shifty eyes that she was fully aware that Ryan was watching. "Fine. But you owe me."

She grabbed Kristen in a hug. "Thank you, Krissy. This means a lot to me."

"Can I go back to bed now?"

"Let me say goodbye to them." She opened the top of the carrier and gave each of her boys a scratch on the head. "Be good for Auntie Krissy."

She moved the carrier into Kristen's living room along with the bag of food she'd snagged from home. "I'll call you with an update of when I'll be back."

"Wait a sec, don't you have to work? And what about

him? Doesn't he have a job? God, Avery, tell me he has a job."

Avery walked back onto the front step, chewing the inside of her cheek as she debated what to say. "We work together."

Kristen perked up fast. She grabbed Avery's sleeve, her eyes as huge as her smile and her hangover clearly forgotten. "He's an ICE agent? I've been telling you for years to hook up with one of the agents you work with."

She didn't bother to mention that Ryan was the first unmarried agent she'd been attracted to. No time for that. "Yep. I finally listened to you. I realized I could use a week of hedonism."

"After what you went through with Zach, you deserve a *year* of hedonism. Have fun. I'll watch Aston and Martin as long as you need."

She gave Kristen an extra squeeze and thank-you, then bounded to the car.

"Hi again, James," Kristen called, giving a flirty little wave. "Take good care of my girl."

Ryan, leaning against the driver's side, waved back. "I'll do my best."

When Avery reached the car, she looked across the roof and smiled at Ryan. Her favorite twitchy-lipped almost-smile was dancing on his face. It hit her that he'd probably never be the kind of man to out-and-out smile or fill a house with laughter—he simply wasn't that kind of effusive personality—but she was learning his subtle expressions, and she took pride in how often she'd been able to lighten his look.

Could she live with a man so reserved? And, more importantly, why was she bothering to ask herself that? Yes, she liked him. She liked him a lot, actually. But she had no idea how the next hour was going to play out, much less the rest of her life.

Ryan pushed away from the side of the car, hunching into the hands he braced on the roof. She allowed a quiet hum of pleasure to escape her throat at the sight of his forearms. She'd never really considered a man's forearms as sexual, but she wanted to work her mouth over every inch of his arms and outline the ropes of muscles with her tongue.

To distract herself from the sudden rush of arousal, she asked, "What are you smiling about?"

He pressed his lips together, fighting a smile so hard that she wanted to scream at him to relax and let it out already. "A week of hedonism?"

So he'd heard, then. No big deal. After all, she *did* deserve a week of reckless, crazy love and fun with a hot guy. Every woman did. "It was all I could think to say. And it worked, didn't it?" She sank into the passenger seat before he could check out the blush she felt rising on her cheeks.

He slid behind the wheel, turned the engine over and pulled away from the curb. "You know, a week of hedonism ranks number one on my bucket list."

Avery swung her face in his direction so fast it was a wonder she didn't get whiplash. "You have a bucket list?" *And a week of hedonism is at the top of it?* But she was too chicken to add that last part.

"You mean a list of things I'd like to do before I kick the bucket?" At her nod, he added, "Of course. Don't you?"

Avery's bucket list had evolved since she and Kristen had sat on Kristen's pink ruffled bed in seventh grade and wrote out their lists with cherry-scented pencils.

Her list was as important to her now as it was then. "Ryan, you're living my bucket list."

Snorting softly, he navigated onto the freeway toward downtown and their ICE office. "Since I'm not living a life of hedonism, you must have a different list than I do. Being an ICE agent tops your list?"

"Not exactly. It's a long story. No need to get into it." After their crazy-cat-lady field trip, he'd think she was nuts for sure.

"We've got about ten minutes until we get to the office." He glanced her way. "I want details."

"Then I'll expect details about your list in return."

"Deal."

She took a calming breath. "I'll tell you, but don't laugh, okay?"

Hitching his elbow on the center console, he frowned at her. "You worry about that a lot."

"What?"

"Being mocked or made fun of. What's up with that?"

She gave it some thought. She hadn't put it all together how often she guarded against being ridiculed, but he was right. She worried about being ridiculed all the time. But she couldn't help it. Some experiences were so emblazoned on a person's spirit that they couldn't break free of them.

How could she not be wary after a childhood of enduring her classmates' teasing because of the type of clothes she wore or how her hair was styled because she knew next to nothing about modern pop culture? She hadn't consciously realized she'd held on to those insecurities, but apparently she was still far more sensitive than she'd been conscious of.

"When you're a kid and you get an invitation to a

birthday party at McDonald's and your parents RSVP by sending the birthday girl's parents a scathing letter about fast-food slaughterhouses, you get a little sensitive about being made fun of."

"Yikes. That really happened?"

She nodded. "Let's just say that was the last invite I got until high school from anyone outside of the other families in my parents' political party."

"What happened once you got to high school?"

"I got a job, so I had money of my own, and I turned into your standard teenage rebel, except that being a rebel in my family didn't mean drinking, drugs, sex and piercings, but—"

"Let me guess. Wearing leather and joining the Republican Party?"

His guess was so spot-on, she laughed out loud. "So, then, you have met my family?"

His chuckle was so quiet, she might not have heard it if she hadn't been so tuned in to Ryan's every nuance. He rubbed her outer thigh with the back of a knuckle. "Except you never turned into a full-blown rebel."

She looked at his hand, wanting to hold it. To thread her fingers with his long, thick, masculine ones and absorb his heat and strength. She folded her hands in her lap to keep from indulging in the urge. "How do you know that?"

"Because you still haven't told your parents where you work."

He wasn't going to let that drop, was he? Yes, she understood what a spineless wimp it made her that she hadn't fessed up to her folks about her dreams or career, but that wasn't anybody's business but her own. She cleared her throat. "Back to my bucket list. I already told you how my secret-agent fascination started, so the top thing on my list is to assist in the capture of an international criminal mastermind."

She braced for a snort of amusement or worse, but he nodded pensively. "Chiara qualifies as that, and you've already been a big help to me. What else?"

She rubbed the watch on her wrist. "I've always wanted to own a spy gadget."

"This is a banner night for your list, isn't it?"

"I'll say."

"Is there more on your list?"

Since the third item on her list involved a dangerous man and crazy desires, she decided it was time to turn the tables. With a shrug, she said, "What? You don't think that's enough? What about your list? Tell me about it."

He snorted, then wedged his hand between her clasped ones. He brought her left hand across the center console and kissed the back of it, much to her fluttering heart's surprise. "If you're going to be a spy, then your powers of redirection are going to need to get more subtle."

"I'll have to work on that in spy school."

He lowered her hand to rest on his leg but didn't let go. She wiggled her fingers, getting comfortable in his solid, warm grip. And it was like her whole body took a cleansing breath and relaxed. She really did love holding his hand.

The car slowed to a stop on the freeway off-ramp, then he turned toward the office a mile or so away. "You're in spy school right now. Field training 101."

"Back to your bucket list, Mr. Redirection."

His eyes got that smiley look again. "My bucket list isn't all that ambitious. Not like yours. A week of hedonism with a beautiful woman tops the list."

"You're such a guy."

"That's not on your list?"

It hadn't been, but she was adding it now. Indulging in hedonism would be a fine way, indeed, to spend a week. "A week of hedonism, sure, but I'll pass on the beautiful woman part. What else is on your list?"

"One of my dreams is to take a vacation that involves sitting poolside with a drink in one hand and a book in the other. Not exactly hedonistic, but it sure would be nice."

"You've never done that?"

"Nope. Not even close. The only time I jump into a pool is for underwater physical condition and combat dive training."

He sounded tired when he said it. Tired like a man sorely in need of a vacation. "What else is on your list?"

He gave a noncommittal shrug and turned right into a narrow alley two blocks from their office.

"Come on—you can tell me."

He turned off the engine and let go of her hand to remove the keys from the ignition. Avery bit her bottom lip, fighting for patience not to press him. After a quiet exhale, he pinned her with a look of sheer, raw conviction. It was, perhaps, the first real glimpse she'd gotten of Ryan's vulnerability. Her breath caught in her throat.

"Marriage. Buying a house." He shook his head. "I don't know if I can. I don't know if this job has left me enough of a good man to—" He swallowed and looked out the windshield. "Anyway, that's the whole list."

Avery studied his profile—the hard plane of his forehead, the stubbed angle of his nose. The marriage comment had her all fluttery and on edge for reasons she didn't have time to wonder about.

"That's on my list, too." Which was true, even

though it was way down at the bottom of the list along with the other things she wanted but couldn't control.

Bucket lists were all about being proactive, about making goals and following through. Finding someone to spend the rest of her life with wasn't like that. She didn't want to force it or go after eligible bachelors like a heat-seeking missile to a target, as she'd witnessed with some of her friends over the years. When she fell in love in a forever kind of way, she wanted it to happen because both she and the man she was with couldn't fathom life without the other. Not because she was trying to cross something off a list.

With another labored swallow, Ryan opened the door.

"Why are we getting out here?" Avery asked.

He grabbed the screwdriver from the cup holder. "I hate to say this because I've grown fond of this car, but it's time to ditch the pimpmobile."

She caught his drift now and agreed with the move. "You mean you don't want to drive a stolen car into a federal agency's parking garage? Why ever not?"

His eyes looked like they maybe almost wanted to smile. Maybe. "Let me get these plates off, then we'll talk about strategy for when we get up to the office."

She followed him to the front of the car, watching, her tote bag slung over her shoulder. "So we're going up to the office? I wasn't sure if you were serious about that."

"I don't think we can get around it now that we've seen Mickle. Plus, it'll be good to get a handle on what they know and don't know."

Hard to believe she'd just been at work the night before. Everything was so much more complicated now. "Agent Mickle thinks we're a couple, but I don't think

we need to act like it at the office or even let on to anyone else that we spent the night together."

Holy smokes, she loved the way that sounded. If
only the truth about what they'd spent the night doing
weren't so unsexy. Then again, there'd been kissing.
With a hint of tongue. Not to mention gun fondling, a
bit of front-to-back grinding and lots and lots of touching. Okay, yeah, maybe the night had been pretty darn
sexy after all.

They set off on foot through the early-morning haze.
The streets of downtown had a stale, sticky smell to
them, like the coastal fog that had rolled in during the
night had picked up the tacky urban grime from the
pavement and walls and painted it on Avery's skin.
Working hard to keep up with Ryan's long strides, she
breathed in the sugary decay from spilled New Year's
Eve drinks and the pungent odor of damp cigarette
butts, sidestepping the occasional sleeping homeless
man.

"We'll get the letter from your car first and drop off
your bag in your trunk before heading upstairs. I have
no idea how long we'll be there, but whatever you do,
don't leave the office without me, not with Chiara and
his men nearby."

It wasn't safe for her to be alone outside, and the realization made her ribs constrict against her lungs. Then
she pictured Agent Mickle's angry, confrontational eyes
in her apartment parking lot. Knowing what she did
about the ICE double agent, was it safe for them to be in
the office? Then again, maybe there was no safe place
for them until Chiara was captured.

"What am I supposed to do while we're here?" she
asked.

"Get your hands on all the intel you can find about

Chiara's San Diego connections. See if there's anything mentioning that FBI agent who was undercover with Chiara's men."

"Got it."

They stopped across the street and down a block from the office, peering at the nondescript, brown four-story building from around the corner, assessing the situation they were about to walk into. All looked quiet, as expected, except that the lights were on in the building.

"What are you going to do in there?"

"I'm going to quit."

Chapter 12

Stunned, Avery ground to a halt in the middle of the street. "You're going to *what?*"

He shrugged. *Shrugged.* "That was always the plan."

Talk about digging himself into a deeper hole. If that was the plan, then how dare he drop that on her at the eleventh hour. "You should've told me."

"It doesn't change anything."

"Like hell it doesn't."

"We need to get in the building. It's not safe out here." It took a tug on her arm to convince her legs to work.

Mechanically, she let him drag her the rest of the way across the street. He was going to quit ICE today. There had to be a good reason, some piece of the puzzle she was missing. Some reasonable excuse why he didn't tell her sooner.

There were two ways to get into the parking garage

on foot—go through the main door of the building, then take the interior stairs down, or take the exterior stairs adjacent to the barred entrance gate of the garage. Either way required a swipe of a key card, and though Avery wasn't aware of any kind of in-house monitoring program or app to track who entered and left the building, it was quite possible that such a thing existed, which would completely remove their element of surprise.

Ryan beelined for the external stairs and swiped his key card. Avery stood next to him, fingering the gadget watch. "What about our partnership?"

He looked her way as he pushed the door open. "I told you—nothing's changed. What I have to do—take care of Chiara, protect you—I can't be locked in to following the rules of the job."

She followed him down the stairs and into the cavernous garage. What he said made sense except... "How are you going to arrest Chiara if you don't work for ICE?"

He stopped at the base of the stairs and, after giving the area a sweeping three-sixty scan, shot Avery a hard, all-business look that said, *You know the answer to that.*

Her heart sank. She did know the answer. He wasn't going to arrest Chiara. He was going to kill him. She focused on a patch of blacktop and let her vision fuzz, breathing and thinking. *Wow.* That made sense.

That made a lot of sense. Whatever supersecret spy organization Ryan actually belonged to, there's no way they'd put a lethal, highly trained former soldier like Ryan—with an entire arsenal of weapons at his disposal—on the hunt for one of the most wanted men in the world so Chiara could have a fair trial. That wasn't how covert ops worked. Not in movies, not in books and, so it seemed, not in real life.

"Are you okay?"

She shook herself out of her trance. "Yes." It was true. She was surprisingly at peace with the idea of the world being rid of one of its worst, most vile people. She braced herself for the usual wave of guilt about her unpacifistic opinion, but it didn't come, which she was going to consider progress.

There were more vehicles parked there than Avery expected. Either every person in the office was on hand to deal with the Mira situation or lots of people from the various businesses that shared the building had done like Avery had and parked there while they rang in the New Year downtown.

"Where's your car?" Ryan asked.

"This way. In the corner." Her car was her most prized possession, and she took pains to park in the largest corner spot on the far side of the garage to avoid dings from other car doors. They fast-walked across the garage, past the gated car ramp. Struggling to keep up with Ryan's long strides, she broke out in a jog so she could stay next to him.

"There's probably cameras in this garage," she whispered.

"Probably, yes."

"Maybe we should stop running. I think we look guilty."

He didn't say a word or make a sound, but his steps slowed. Avery turned her jog to a walk and took a big breath—a breath that caught in her throat when Ryan touched the back of her hand with his fingers, then took it firmly in his.

She had to consciously choose not to make the sound of contentment she felt welling inside her because of his touch. She loved his hands. They were huge and strong and rough in a way that was so inordinately masculine that his every touch reminded her that she was a woman in a way that was almost erotic.

She'd never taken the time to study his hands in the office; she'd been so wrapped up in the way he filled out a pair of slacks and the ever-somber expression in his eyes. But since those hands had given her a tour of the Remington sniper rifle, she couldn't stop imagining them touring her body.

"Which one's yours?" he asked

"The black one."

He stopped so fast her arm felt like it might get tugged out of its socket. "Wait…that's your car? The Carrera?"

Apparently he'd never seen her pull in. Then again, she was the one who opened the office every morning and Ryan walked to work, as far as she knew.

She studied her shiny, black Porsche Carrera with pride. It'd taken most of her life savings and a generous inheritance from her aunt Judith to pay for the gently preowned car, money she probably should've used as a down payment on a condo or house, or to travel the world, but driving a tricked-out speed machine was the one aspect of spy lifestyle she could flaunt without her family lecturing her on the evils of violence.

Yes, they lectured her on fuel efficiency and the limited natural resources she was squandering, but it was worth it.

"Ryan, meet Nikita."

This time, she thought he might actually smile. "You named your car?"

Nope. No smile. Just those twinkling eyes that made her heart flutter.

"This isn't just a car. It's a Porsche 911 Carrera 4S

coupe with a seven-gear transmission and three-fifty horsepower named Nikita."

He stared at Nikita, his brows raised.

Avery took the opportunity to get her car key out of the concealed carry belt and had barely gotten her shirt back down over her stomach when Ryan swung his gaze around to her. He was wearing the oddest jumble of expressions on his face—amusement, surprise, desire. "I thought you said you weren't into acts of hedonism with beautiful women."

She tossed her hair in what she hoped was a sexy, flirty, secret agent way. "For Nikita, I make an exception."

She swore she saw him smile as she walked to the front of the car to retrieve her gym bag from under the hood.

"Avery?"

She poked her head around the side of the open hood. "What?"

Her breath caught. Sweet surrender. Ryan Reitano really was smiling. And for the first time she noticed the dimple on his left cheek. He walked her way and propped his forearm on the edge of the open hood. "I think you're incredible."

"You do?"

He nodded.

She rose to her full height, holding his hungry gaze and imagining her tongue licking into that dimple. She bet his skin tasted delectable. "I think you're incredible, too."

He huffed, his smile falling. "Hardly. But I wish this all wasn't happening and I was free to ask you out. I just thought you should know."

He wanted to ask her out? The gym bag fell off her

shoulder, back into the under-hood storage. That wasn't what she was expecting him to say at all. Frankly, she'd expected more teasing questions about what her family thought of her choice of vehicles. "Why aren't you free? Because of your job, whatever it is?"

He gave a slow nod. "My life isn't my own. Not until I complete my mission."

"Chiara," she whispered, like saying his name too loudly might conjure him.

"Chiara, yes. And he's not going to go down without a fight."

She covered his hand with hers. "We're partners, remember? Your mission is my mission."

He pressed his lips together and his eyes were sad, regretful.

"That was quite a show you put on at the Mira last night. You never fail to disappoint me, Ryan."

Avery's and Ryan's gazes locked. The man who'd spoken had an unmistakable Italian accent. He knew about the events at the Mira. A stab of fear hit Avery's insides. Vincenzo Chiara.

Avery's heart immediately began hammering, and her insides got queasy.

Ryan pulled his hand from under hers, reached into his pocket and withdrew a cell phone. He set it on her tote bag. "Call upstairs," he whispered under his breath.

She nodded and took the phone in hand.

Ryan turned his back to her and walked a few steps forward until he stood even with the passenger-side door. "I wish I could say the same for you, Enzo. Though I gotta say, it took balls for you to waltz into a federal agency's building."

With shallow breaths and a hammering heart, she punched the volume on the phone to mute, then pressed the text message button. With trembling, sweaty fingers, she typed 9-1-1 in the—

"She's back there, your girl. The one you were with last night. She needs to close the hood so you can introduce us properly."

Avery froze, her finger on the touch keypad.

Ryan didn't budge from his soldier-at-rest pose. "What are you doing in San Diego, Enzo? You knew I'd be here. It's almost like you want to get caught."

She wiped her finger on her shirt, then resumed typing parking garage. Chiara.

"I was supposed to meet with some friends at the Mira, but you ruined all my fun." Chiara's voice was lilting and light, the confidence of a man who thought himself indestructible. Avery entered Agent Tau's cell-phone number, then hit Send. "Tell your woman to close the hood and move so I can see her. Or else I'm going to come and get her."

She wedged the cell phone in the concealed carry belt and her hand brushed over the flash-bang grenade lodged there. She pulled it out. Now that she thought about it, she had all kinds of gadgets at her disposal. But what could she do with them to buy time before Tau and the other ICE agents rushed in to save them?

It was an easy trick of the mind to visualize herself leaping into view and lobbing a grenade in Chiara's direction, scaring him enough to open a window for Ryan to act, but the cold, hard reality was that she stood a greater chance of getting herself and Ryan killed by acting on the fantasy.

"You should be less concerned with her and more concerned about what I'm going to do to you," Ryan said. His words were laced with steel, and she could well imagine the hard glint in his eyes, the absolute focus.

His hands were by his side, inches from the gun in his pocket. The only reason Avery could figure that he wasn't drawing his weapon was because Chiara had one aimed at them. Or his bodyguards did.

It was impossible not to feel like she was deadweight to Ryan. There she was, with an impressive stash of gadgets, and she didn't know how to best use any of them.

Where the hell is Tau?

What were they going to do if he didn't show? She gripped the grenade, an idea taking shape in her mind.

"It's okay, Emma." It was Ryan, his tone flat. "Come here."

Avery's nerves were getting the better of her. She swallowed back her queasiness and pinched the grenade's pin between her fingers. Ryan had to have a backup plan, didn't he? But if she gave up the element of surprise by walking into the path of the guns Chiara most certainly had aimed at them, then what could they possibly do to defend themselves?

If the other ICE agents never came to their rescue and they were on their own, then there was only one skill Avery possessed that might get them out of this jam, depending on what kind of firepower and manpower Chiara had with him. She pressed the unlock button on her key chain.

The faint click from inside the car sounded as loud as a rock through a window to her ears, but hopefully Chiara was too far away to register the sound. Ryan showed no outward indication of hearing it either, but she hadn't expected him to.

She stuffed the grenade in her bra for easy access,

then stuck her hands in the air. "Coming." Rather than walk to the passenger side to stand next to Ryan, she chose the driver side.

Enzo Chiara did not have a gun drawn. Three huge men behind him did.

He looked perhaps in his mid-forties and was impeccably dressed in a tailored black silk shirt beneath a charcoal suit, his black hair slicked back, diamond earrings adorning his ears. If he hadn't been a mass murderer and human trafficker, she might've thought of him as handsome and charismatic.

When he saw her, he smiled a bully's smile, hard and menacing. "Hello, Ryan's lady." He shifted his attention to Ryan. "I've never met any of your ladies before. She's nice, no? Are you in love?"

Ryan's jaw rippling was the only movement from him Avery could see.

Chiara waved his arm in a beckoning gesture. "Keep walking, Ryan's lady. Let's shake hands."

"No, thank you." Her plan to jump in and peel out of the spot, hopefully running over Chiara in the process, wouldn't work, not with all the armed bodyguards Chiara had brought. By the time the driveway gate opened, they'd both be dead.

Chiara looked annoyed by her response. He lifted a finger. "Andre, if Ryan's lady doesn't come to shake my hand, shoot her."

"Yes, sir," said the black-clad muscle head on the left.

Avery willed her legs to move. She couldn't see how she had a choice.

Chiara beckoned her with a wave again. "Don't be shy. My name is Enzo. What's yours?"

She inched forward, slowly, giving ICE time to get their butts down to the garage to save them before Enzo's bodyguard got the orders to mow her and Ryan down. She opened her mouth and tried to speak, but it came out as a squeak. She cleared her throat and tried again. "Emma. My name's Emma."

"Very nice to meet you, Emma. Get on over here. Andre loves to shoot blondes, so let's not give him a reason to, shall we?"

"Who's your ICE contact?" Ryan asked, cool as a cucumber.

"I'm not going to talk business in front of a lady. That would be rude."

"And threatening to have me shot isn't?" Avery said, feeling stronger and more capable with every word she spoke and every small step she took.

Chiara's smile turned into a sneer. "I hate women with smart mouths." To Ryan, he added, "How can you stand that?"

The venom in his voice turned her blood cold. Her step faltered.

Sniffing, Chiara bridged the distance to her in three long strides. He grabbed her chin in his hand, squeezing hard. "A smart mouth and you can't follow directions." He tipped her head to the side. "You wouldn't even make it as a whore with an attitude like this. Worthless, girls like you are. Pennies on the dollar. Your organs would be worth more than your life as a whole."

Avery didn't think she'd ever been so frightened in all her life. It was worse than being held at gunpoint in the parking garage last night or being shot at in the Mira lobby. She hadn't forgotten about the decoy grenade or the other gadgets in her possession, but if she tried using any one of them, she was sure Chiara's men would shoot to kill.

"That's what I'm in the business of, wouldn't you say,

Ryan? You've known me long enough. Finding a profit where no one else can. That's what I'm all about. Making the world bleed money straight into my pocket."

With another dramatic sniff, he seized her shoulders and spun her around. His arm snaked across her ribs below her breasts. For the first time since she'd started the long walk to Chiara, she looked at Ryan.

He had a gun in his hand and an intense look of focus on his face, almost as if he was absorbing the scene in front of him, taking it all in, waiting for the right window to strike. At least, she hoped he'd strike. *Please, Ryan. Strike soon.*

"Aren't you going to tell me to get my hands off her?" Chiara asked.

"Get your hands off her," Ryan said in a flat tone.

Chiara laughed and tightened his arm around Avery's middle, making it hard to breathe. "No. I don't think I will. Not until we've talked."

"What do we have to talk about?"

"I have some questions about events, perhaps, how do you say…secrets?"

Avery was done with this being taken hostage situation. Chiara smelled like menthol cigarettes and she didn't want him touching her anymore. Ryan might be waiting for his window to strike, and perhaps she could help him with that. Though Chiara had her arms pinned at the elbows, she was able to reach up and grab the decoy grenade.

She yanked the pin out, held the grenade close to her body and said the first thing that came to mind. "Ryan, save yourself. I'm taking Chiara with me to the grave."

Chiara shoved her away and stumbled back.

A gunshot sounded, then another. Avery jerked her head up in time to see Ryan dash past her, firing. He ducked behind a parked car as Chiara's men returned the shots. Avery chucked the grenade in the direction Chiara had run and dropped to her hands and knees. As the flash-bang filled the air, she scrambled behind the nearest car.

Another rapid succession of shots rang out, this time from the direction of the stairs to the lobby. ICE agents were finally on scene. *Thank goodness.*

The screech of tires had her poking her head around the back bumper of the car she hid behind. The gate was opening. She caught a glimpse of Enzo Chiara's hair and suit as he disappeared into the backseat of a black sedan.

Ryan, two cars in front of her, fired on Chiara's getaway vehicle. The shooters near the stairwell fired, too. But they were all too late. When the gate was open wide enough, Chiara's car lurched forward, tires squealing. Then it was gone.

"Let's go after him," Avery said. "My car could catch him for sure."

Ryan stood. He held out his hand. "Give me your keys."

Avery didn't do a whole lot of adventuring, but she loved to drive fast—and had the speeding tickets to prove it. "No way. I'm driving."

She took off in a flat-out run to Nikita.

"We don't have time for this. Give me your keys," Ryan commanded.

She reached the driver's side at the same time as him and poked him in the chest. "Listen, Mr. Secret Agent. You need your hands free to shoot or lob a grenade at them. I drive—you shoot. That's the way this works. Haven't you ever seen *You Only Live Twice?*"

Ryan sucked his cheeks in, considering. "Fine. Let's roll."

She dropped into the driver's seat, cranked the engine over, set her feet on the pedals and threw it into Reverse just as Ryan slid into his seat.

"You sure you know how to handle this beast?"

She peeled out of the spot. "Guns might be your thing, but driving? Driving's mine."

She roared out of the parking lot, banking right as the rear bumper of Chiara's car disappeared around the corner four city blocks down the road.

Chapter 13

Behind the wheel of Nikita, Avery was confident she could catch up with Chiara's Lincoln Town Car in no time flat because Town Cars were not exactly built for speed. This only left her with one whopper of a question. "Um, Ryan? What are we going to do when we catch up with Chiara?"

"That is an excellent question. How about we kill him and his bodyguards?"

"Sounds good to me."

They roared through the quiet downtown streets and it wasn't long before Chiara's driver realized they were being followed. Avery could tell because that was when the Town Car started weaving, then shot left, going the wrong way down a one-way street. Avery gave chase, swishing around a slow-moving car, which aimed her straight at a bus with a honking, irate driver.

Avery threw on the brakes. Nikita fishtailed, then

spun out. Amid a nonstop bleat of the bus's horn, she downshifted and got them moving again in the same direction they'd last seen the Town Car head. The trouble was that though the sky glowed navy blue with the promise of a rising sun within the next hour, the darkness provided too many opportunities for a black car to fade into oblivion.

It nearly did just that as it sped under a plastic sign strung over the road advertising the annual "Run Your Resolution" half marathon.

"Ryan, that's today. At dawn."

"What?"

"The half marathon. There's going to be pedestrians, and streets closed."

"Well, they're not closed yet. Keep going."

They found the closed-off streets around the next turn when they realized they were heading toward a barricade and had to make a hard stop. A smattering of marathon runners and volunteers jumped out of Nikita's path. One volunteer grabbed a water cup from a table and tossed it in their direction. There was no sign of Chiara's car anywhere. Cursing, Avery flipped a U-turn and retraced their path.

Back on the main road, they both scanned the streets, fearing that they'd lost their first good lead on Chiara. "Which way?" she asked Ryan.

"Try left. Toward the freeway."

She took his suggestion as downtown chic gave way to graffitied, run-down buildings and sleeping homeless. It wasn't long before a flash of taillights signaled a sedan ahead. She gunned the engine and sped up close. It was the Town Car, with Chiara's greasy hair visible in the glow of Nikita's headlights. Ryan hung his head out the window and fired.

The car's rear window shattered. Chiara and the other man in the backseat ducked. They were running out of road, with a T intersection approaching. Ryan fired off three more shots. The Town Car swerved, jumped a curb, then bumped over a vacant lot.

Avery shifted gear, reversing while spinning to angle them in the right direction to intersect the Town Car on the far side of the lot. They were nearly there when shots were fired. A crack of glass told her some part of Nikita had been hit. She glanced in her rearview mirror and saw a bullet hole in the rear windshield. Wherever it lodged in her car, at least it hadn't hit one of them.

Ryan shouted orders to keep going, to get Chiara, but Avery looked through the rearview mirror and saw who was doing the firing. A second black car, this one looking smaller and swifter. Chiara evidently called for backup.

More shots fired. Nikita rocked from the impact. Avery jammed her foot hard on the gas pedal, shooting forward in a screech of burning rubber. She still had Chiara's Town Car in sight, but barely. She roared ahead, eating up the ground between Nikita and Chiara's car.

"It's gone," Avery said. "Where did it go?"

The smaller car swerved into view behind them. Avery kept her speed up, looking for Chiara's car, but it was hopeless. Street after street, they saw nothing. And now they had themselves in a tricky situation because the car following them continued to fire every chance they got.

"Damn it," Ryan said. "They're not letting up."

"I know."

"It's time to stop looking for Chiara's car and get the

hell out of here. You need a section of road to test Nikita's speed limits on."

How right he was. She made a sharp left turn and
caught sight of a freeway sign. The other car would follow, she knew, but she was counting on Nikita's speed
to put some distance between them.

She floored the gas pedal on the southbound on-
ramp, cresting the ramp at speeds topping eighty. To
her shock, the other car kept up. During a section of a
deserted freeway, Ryan ducked his head out the window
and fired shots at the follow car. It fired back.

Road signs told Avery she soon had a choice to
make—continue south or take the ramp west, over the
Coronado Bridge. If she had her druthers, she'd never
stop driving. She could have them across the Arizona
border in three to four hours, tops. She had a full tank
of gas in a car that was built for this. But that wouldn't
help Ryan with his plan and it wouldn't save them from
Chiara's wrath.

Then Avery had an idea.

It was risky but would be worth it if it allowed Avery
and Ryan to live to fight another day. They sped like a
rocket over the San Diego Bay on the four-lane bridge,
soaring at close to two hundred feet in the air.

She pushed Nikita to over a hundred miles per hour,
trying not to think about how high up they were. Trying not to look down into the watery abyss. When they
crested the peak of the bridge, Avery slowed.

"What are you doing?" Ryan asked.

"You'll see. I have a plan."

"You're not supposed to have plans. I'm the one with
the plans." Ryan's voice was tight, as if he wasn't crazy
about being this high off the ground, going this fast.

But Avery was confident in her skills. "Not this time.

You shoot. I drive. Remember? You're going to have to trust me."

"This is me trusting you."

She glanced his way, then scoffed. "You have a death grip on the door."

"I've never been driven like this by a woman before."

"I bet you say that to all the girls." The spot she was waiting for was dead ahead. She narrowed her eyes and slowed her speed even further. Steady…steady…

The chase car was catching up to them. It was close enough now that she could see the two men in the front seats as well as the silhouette of a man in the back. Under her breath, she counted down the seconds. She set her hand on the gearshift. Her foot twitched, ready to react the instant her brain sent the signal to.

At the exact right moment, right before the concrete partition separating the two directions of traffic turned into orange, water-filled trash cans, she hit the brakes. Nikita spun, crashing gently into the trash cans as she stopped, facing oncoming traffic.

Facing the follow car.

It slammed on its brakes, fishtailing. Avery pressed the gas, shooting toward it in a high-elevation version of chicken on a bridge, just like she'd seen in a movie one time.

Ryan was visibly nervous. "Avery…"

"Trust me."

The follow car made to swerve around Nikita, but Avery's handling skills were far superior. All it took was a nudge of Nikita's bumper to the speeding follow car and it crashed into the outer rail of the bridge, buckling the railing.

Avery reversed it, then plowed forward again. This

time, the follow car tipped over the edge and disappeared.

Ryan jumped out of the car and peered past the twisted, broken rails. Then he ran back and took his seat. All Avery could do was blink and try to catch her breath.

"We need to get out of here. We can't give the police or any witnesses a view of your license plates."

Avery managed a nod and shifted into Reverse.

"Would you like me to drive?"

"I'm good." That was one whopper of a lie, but she hated riding shotgun in Nikita. Nikita was her instrument to wield.

She wiped her clammy hands on her pants, then reversed Nikita while turning to point her in the direction of traffic. They drove over the remainder of the bridge and onto Coronado Island in silence except for their heavy breaths.

Avery felt her adrenaline crashing, but she was getting used to the way that felt and had an easier time compartmentalizing the sensation of bottoming out. As she drove, Ryan made an anonymous call to the local police using one of the untraceable cell phones he got from his secret lair, reporting seeing a car go over the bridge after a drag race with a white Audi.

Coronado Island wasn't a real island, a fact Avery had always thought was weird, but it certainly served her purpose this morning because there was no way she wanted to brave the bridge again. She navigated through the vacant streets, heading south, toward the strip of land connecting the so-called island to the mainland while she struggled to keep from freaking out over what she'd just done.

Ryan tapped the phone against his knee. "Where did you learn to drive like that? More importantly, why?"

Normally she would've preened at the compliment, but she was still in shock about what had just happened. "Driving schools, amateur races at local tracks and lots and lots of practice," she murmured absentmindedly. "But it didn't do us any good. We lost Chiara."

"He's not going to stay lost for long, and anyway, I think you did terrific. We're alive, aren't we?"

Funny he should mention that. During the past twelve hours, Avery felt more alive than she ever had. And that was what scared her the most.

Adrenaline rushes always left Ryan feeling randy, but he'd never in his life been so scared out of his gourd yet turned on at the same time. Like, pull-Avery-across-the-seats-onto-his-lap-and-take-her-against-the-dashboard turned on. He might've even done it except Avery didn't seem to be experiencing the same car-chase afterglow.

She had a death grip on the steering wheel and her face had gone pale.

"Pull over. Let me drive us back to the shipyard."

Mashing her lips together, she shook her head. He was about to get more insistent with his offer when she took the next exit off the freeway. She wound the car through a hilly maze of corporate business buildings tucked into one of San Diego's innumerable valleys, vacant because of the holiday.

He motioned to a driveway that looked like it was the start of an alley that ran between a steep, grassy hill and a long row of cream-colored two-story office buildings. "Back there, that looks like a secure place to stop. Easy escape and out of view."

She took his suggestion and pulled around behind the building.

The second the engine shut off, she thunked her head on the steering wheel. "Oh, my God. I did it, didn't I?"

He almost said, *Yes, you did pull off some secret-agent-worthy driving skills,* but the anguish in her tone said she wasn't fishing for a compliment about her driving. She was thinking about the violent act she'd committed.

He had no idea what she needed from him to be okay with what had happened, but in the Mira stairwell his touch had soothed her. He set his hand between her shoulder blades, his fingertips touching the skin of her neck. Her pulse was racing. "Yes, you pushed that car off the bridge."

"I killed those men."

He'd peered over the bridge after the car jumped the rails, at the mangled wreck floating in the water, and he respected her too much to downplay the odds. "There's a hundred percent chance that's what happened."

"I need air." She poured out of the car. After a few steps, she bent over, her hands braced on her knees and her eyes closed.

Watching her suffer like that and knowing he was indirectly responsible gave Ryan a nasty ache in his chest. He sat in the car, giving her a few moments to simply breathe and be. When he could no longer stand to sit there helplessly, he stretched out of the car and went to her side. He looped an arm around her back. "Come here."

She drew a ragged breath and allowed him to pull her into his arms. He tucked her head beneath his chin and held her as tightly as he could, grieving along with her over her loss of innocence. Her first killing. *Damn.*

After several minutes, her breathing slowed. He pressed his fingers to the side of her neck. Her pulse no longer raced. *Good.* He'd made the right choice in comforting her by holding her. It was a small consolation, but a start.

She nuzzled into his shirt, then flattened her cheek to his chest and sniffed. He adjusted his hold on her to stroke her hair.

"Did you ever use that Remington sniper rifle to kill?" she asked pensively.

The question came as a shock. She must've been holding that inside her since last night when he'd introduced her to the weapon. He drew a breath, considering how much he could get away with telling her without the risk of revealing too many details about his past.

Then he decided *screw it.* He'd kept so many truths from her, but not this. She was the newest member of a club that no decent human being wanted to be in. The least he could do was let her know she wasn't alone. "Three. I've killed three men with that rifle."

"I killed three men in one morning."

He took her hand from where she'd splayed it over his heart and guided it to the outside of his pants pocket, cupping it over the gun inside. "With this S&W, dozens. I've lost count of how many people I've killed with it. I wish I knew because it feels like…"

He swallowed. He hadn't realized until this moment how much it bothered him, that the details had faded, that he'd gone so numb to the violence he was a part of. "It feels like a loss of humanity to have forgotten. Sometimes I think I must be losing my respect for life, that I can't see the faces of the men I've killed. I can't remember how many or what every circumstance was."

Maybe she sensed his sorrow and frustration because

she brought their joined hands between them and kissed the backs of his. But she said nothing, just pressed her lips to his skin and held them there.

Standing there with her like that, their bodies and souls wrapping around each other for comfort, he was floored by the most profound sensation. He couldn't even put a name on it because he'd never experienced anything like it before. He closed his eyes and wallowed in it, drinking in the scent of her hair and her skin, the feel of her soft lips against his hand.

Yet, despite all of that—or perhaps because of it—his need to kill Chiara swelled up to taint the moment like a festering wound, marring his ability to be the man he wanted to. To be with Avery like he wanted to.

Avery shivered, then tucked their joined hands below her chin. "The hardest part for me is that I liked it, sending that car off the bridge. Watching it go felt satisfying. And that scares me so badly."

"Sometimes, that's the worst part for me, too. When it feels good to do damage. You have to keep reminding yourself they would've killed us if you hadn't been so skilled a driver. If not for that, then we might be dead. Look at poor Nikita."

She brushed her face over his chest as she turned in his arms to look at the damage her once flawless Carrera had sustained. Bullet holes, gashes and dings covered its body. It was a silly connection to make, but he couldn't help but think about the destruction of Avery's sexy New Year's Eve dress, too.

Good thing Ryan had a lot of money in the bank to replace all the beautiful things she'd lost during this ordeal. The money was one of the greatest ironies of his job. The pay was phenomenal, but he never stopped moving long enough to buy anything with it or even properly invest it. He'd bought his parents a new house and cars several years back, but that was the extent of it. The rest just accumulated interest in the bank.

Avery made a mournful sound and walked to the car. She smoothed a hand over the hood, petting it. "Do you think my car insurance covers bullet holes?"

He joined her, marveling at her resilience. Not only was she pushing past her dark emotions, but she was making a bold attempt at levity. It was one more thing to love about her. "Actually, I think Nikita looks even cooler with her combat wounds."

She offered him a small smile. "I kind of think she does, too."

He touched her cheek. "Promise me you won't lose that."

"What?"

"You're like this ball of light and optimism. You shine that light on everybody around you." He smoothed his hand over her hair. *You shine it on me.* "My best friend used to have to remind me that, every time you take a life, you should take the opportunity to get right with yourself again and remember you're one of the good guys. You've got to accept the pain involved in ending someone's life and hold on to that, at least a little, so it doesn't destroy who you are. I don't want to think about you getting jaded or letting the job harden you. You're too special to let this bleak world change you."

She looked at him searchingly. "I've heard you talk more in the last twelve hours than the last six months combined. A girl could get used to the sound of your voice."

He huffed. She was right. That was some effect she had on him, turning him into a motormouth. When his mission was over, if he survived his battle against Chiara, maybe he would settle in San Diego. He would ask Avery out on a proper date.

A thrill of hope snaked through him, and he pushed it away. If Chiara slipped through his fingers this week and he had to go abroad on the hunt, then he had no idea when he'd return or what trouble with the government he'd be in when he got back.

And who knew where Avery would be? She should be enrolling in the ICE academy, or the FBI. Even if she stayed in San Diego, the odds of a woman like her staying single for long were not in his favor. If the male gender had any kind of clue, they'd be lining up for miles hoping to catch her eye. The realization added a new level of frustration to his already despairing heart. He'd never ask her to wait for him; he'd never hold her back like that.

But, damn it all, he wanted to.

He wanted to be her shepherd through this dangerous world she dreamed of being a part of. He wanted to be everything she needed to embrace how strong and capable she truly was. He wanted to help her fly.

She flattened against the car and smoothed her palm over his cheek. In her eyes, he read tenderness, desire. Need that mirrored his own. He stepped into her, pinning her against the car with his hips. Her smiling lips parted on a hungry sigh.

"You're going to kiss me," she breathed so softly that if his gaze weren't already transfixed on her lips, he might've thought he'd imagined it.

He brushed his hand along her jaw, past her ear and into her hair. He brought their faces together, breathing into each other, noses rubbing. "Yeah, I am."

A tilt of her head and her lips skimmed his lower lip with a touch so feathery light a ripple of electricity washed over his skin. A growl of pleasure rose up from his throat like he was some sort of damn animal, but he couldn't temper the intensity of his hunger for her. To take her and make her his.

Her eyes cracked open and met his gaze. And it was the strangest thing because it was like she was looking inside him, at the real Ryan that he only showed to maybe a handful of people the world over. He hadn't even meant to show that side of himself to her, but she'd stripped his defenses handily, effortlessly, by stripping off her own defenses and inviting him into her world, to bear witness to the glories of her spirit.

He felt like he could hang in that moment with her forever, hip to hip, nose to nose, getting high off the knowledge that they were going to put their mouths on each other and it was going to be fireworks.

With Avery, everything was fireworks.

He took a breath, then closed his lips over hers. The jolt he felt at their mouths touching wasn't fireworks; it was lightning. A sizzle of raw pleasure. She made a little whimper in the back of her throat that told him she was feeling it the same way he was.

He wondered if she felt what came after the first lightning bolt—the shock wave of profound relief, like a craving satisfied by that first bite of a chocolate bar or that first step through the doorway of his parents' house after a particularly bloody mission. This wasn't their first kiss, but midnight felt like a lifetime ago and they'd barely known each other then.

Now he knew her. This time, he wasn't kissing the hot, vivacious secretary he happened to find himself with when the clock struck midnight. He was kissing Avery Meadows, in all her many glorious, beautiful nuances. He did his best to tell her with his tongue and body how crazy happy she made him. How she'd breathed vitality into his soul again. For all the world, he didn't understand how he'd survived for so long without her presence in his life.

Hooking his hand behind her knee, he brought her leg up as he forced her mouth open wider, plundering her depths, showing her he could generate some lightning of his own. Telling her that soon, very soon, they were going to do a whole lot more than kiss.

When he felt like he was in danger of drowning in the hunger their kiss evoked, he pulled his mouth from hers and gathered her tightly in his arms once more.

She splayed her hands over his chest and dragged her lips along his jaw. "Tell me who you are. Please."

He hated that it had to be that way, when she kept herself so open and vulnerable to him. "ICE Special Agent Ryan Reitano."

"And before six months ago?"

He dropped his face to her shoulder and inhaled that intoxicating shampoo and Avery scent that drove him wild. He wanted to tell her everything about himself. And while he couldn't go that far, he could get pretty close.

"That's my real name and my real job title. I was sworn in as an ICE special agent thirteen years ago."

"Why did you quit the SEALs?"

"I didn't quit. I was recruited by the Department of Homeland Security after 9/11." It was the oddest feeling, saying this stuff out loud. When had he ever had occasion to lay it all out like this? Not for years and years. Everyone in his life either already knew his story or had no business knowing.

"Recruited for what?"

"Black ops. I was part of a team that went into situations nobody else could and took care of situations and people—whatever needed to be done to further the interests of the U.S. in the global theater."

Her eyes widened. "You really are a secret agent for the government? Like, in the actual, literal sense of the term?"

Despite everything, he felt a smile tugging at his lips. "Yes."

"You said you were part of a team. What happened to it?"

"After our last mission, Diego, the team leader, quit black ops to follow the woman he fell in love with." Which was true, but not the whole story.

"He quit his job in black ops for love? Why would she make him quit? It's who he was."

He caught himself wanting to smile again. Of course she'd think that. She lived and breathed covert ops and secret agent stuff. Then again, so had Ryan for his whole life. Could he have quit the job for love? If he had killed Chiara years ago like he'd tried to, and met the right woman, would he have been willing to walk away from his career? He hoped so. But it had never come up the way it had for Diego.

"Diego's situation was more complicated than that. She didn't make him. He quit willingly—it was something I advised him to do. Love doesn't come easy to guys like us. Love's damn near impossible, actually."

Since the team split, he'd planned to quit anyway after he killed Chiara, but now he wasn't so sure. Blacks ops alongside Avery was reminding him of all the parts of his job he loved. The adrenaline, the chase, the camaraderie of being part of a team. It was reminding him of how good he was at combat like this, and it satisfied the ultracompetitive gene he was born with to be the best at something so challenging.

"What's the real reason your black ops team split up?"

Man, she was smart. The image flashed through his mind of his teammate Alicia's prone, unconscious body on the wooden floorboards of the boathouse where he and Diego had found her lying in a pool of blood.

That was the part of his past that still burned hot and fierce inside Ryan, as it surely must in Alicia. It was yet another reason that finding the double agent in ICE ranked so high in his mission objectives.

"Another one of our teammates, Rory—" and maybe John, too, though no one would ever know for sure "—sold out our team and our mission to the Chiara brothers. And our teammate Alicia nearly paid the price with her life."

The air whooshed out of Avery on an exhale, crumpling her forward. She dropped her forehead to his chest. "Enzo and his brothers had a member of your black ops team in their back pocket? Oh, my God. It makes sense now, why you're here going after Chiara."

It would've been easy to agree with her and let the matter drop, but he'd be a bastard for letting her think that was the whole reason for his focus on Enzo Chiara. "There's more to my history with Enzo than that— things I can't tell you—but you're right that what he did to Alicia and our team is part of it."

She raised her head and locked her gaze with his. "He deserves what you're going to do to him, Ryan. I've read the reports of all the evil he and his brothers have done. I know it's not PC to think like that, and my parents would never forgive me for saying it, but all three of the Chiaras deserve to die."

The conviction in her words and eyes slayed him. She supported him in what he had to do…and she didn't even know the worst of Enzo's crimes. If Ryan had anything to say about it, no one would learn the truth.

He kissed her hair, and all he could think to say was, "Thank you."

"Where are the rest of your teammates now?"

"Diego moved to Vermont with his bride, Alicia moved home to Arizona after she got out of the hospital and Rory went to maximum-security prison to rot for his crimes against his team and his country. As for John, who may or may not have been working with Rory, nobody knows where he is. And nobody really cares to find out."

The only member of the crew left standing was Ryan. A wolf without his pack. Since the dissolution of the team eight months earlier, Ryan was alone for the first time since joining the navy as a shy, gangly eighteen-year-old. Until Avery had stormed into his life with a bright pink cocktail dress on and a martini in her hand, he'd felt that loneliness all the way to his core.

"After you kill Chiara, what will you do next? You said you're quitting ICE."

The feds, including ICE, wanted to bring Chiara in alive. They wanted to mine his secrets and offer him a plea bargain, as they had his brothers, to give up the names of the corrupt world leaders and criminals who'd done black-market business with the Chiaras. When Ryan killed him, he'd be going against a direct order.

If Ryan got caught, he'd be sent to rot in prison alongside Rory. He took one last inhale against her neck, one last stroke of her soft, pretty hair. "I need to see that letter."

She straightened. "Sure. It's in my gym bag."

He walked to the front of the car while she popped the hood. From the under-hood storage, he found Avery's gym bag and unzipped it. The thick, white cardboard envelope from Paolo Hawk sat right on top.

He tore it open. A single white, unlined paper was inside, confirming his worst nightmare. He froze and held his breath, waiting for that first wave of panic to pass. Avery was watching him, and it wouldn't do to let her sense his fear.

Enzo Chiara's men had been to Choluteca, Honduras, in the past month asking questions. It was only a matter of time before the truth came out and Ryan's family paid the price. Dizziness made it hard to think. He let his breath out on a slow, steady exhale and fought to get a grip.

"Will you tell me what it says now? Whatever it is, it's bad, isn't it? I can see it in your eyes."

So much for his poker face. He tossed the letter and envelope on top of the gym bag and closed the hood. The panic and nausea were gone now. He didn't have time for frivolous emotion from here on out. Determination pounded in his heart like the song of a war drum.

"It's nothing. A letter from an old friend."

She stared at him, her expression hard, frustrated. "How about this? When you can't tell me something because it's classified, just say that. Don't lie to me anymore. We're past that now."

She didn't wait for a response before climbing into the driver's seat, and it was a good thing, too, because Ryan had no idea what he should've said. She was right about them being past the lies and was justified in getting pissed.

He didn't want to think about how she'd react to his plans for her tonight. Because Diego and Alicia were en route to San Diego. They were going to take Avery and Ryan's family somewhere safe. Avery would be spitting nails. She'd try to talk him out of it—he knew she would—but Ryan had to stand firm. Only after he could be assured of Avery's and his family's safety would he be free to do whatever it took to stop the rest of his nightmare from coming true—even if it killed him.

Chapter 14

Because she'd been awake for more than twenty-four hours, and they'd left Ryan's lair before the sun rose that morning, time was starting to get jumbled up in Avery's head. She would've sworn it was midday, but the gadget watch and Nikita's clock both read seven o'clock.

As she drove them to Ryan's sister's house, where he'd asked her to go for reasons he told her he couldn't explain, annoyance and affection warred in her heart. The blatancy of Ryan's lie about the letter made her want to strangle him, yet her lips and heart still tingled from his kiss and the power of their connection.

At least Nikita didn't seem to be damaged beyond her body and the rear window. Avery had been worried about an engine component or the gas tank getting punctured, or even a tire, stranding her and Ryan in the corporate industrial park, but Nikita's engine purred like it always did and handled as usual.

The streets and highways mirrored the deceptively early time and were, for the most part, empty. Yet she couldn't shake the feeling that they were being followed. A few times, she caught glimpses of a white, nondescript sedan. It might not have even been the same car because there were a zillion white sedans in San Diego, but she confessed her suspicions to Ryan anyway.

Though neither of them noticed anything out of the ordinary, they wove an unpredictable and circuitous route that involved several lengthy, straight sections of highway in which they could see for miles behind them before heading through the heart of an aging suburban neighborhood.

Ryan's sister's house was a cottage-style one-story, with a small, neat, middle-class feel to it that reminded Avery of her childhood home, except that Avery's parents grew vegetables in the front yard because they thought lawns were bad for the environment and a waste of arable land.

No sooner had they pulled to the curb than a man pushed the front door open and walked their way, his expression worried. "This is my brother-in-law," Ryan said under his breath before approaching the man.

He looked Hispanic and in his forties, with a thick black mustache and a full head of dark, glossy hair.

"Hi, Fernando," Ryan said, his hand extended in greeting. The men shook; then Ryan gestured to Avery. "This is my friend Emma Peel."

"Clever," she whispered out of the side of her mouth.

Fernando gave Avery a once-over with a strictly business expression. But when he looked past her, to Nikita, his face paled.

He tipped his nose to Ryan. "Is everything all right?" His voice was tight.

"Let's talk in a minute. First, we need to park in your garage." Out of sight, was the unspoken reason.

Fernando's inhale drew him up several inches taller. The worry lines in his face deepened. "What's going on?"

"This first. Is Linda here?"

"No. She and Michael went to get doughnuts."

Ryan nodded. Avery returned to the car and turned the engine over while Fernando went in the house. A few moments later, the garage door opened.

Avery backed Nikita into the garage, working desperately not to stick her head out the window and ask any of the dozens of questions pinging around in her brain.

Fernando stood in the open doorway leading from the house to the garage, watching with a grave expression. Once Nikita was settled, he closed the garage door, then bade them to follow him into the homey living room done up in sage greens, beiges and browns.

"Like I asked before, is everything all right?" The way he said it made Avery think Fernando knew all about the danger inherent in Ryan's job and what he and Avery had gone through overnight.

Ryan's face gave nothing away. "No."

Fernando sat back against the cushions, swabbing a hand over his mouth and chin. "We heard reports on the news last night and this morning about what happened downtown. It's him, isn't it? Chiara."

Avery's diaphragm gave a jump, like a hiccup. What did Ryan's brother-in-law know about Chiara? Why was he so worried? Enzo Chiara and his brothers were a problem for federal and local law enforcement, not a shipyard owner.

Ryan inhaled. The muscle in his jaw rippled. "Yes."

"You warned us, but we prayed it wouldn't happen. It's been so long, we thought God heard our prayers."

"He might have," Ryan said. "Time will tell."

"What do we do now?"

Avery didn't understand the fear. Why did Fernando and Ryan's sister have to do anything? Ryan's expression was like stone. "We do what we talked about."

"When is that going to happen?"

"This afternoon."

"Wouldn't we be better off leaving town right now? I mean, Linda and Mikey are just at the store. I could call them and we could be gone in less than a half hour."

The suggestion threw her for another loop. Fernando didn't simply care about Chiara—he was ready to pack his family up and leave town. Whatever it was Fernando didn't want Chiara to figure out, it had to be huge. Huge and dangerous.

"We've talked about this. Skipping town makes the bull's-eye on the runner's back even bigger, unless they have professional help from someone who knows how to disappear. That's why we're waiting. I have some friends coming into town. Diego and Alicia, who I told you about."

Fernando nodded. Though he seemed pacified, his hands still shook and his breathing remained uneven. "Until this afternoon, what do we do?"

"Stay calm. We'll call Linda and get her and Michael home where I can watch over you all until Diego and Alicia arrive. All Chiara has right now are vague suspicions, and it's going to stay that way."

Fernando pushed off the sofa and paced to the window. "How can you be so sure?"

"Because this is my job. My life. More important than my life." For the briefest moment, his shuttered expression opened and she saw the raw fear and determination in his eyes. In that instant, she had no doubt that whatever was going on between Chiara and Ryan, Ryan's brother-in-law was involved. The stakes for Ryan were personal.

Fernando shook his head at the ground. "Sooner or later, he's going to figure it out."

Figure what out? It was killing her not to ask. She clamped her teeth together and held still lest they remember her presence and clam up. What was she missing? A huge piece of the story with Chiara, obviously.

Ryan stood and snagged Fernando around the shoulders for one of those guy hugs that looked like a wrestling move. "I'm handling it. You need to trust me."

Unease slithered into Avery's awareness. There was a lot more she didn't know about Ryan and the situation she'd been thrust into than she'd previously believed. He could claim all he wanted that he really worked for ICE, that he was a SEAL, but she had no proof. Nothing but a handful of facts and Ryan's word. He wanted her to trust him. He wanted his brother-in-law to trust him.

She looked at the gadget watch on her wrist.

Yeah. Their current arrangement of blind trust wasn't going to work, not anymore.

Mickle's words from earlier that morning echoed in her mind. *There're things going on here that you don't know about, and I'd hate to see you get hurt.*

Judging by Ryan's conversation with Fernando, there was a hell of a lot more going on than she'd been led to believe. Every time she thought Ryan was opening up to her, she was hit by evidence that there was even more he was concealing—a proverbial iceberg.

"Ryan, may I talk to you out back?"

He nodded and walked to the sliding glass door that

led to the backyard. Fernando pinned her with a look of distrust before turning and walking away.

Avery watched him go, her ribs feeling tight, her head spinning.

The backyard was a tidy place, with a neatly trimmed lawn edged with flower beds. A red-and-white soccer ball sat in the middle of the grass.

Ryan followed Avery away from view of the door. He stood, looking at her with an intense, yet business-like gaze, his emotional iron curtain erect, waiting for her to speak. Fine. She had plenty to say.

"It's personal." The tightness in her ribs hushed her voice. "Whatever's going on, whoever you really are, this mission you're on against Vincenzo Chiara has nothing to do with ICE or your black ops team. You lied to me again." It wasn't a question, and she made damn sure she didn't phrase it as such. She didn't want to give him any wiggle room to evade the truth. "You're not on a government-sanctioned mission. This warpath you're on against Chiara is a personal vendetta."

He blinked and wrenched his gaze away. "No, it's not."

She fingered the gadget watch, considering, yearning to know the truth, yet scared of what that might be. A part of her—the old Avery—wished that she could be spared the dark, unsavory reality of who he was so she could go on believing he was her secret agent hero. The man of her dreams.

Zach's deception coupled with Avery's new aware-ness after all she'd seen and done since New Year's Eve had transformed her completely. No more meek, trust-ing girlfriend, no more ordinary secretary playing it safe behind her desk.

"What did Chiara do to your family? Did he hurt Fernando? Kill his parents or something?"

He squinted at the sky. She watched his Adam's apple bob beneath the dark stubbled skin of his neck. "I told you—this is not a vendetta. Revenge is reactionary. What I'm doing is strictly preventative." Conviction and honesty poured from every cell in his body, but he still wasn't spitting the whole truth out.

She mashed her lips together. How dare he feed her vague answers, after the trust she put in him. She yanked the end of the watch strap, unlatching it.

He cuffed a hand over the watch, encircling her whole wrist. "Don't do that. Please. My family's in danger. You're in danger, too. Be as mad at me as you want, but let me protect you. It's the only way."

Before she had time to formulate a thought or figure out how to feel, the slider opened. Fernando poked his head through. If he'd looked worried before, he looked downright terrified now.

"Four black cars just pulled up out front."

Ryan shot a glance in Avery's direction, then sprinted through the house, his gun drawn. He stopped in the kitchen, leaning around the edge of the window to look out front.

Avery stood behind him.

"It's ICE."

"What?"

She rocked onto her tiptoes and peered around Ryan's shoulder. Sure enough, four unmarked black cars Avery recognized as ICE department-issue vehicles were piled on the street in front of Fernando's house. One had parked in front of the driveway like a barricade. Director Tau stood next to it. Agent Mickle and five other agents had spread out along the sidewalk, and Avery wouldn't be surprised if agents were outside the backyard fence, making sure no one fled the scene.

"Do you think they're here to arrest us or because they were worried about our well-being after the garage ambush?"

"Yeah, they're real big on gathering all the agents to come check on people when they're worried." Ryan screwed his mouth up like he was reading a menu and couldn't decide what to order. She wanted to grab his shirt and shake him until he was as freaked out as she was.

"You know what this means, right?" he asked.

She was putting the pieces together fast—and this particular piece had only one viable explanation. "My car was bugged by the double agent."

"Bingo."

He swung around to face Fernando. "We're going to get the agents out of here, but we're probably going to have to go with them. You call Linda. The three of you go to the shipyard. My apartment security has a key code override located in the inner wall between your office and my room behind the boat-knot picture. You'll have to smash the drywall to get to it."

He grabbed the magnetized pad of paper from the front of the refrigerator and tore a sheet off, then wrote a long, seemingly random sequence of numbers and letters in neat, compact printing. "We'll be there as fast as we can. And I'll bring my friends to get you out of the city."

Avery was happy to let Ryan take the lead as they walked out front. He strode to Tau. Between the director's disheveled shirt and dark smudges under his eyes, Tau looked beat.

"Sir, what are you doing here?" Ryan said.

Avery stood shoulder to shoulder with him, ignoring Mickle's stare.

Tau narrowed his eyes. He crossed his arms over his chest. "You fled the scene."

Ryan shrugged. "If that's what you want to call it. We didn't flee, though. We went after Chiara."

"We were handling it," Mickle said, joining them.

Ryan raised an eyebrow, looking skeptical. "Yeah? I didn't see you going after Chiara. And that still doesn't explain what you're doing here and why you brought so many cars and personnel when we finally have concrete proof that Chiara's in the city."

"First you don't call to check in or call for backup while you're driving all over creation in a high-speed chase. Then we get a report that a car with three men jumped the Coronado Bridge. An anonymous caller mentioned a white Audi, but eye witnesses saw a black Porsche near the scene. Makes us wonder what you two are up to and where your loyalties lie."

Avery decided to ask the question that had her feeling queasy. "How did you know where to find us?"

Tau gave her a patronizing smile. "Never mind that."

"No," Ryan said, his scowl intensifying. "I'd like to know, too. Are you tracking us?"

Mickle rubbed the sides of his mouth, looking annoyed. "Where's your car, Ms. Meadows? The one you two drove on your little high-speed chase. We need to have it towed and processed for evidence. I know you want to help us in any way you can."

She didn't want to give up Nikita. Cars taken in as evidence weren't returned to their owners for months or more and, besides, by the time they mined Avery's car for any evidence, Chiara would be long gone, either killed by Ryan or disappeared into the wind. But beyond that, there was something about the request and the way Mickle said it that raised the hair on her neck.

Two days ago, Avery would've done almost anything the ICE agents at her offices asked. She'd loved being part of the support staff that helped put away dangerous criminals. But today everything was different. Someone in the office—Tau or Mickle or one of the other agents present—had put a tracking device on her car. When she thought about that, only two words came to mind: *deal breaker*.

She stood shoulder to shoulder with Ryan and looked Agent Mickle full in the face. "Do you have a warrant?"

His brows flickered up. "Is that the road you really want to go down, Ms. Meadows? Because I don't recommend it. I'm trying to protect you, but you're making yourself look bad."

Maybe I am bad. She'd killed men that day. She'd participated in a high-speed chase that could have hurt civilians; then she'd led three men to their deaths. Granted, they were bad men who would have killed her and Ryan and done something terrible to Ryan's family. Now that she was over the initial shock of having committed the act, she didn't regret what she'd done. It was at once freeing and terrifying.

"When you have a warrant, I'll give you access to my car."

"Is that the only reason you're here, Mickle?" Ryan said. "Or is there something else we can do for you?"

Mickle's eye twitched. Director Tau lifted a hand in a cease-and-desist gesture. "You two are the only people who've come face-to-face with Vincenzo Chiara since the intel came through about him being in the area. We need to question you both about what happened this morning in the parking garage as well as the events of last night."

The events of last night. How much did they know about Avery's involvement? They'd already bugged her car, which begged the question—what else had they done? Relief swept through her that she'd heeded Ryan's command to ditch her cell phone.

"How about we follow you to the office?" Ryan said.

"I don't think so. Ms. Meadows, you're driving with me."

No way. Getting in a car alone with a possible double agent was as appealing to her as getting in that trunk at the Mira. "I'm sorry, but unless you're arresting me, I'm afraid you can't make me do that."

Mickle let out a hard burst of laughter and withdrew a pair of handcuffs from his pocket. "All right, then. We'll do it your way."

Chapter 15

"Ms. Meadows, we appreciate your loyalty to Agent Reitano, but you're only shooting yourself in the foot. This is a matter of national security and we need answers."

"I didn't do anything wrong."

"Then you need to help us out here, because the way this is looking, you might go to prison for a long, long time."

Avery loosened her grip on the arms of the chair she sat on in Director Tau's office and tried to relax. It wouldn't do to lose her cool now, not when they already thought she was capable of subterfuge and law breaking. Which she was, but that was beside the point.

She stared at a spot on the front of Tau's cherry-stained desk, listening to the comforting flurry of sounds beyond the closed office door. The department had gone into crisis mode; Director Tau had explained it to her when they'd arrived in the middle of the controlled chaos. Because of the shooting in the parking garage and the inexplicable crash of the office's computer network, everyone was clearing out, transferring to the local FBI building until it was determined why, of all the various law enforcement entities hunting Chiara, he was specifically targeting ICE.

To complicate matters more, the office was also preparing for a joint press conference with the FBI, ATF and San Diego Police Department to calm the mounting fears of the public. Normally Avery would be assisting in the prep work and gathering media contacts for the press conference, but instead she was being subjected to what Tau was calling an interview. To Avery's thinking, the only way that was accurate was if the word *interview* was code for interrogation.

"Go to prison for what?" she said. "You have no evidence of anything, including any crimes you think I committed."

Tau could threaten prison all he wanted, but as of yet, despite Mickle's threat, Avery hadn't been arrested. While still at Fernando's house, Ryan had stepped in and smoothed things over. After some debate, he'd persuaded her to ride with Agent Montgomery to the office. Avery knew Ryan and Agent Montgomery had both been involved in the Chiara brothers' arrest the previous spring.

Of all the agents present, Avery's gut was telling her she could trust him, and it must've been telling Ryan the same thing. True to their instincts, the ride to the office was uneventful. She wished he were in the room with her now, but she and Director Tau were alone.

Tau sat at his desk, his fingers templed near his chin. To the right of his elbow sat a stack of files, and Avery took note that the top file was the one that'd been missing the night before. "Let me spell this out for you. We know the office received a call last night at 9:58 p.m. from Agent Reitano's cell phone. We know you answered that call. We also know Agent Reitano was at the Mira when the gunfire occurred, and we suspect you were with him."

"Okay, whoa. I don't understand why you're spying on me. Sending Agent Mickle to my apartment this morning, tracking my car, tracking my phone calls. What else? Do you have a surveillance camera aimed at my desk? I'm the secretary, not some rogue, double-crossing agent."

"Agent Mickle went to your apartment this morning? I was not aware of that."

"Maybe you should be talking to him instead of wasting your time with me."

Tau didn't respond but paced between his desk and the window, looking somber.

She hadn't seen Ryan since they'd been taken into separate rooms for questioning. She hoped what she said matched what he said, because if they had different stories, then that could cause all kinds of problems.

Tau cleared his throat, then strummed his fingers on the stack of files. "Be careful about what you deny, Ms. Meadows. We recorded you on surveillance video last night. After you talked to Agent Reitano on the phone, you walked into my office several times, then around the rest of the office, rifling through desks and file cabinets. What were you looking for?"

A chill swept through her. They'd been watching her. They'd seen her in her undergarments and struggling to zip her dress. They were monitoring her phone calls. Did they have her home line tapped, too? "I can't believe you've been spying on me."

"Spying's such an ugly word. I prefer to think of it as protecting the country's interests. Now tell me, what were you looking for?"

There was no sense denying it because they had her on tape. "File LM1204. Agent Reitano asked for it over the phone. He wanted me to email it to him, but his computer wasn't working, as you know, so I went looking for the hard copy. Why do you have the office under video surveillance?"

"I'd say it's not your concern, except with all you're guilty of last night, I'd say it's very much your concern."

"What, exactly, am I guilty of?"

"Lying, for one."

Avery's stomach lurched. She didn't like this. Not one bit. "Lying about what?"

Tau walked around his desk and leaned against the front edge, looming over Avery. He offered her an oily smile. "How much do you really know about Agent Reitano?"

Despite that she'd been asking herself that question ever since they'd left the Mira, protectiveness flared inside her. She and Ryan might've gotten off to a rocky start, but they had an agreement now. They were partners, and she'd protect his secrets and his mission. No, she wouldn't just protect him, she'd do everything in her power to help see his mission through and figure out who, if any, of the men or women she worked with were double agents. Could it be Tau?

"What are you getting at?" she said.

"Are you two lovers? Is that how he got you to do his dirty work here—he seduced you?"

The question was so offensive and sexist, Avery had

to visualize a basketful of kittens so she didn't show any outward signs of her outrage or, worse, give in to her urge to slap him. How dare he treat her like some easily impressionable, wide-eyed innocent, duped into a life of crime, or whatever conclusion he'd jumped to. Clearly, Tau was trying to get under her skin, get her off balance so she'd start talking. She'd seen enough interrogations in movies and books to know that trick.

"I don't know what you're talking about."

Then again, she'd questioned Ryan's motives for coming on to her, too. She touched the watch on her wrist.

I came on to you because you're hot, smart and funny. But I'm asking you to hold on to my watch because I want you to help me.

"He lured you to the hotel, isolated you. Maybe he insinuated a romantic attraction to you, some ruse to gain your loyalty, but the cold truth is that field agents like Agent Reitano are trained to make their targets trust them any way they can."

Their targets? She certainly felt like a target now, and she'd been a target of many of Chiara's men's bullets, but Ryan had never once made her feel like a target, an objective.

"I don't know what to think," she said blankly.

"Agent Reitano is the best of the best. Don't feel bad that you fell for his act. Any honest, trusting person might." But that was just it. She didn't feel like a trusting person. She felt like she'd put Ryan through his paces before she'd given him her trust. She was post-pole-dancing-instructor savvy, or so she'd thought.

He came clean about his past, with his dad. He'd given her his gadget watch.

Oh, damn. He'd given her exactly what she loved—

what she'd *told him* she loved—and he made it seem like he loved it, too. Did he actually? Or was Tau right and that was part of his act?

She didn't want to be that woman, the one who fell for a pretty face and a hot body, for a man who fed her a line all the while mocking her behind her back. Ryan wasn't like that. Was he?

He'd wanted her to trust him and admitted immediately that he'd used the gadget watch to bribe her, so that meant he was being authentic, right?

Right?

Agent Tau leaned in, his lips in a thin, flat line, gravitas written on his every feature. "You have to ask yourself, would a thrill-seeking, high-ranking black ops special agent really be interested in the office secretary?"

Whoa, now.

That was one rotten negotiating tactic, insulting her to get her to help him. The sad thing was, she bet it worked on people with low self-esteem, women in particular. But it wasn't going to work with her.

She might have had to endure the teasing and putdowns of other kids while growing up, and, yes, it had made her paranoid that people were regularly smirking at her behind their hands, but it had also toughened her. Rather than absorbing the put-downs and jokes at her expense as the truth, she'd thought, "How dare you." She got mad. She got proud. Regardless of her private doubts about Ryan's motives, nobody got to talk to her like that and get away with it.

And now that she was thinking about it, how did Tau know Ryan was a black ops agent? That didn't seem like information that would trickle down to a regional office director.

As much as she wanted to tell Tau off for implying she wasn't worthy of Ryan's affection and interrogate him on how he knew so much about Ryan's true purpose in San Diego, Ryan had taught her that there was a time to kick butt and a time to hang back. Manipulating Tau would be far more satisfying than a verbal smackdown and yield better results.

"Oh, my God." Channeling the way she must have looked when she caught Zach getting his own private pole-dancing lesson, she faked her best horrified expression and curled over, cradling her head in her hands. "That jerk. He used me."

Tau pressed his hand to her knee. It was probably meant to be consoling, but it felt like sexual harassment. He would've never done that to a man. She pushed her chair back, stood and walked to the window.

"Like I said, he's an expert. You can't beat yourself up over it."

She stared out the window, pensive. "What should I do? How can I help you catch Agent Reitano at his own game?"

Tau nodded. A smile spread on his lips. "I'm glad you asked."

Because Tau was interrogating Avery in his office, Ryan sat in a small auxiliary conference room with Agent Dreyer and Aaron Montgomery. Ryan had worked with Montgomery more than once and Dreyer innumerable times over the life of Ryan's career, but neither man looked at him with a modicum of respect or acknowledgment of their history.

More than anything he wished he knew how Avery was faring. He hated being separated from her like this, not knowing who in the office was on Chiara's payroll.

For the fourth time, they were rehashing the events in the ICE parking garage that morning. Ryan wasn't sure how much longer he was willing to sit there, especially knowing that Chiara was out there, somewhere close. So very close.

"You're telling us that when you and Ms. Meadows arrived at the office, Vincenzo Chiara was there waiting for you?" Montgomery asked.

Ryan leaned in, speaking directly into the digital recording device at the center of the table. "Like I said the first three times, Chiara approached us within minutes of our arrival in the parking garage."

Montgomery sighed and rubbed his chin. "How did you know it was him?"

Ryan had the urge to reach across the table and slap him for that question. He fisted his hands beneath the table and was careful to wipe any expression off his face. No one at the San Diego ICE office was aware of Ryan's singular focus on Chiara, but Dreyer and Montgomery knew good and well that Ryan had been chasing the Chiara brothers almost his whole career. Living and breathing them, dreaming of them.

He and Enzo Chiara had stood face-to-face three times, always with guns and viciousness between them. Always with the intent to kill the other. In his mind's eye, he never stopped seeing the taunt in Chiara's hazel eyes, so achingly familiar it hurt Ryan's heart. "I'd know Chiara anywhere. I'm the leading authority on him in the world. You know that."

Montgomery tapped his pen on the table to reclaim Ryan's attention. "Moving on. When did your relationship with Ms. Meadows begin?"

Yesterday. But it feels like I've been waiting for her

for a lifetime. "That's none of your business. Human Resources can ask me about it if they want to."

Dreyer cleared his throat. "I'm sure they will. For now, I'd like to move and talk about several other inconsistencies we've uncovered."

Ryan had no idea what he was talking about. "Whatever you want to talk about, sir."

"Okay, good. I'm going to cut right to it here. Part of our intelligence gathering in preparation for the Jade Rose operation was pulling all the information on Vincenzo Chiara our department has amassed in the last thirteen years." Dreyer shuffled papers within a file perfectly positioned on the table in front of him. He cleared his throat, then adjusted his tie. "Let's talk about Honduras."

A buzzing started in Ryan's brain, loud like thousands of cicadas. So that was how it sounded when a man's world imploded. Because that was exactly what was happening here.

"Sir, that mission was ten years ago. I doubt the massacre has any bearing on Chiara's actions here in San Diego."

Dreyer set his hand on the table, his long, thin fingers spread wide. He tapped his fingertips quickly as he spoke, punctuating his words. "We got a report yesterday on the wire from the CIA that Vincenzo Chiara's men were spotted in the area."

"In Choluteca?"

"Affirmative."

The buzzing in Ryan's head grew louder and swirled with the hard, fast beating of his heart. "When?" His voice was thin. He exhaled, forcing himself to relax.

"Last month and again three days ago."

"Why wasn't I told about this?"

"You were sent to the San Diego office because of your understanding of Chiara and your history with the brothers, but we are in no way obligated to share sensitive intel with you if we don't deem it necessary."

Ryan hated that answer. "Yes, sir."

"What do you remember about the HAWK operation?"

Easy question, but Ryan's mouth had gone dry. He sipped from the glass of water Dreyer had insisted on providing. "Everything."

"Good. Then you'll recall that Chiara's mistress was going to testify. I, myself, had convinced her to travel to the U.S. to testify in front of a grand jury. The night before your team was supposed to extract her, she along with her unborn child and every last family member and staff in her household were killed."

"Did you hear me? I remember, okay?" He could see it in his mind as clear as the day it'd happened. The mangled wreckage, the worst he'd ever seen, bodies and rubble everywhere—the aftermath of Chiara's rage.

"You did not fly back to the United States at the same time as the rest of your black ops team."

So it began. "Show me the proof."

Dreyer slid two papers across the table. The first was a flight manifest dated seven-thirty in the morning on the day after the massacre, for a direct flight from Tegucigalpa, Honduras, to Washington, D.C., and listed the standard travel aliases of Ryan's four teammates. The second paper was another manifest dated that same day, but at seven-fifty that evening—with Ryan's standard traveling alias and listing a five hour layover in San Diego.

There was no good excuse he could give, but he had to try anyway. "That means nothing. I had personal business in San Diego. Family." Which was true. "If that's all the proof of wrongdoing you have, then I'd say you don't have any real case against me."

Dreyer slid another paper across the table. Another flight manifesto. "An anonymous whistle-blower passed this to me a few days ago and Agent Montgomery and I have confirmed its legitimacy. The day before Chiara committed the massacre, you flew into Honduras—alone."

No, Ryan hadn't. The manifest looked identical in authenticity to the others, but someone had manufactured it. "You ought to check your source, because that's a fake."

"Our source is legitimate. It's you who's not."

"You're going to have to come up with more proof than that if you expect any charges to stick." He knew that made him sound guilty, but he no longer cared. Unless they were going to arrest him, he'd let them finish laying out their evidence, then he was out of there. None of this mattered, his future didn't matter, until his family and Avery were safe.

He checked his watch. Two hours before his rendezvous with Diego and Alicia. Two hours before he was free to initiate the final phase of his mission.

Dreyer set a color photograph in front of him. "If you want to see more of our proof, then here you go."

The photograph was one of those shots where angle and opportunity were everything. The photographer must've had his or her camera trained on Ryan from the moment he'd set foot in the Mira lobby. They must have been snapping a continuous stream of photographs because they got this one just right. Ryan was facing the bellhop at that exact moment when the man had said a greeting to him. Except in this picture, it looked like the two of them were meeting in the shadows. The photo had been manipulated so in place of the bellhop's face was the face that haunted Ryan's dreams. Enzo Chiara.

Goddamn.

"If you're not the double agent, then how do you explain this?" Dreyer said.

There was only one explanation—whoever the real double agent was in ICE, he was good. So good, in fact, that he'd succeeded in the perfect setup, and now Ryan was being framed.

A sense of calm flooded him. The charges, a mix of truth and fabrication, were too much to deal with now that the clock was ticking down on his window to kill Chiara. He stood. "Are you going to arrest me?"

Dreyer stood, too. "No, actually. I have a proposition for you. Off the record, of course."

Chapter 16

Ryan was interviewed in the conference room for a long time. Long enough for Avery's anxiety to balloon into a barely manageable feeling. Her fingers never stopped trembling with adrenaline and nerves and she wasn't sure she ever drew a full breath.

Though she couldn't stop from darting looks at Ryan's desk, the nonstop stream of phone calls ranging from media personalities looking for private interviews with Tau to the Pentagon coordinating efforts for Chiara's capture kept her too busy for her nerves to completely take over. Whichever ICE or FBI official was tasked with listening to that part of the recording picked up by the hidden microphone she wore would be terminally bored. The rebellious thought gave her a modicum of satisfaction.

After what seemed like ages, the conference room door opened and Ryan walked out, followed by Executive Director Thomas Dreyer and Agent Montgomery.

From the memos that came across Avery's desk, she knew Dreyer and Montgomery had both been involved in the Chiara brothers' capture in Panama, the same as Ryan had, and she had to wonder if their shared history made any difference in their opinions of Ryan's actions. She had to hold out hope.

Ignoring Agent Mickle's glare, Ryan walked straight to his desk and sat. He pushed papers around, his blank expression firmly in place. She knew that look—in fact, she was learning to read all his looks, they'd spent so much intensive time together. He was still the same tall, dark and droolworthy office crush he was a few days ago, but she was starting to appreciate the complicated, beautiful spirit he possessed. This particular look was his game face when confronting danger. Something bad had happened in that conference room.

She wondered what Dreyer had said to him and if it was nearly as outrageous and insulting as what Tau had said to her. Most of all, though, she wondered if he'd quit, as he'd told her he would. Then he stood again. He didn't look her way but continued on to the break room.

Tau came up behind her and set a memo on her desk. "Now's a good time," he whispered.

She wished she were in a position to speak her mind on that topic. She would've come back with, "Is it ever a good time to betray the trust of people you care about?" Like Tau cared about her feelings or future. He could attempt coercion with her until his self-satisfied face turned blue, but the truth was that the only person Avery planned to betray today was Tau.

Even though she had no idea what the memo Tau had left her was about or if copies were even needed, she picked it up and walked to the copy machines, which stood along the wall in the break room. She figured it was a good guise to get her in Ryan's vicinity without looking obvious. Ryan stood at the break room counter, moving a stir stick in a mug full of coffee. He glanced her way over his shoulder and she glanced back.

Working by rote, she set the memo in place and programmed the machine to make a hundred copies. A glance over her shoulder revealed Tau in his office, standing behind his desk watching her.

She pressed Start on the copy machine, then slipped into the ladies' lounge. There were only a handful of women in the office, and over the years they'd countered the testosterone overload of the rest of the office by transforming the women's restroom into a cozy, shabby-chic oasis complete with pale green walls, scented soap and a sitting area used for everything from breast-feeding to sneaking a few minutes of reading a favorite book.

As she knew he would, Ryan followed her in and locked the door. He still had his game face on and his eyes swept over her from head to toe, as if checking to make sure she was unharmed.

"How did your interview go?" he asked.

She walked to him and took his cell phone from his shirt pocket. His brows furrowed in question as she navigated to the text screen. "They don't like that I demanded a warrant to see my car."

"That was a ballsy move, Meadows." She glanced up from the message she was typing to see an almost-smile appear in his eyes.

"Well, the law is the law." When she was done typing, she held up the phone so he could read the unsent text: I'm wearing a wire.

His smiling eyes turned to ice as he nodded.

"It was a surprise to see Agent Dreyer today," she

said, deleting the unsent text. "He wasn't due until tomorrow."

She typed a new one. Did you quit ICE?

He shook his head.

She typed another message. Why not?

"Things change," he said aloud, then added, "Dreyer flew in early because of what happened at the Mira last night. He's asked me to help with the Jade Rose operation."

"I thought you were already helping."

"This is a new job, something I can't tell you about. You're innocent in this whole Chiara mess, and I hope Tau and Dreyer know that. If they want my help in this, then they'd better not punish you for something you had no involvement with and no knowledge of or the deal's off."

It sounded as though he was talking straight to the wire, sending a message to his bosses that Avery was not to be dragged into whatever conflict had arisen in that private meeting between Ryan and Dreyer.

"Thank you," was all she could think to say in response. Taking a fortifying breath, she replaced the phone in his shirt pocket before asking the first leading question Tau had prompted her on.

Before she could, Ryan stepped into her personal space, somber intensity radiating from his every cell. His arms encircled her waist and held her close, mashing the wire threaded into her bra against her chest. "The answer to your question is that it's real," he said quietly.

"I didn't ask anything."

"You want to know if what I feel for you is real." His hands splayed over her back, his touch tender and soothing. His lips brushed her forehead. "It's real. I'm real. I'm not faking this so I can manipulate you, no matter what Tau tells you."

He was spot-on. She'd been asking herself that question since he'd given her his gadget watch. In this game of double agents and espionage, where reality kept bending around secrets and betrayals, she was losing perspective on what was true and what wasn't. And yet, there were still absolutes that she didn't doubt, despite the turn her life had taken in the past two days.

Moving forward with her life, whenever that became possible, her drive to transform herself into some kind of agent was real. She wanted the thrill, the danger, the running down bad guys to make the world safer.

The love she felt for her family was real. She'd have to figure out a way to show her parents she honored them and her upbringing despite her break with their values. And then she was going to have to find peace with her choice—guilt be gone.

There were moments between her and Ryan that she knew without doubt were real. When he kissed her, when he held her. His fear for his family. Those smiling eyes that said he found her charming.

He knew she was wearing a wire, so he also knew his every word was currently being recorded. But Tau did tell her to fake that she was still buying Ryan's lies, so hopefully Tau thought she was acting when she said, "I believe you."

She lifted his cell phone from his pocket again and typed out another text. Want to get out of here?

He circled his index finger like stirring a pot and mouthed, "The office?"

At her nod, he took the phone from her. If we leave, ur breaking the law. "Are you sure?"

They looked into each other's eyes. She could tell

he was testing her resolve, looking for a sign of hesitancy, as if maybe she didn't wholeheartedly believe in her own idea, so she tried to impart to him without words that she'd already made the choice to follow this mission through, even if it meant her job. She could get another job, but this two-day window was their best chance—and maybe their only chance—of catching and killing the criminal who threatened Ryan's family and who would likely try to kill Avery and Ryan if he remained on the loose.

She took the phone from him, erased the message and wrote her own. I'm all in.

When he finished reading her text and looked up at her, still questioning, she mouthed the words, "You and me, partners, remember?" She jangled the watch to back up her point and mouthed, "Your family needs our help."

Tenderness warmed his gaze as he nodded, then took the phone from her. Then let's get that wire off you.

With the phone returned to his pocket, he turned on the sink faucet full blast. She assumed because the noise of it would help muffle the sounds of their movement. She got close to the sink for the maximum noise level.

Ryan took hold of the bottom hem of her short-sleeved black shirt and pulled it off over her head, then peeled up her long-sleeved baby-blue shirt, taking care to pull it away from the wire so it wouldn't rub as he lifted. Once that shirt was off, discarded to the chair in the corner sitting area, his focus locked on the wire clipped to the edge of her black bra.

To keep Tau from getting suspicious about why Ryan and Avery were dead silent with the water on, she decided to start asking the questions she'd agreed to.

"Can we talk more about Chiara?"

He slid her right bra strap over her shoulder to hang on her upper arm, loosening the bra cup onto which the wire was secured. "What about him?"

"Why was gunfire exchanged at the Mira on New Year's Eve? Who was being targeted by Chiara's men?"

He followed the line of the wire along the inside of her bra around to her back. "You know that undercover FBI agent who Mickle said was there? Chiara doesn't take kindly to that sort of thing."

"I bet. How is he going to get at the Jade Rose? The Mira's security is so tight now, even more so after the shooting. It seems impossible."

She felt his fingers behind her bra strap, working the top latch gradually from its eyelet. Was the microphone picking up her speeding pulse? Because it sounded deafening to her ears.

"Nothing is impossible for a man who's determined."

The second latch slipped free and the bra fell to either side of her spine, though the cups remained more or less in place. She closed her eyes, fighting to remember the other questions Tau wanted her to ask.

She gave up the fight at the feel of Ryan's lips on her neck. Her mouth fell open with a silent expression of surprise and pleasure as she arched into his kiss, suppressing a groan.

He walked around to the front of her and his hands—those huge, thick hands she was half in love with all on their own—covered the lace of her bra cups. Pinning her with a dark, intense gaze, he peeled the cups away from her breasts along with the microphone.

She tried to work up some modesty about him looking at her bared flesh as he slowly and carefully pulled her bra away, but it was a lost cause between the relief of having the wire removed and the desire he'd evoked with his provocative touches and kisses. She held her arms out, still and straight so that the straps pulled off along with the rest of the bra. Slowly, silently.

To her shock, the moment the bra was away from her body, he wrenched his face to the wall beyond her head. He carried the bra as cautiously as one might a handful of eggs and set it on the little shelf behind the sink. She turned to track his movement, and though she considered covering her nipples with her arm, she realized she didn't want to. Already, she was bared to him in spirit and saw the physical exposure as a symbol of their intimacy, a gift of her trust.

While she stood watching, waiting in vain for him to acknowledge her nudity, he removed the wire from her bra a piece at a time, his focus never straying from his task. He didn't look up until the wire had been completely removed and set on the back of the toilet. Then, eyes fixed at the rush of water from the faucet, he thrust the bra in her direction.

She heard splashing and lifted her gaze to see Ryan rubbing a wet hand over his face.

Once her bra was back in place, she took the time to fish the smoke grenade and a vial of white powder from her conceal carry belt and tuck them in the elastic waist of her yoga pants before pulling her shirts on. She couldn't decide how to feel by Ryan's disinterest in her gift—abandoned, confused.

She tiptoed to his side, not sure why she was compelled to be sneaky about it, but it was creepy thinking someone was listening in. Ryan was busy drying his face with a paper towel, but he saw her coming and tossed the towel into the trash. He braced his hands on the sink and watched her approach through the mirror with a fierce, hard gaze that might've been intimidating if she didn't have such a clear understanding of his kind heart.

She got up close, resting her butt on the sink so it touched his pinky finger.

"You didn't look at me," she said under her breath.

He lifted his hand and skimmed her hip, then pulled her between his body and the porcelain lip of the sink and put his mouth so close to her ear that his breath sent shivers coursing over her skin.

"When you take your clothes off for me and show me your body, it's going to be because you want me to touch you. Not because a bad situation forces you to."

Need pooled low and hot in her belly. He captured her chin in his hand and stared at her lips, his nostrils flared, a vein in his neck popping. Then his gaze settled on her eyes and he swallowed hard. "We have to get out of here. Are you ready?"

She was already breathing hard, already feeling strung out with heady desire. She collapsed forward and dropped her head to his chest. Breathing and getting a grip.

"I'm going to set a ruse at my desk," she whispered. She pulled her shirt up to show him the tops of the grenade and vial.

"Set the ruse. Then go to the window by my desk."

She'd been thinking they'd escape via the stairs. "The window?

"You'll see. It'll be fun."

As nerve-racking and intense as this escape idea was bound to be, she agreed with him. Secret agenting was fun. Thrilling, even. "What are we going to use as a getaway car?"

He smiled a full-out, toothy, dimple-revealing smile. "What do you think the odds are that the pimpmobile is where we left it?"

* * *

Avery gave Tau a not-so-subtle thumbs-up as she filed out of the bathroom a couple minutes after Ryan. Tau didn't look as though he was wearing an earpiece, so Ryan had to hope that neither he nor anyone else was actively listening to the wire that was still sitting in the bathroom, but that their conversation was being recorded for analysis later, as was the department's usual policy. Otherwise, Avery would have to get on that ruse of hers posthaste.

He hadn't pumped Avery for details about her plan, having learned that, if nothing else, Avery was competent and creative. She understood the stakes of this risky move she was determined to make, and he admired her all the more because of it.

And her willingness to risk everything in order to help him keep his family safe, despite not knowing exactly why they were in danger? It blew him away. She was hands down one of the bravest, most loyal people Ryan had ever been lucky enough to know. The worthiest of partners.

What she was doing today in support of him and his cause meant everything to him. She was coming to mean everything to him.

Back at his desk, Ryan watched Avery chatting with Tau and Mickle, wondering how long it would take ICE to figure out the wire wasn't on her. Minutes, max.

Good thing Ryan was paranoid about maintaining escape plans in every situation he was in. He'd set up this particular escape plan the first week on the job in San Diego. He sensed Dreyer's and Montgomery's eyes on him.

The fool men expected him to deliver Chiara to them—alive—in exchange for Ryan's freedom. Right.

Solid plan, guys. Way to think outside the box. From across the room, he saluted Dreyer. Then he walked past Avery's desk.

He smiled at her like he figured Tau thought Ryan would smile at her, then met Tau's concentrated gaze.

"Where are you off to?" Tau asked.

"There's a package I've got to pick up. I'm sure Dreyer told you about it. I'll deliver it to you at FBI headquarters before this afternoon's briefing." He felt like an idiot using schlocky, clichéd secret agent speak like that, but Tau and Dreyer and the rest of the federal stiffs ate that stuff up.

Avery offered him a plastic smile. "See you there."

With a little wave, he pushed open the main door and left.

Chapter 17

The second the main door swung shut, he launched into a sprint, pushing his legs to their limit. He burst through the building's front doors and around the block, his eyes taking inventory of the surrounding streets and building. Just that morning, Chiara had ambushed them in the parking garage. What was to say he wouldn't again?

He put the brakes on when he stood below the back side of the office, slightly offset from the second-story window he'd arranged for Avery to walk to. From his pocket, he withdrew the remote detonator and held his finger over the button. Anxious and jumpy, he kept his gaze moving, sweeping the streets, then the window, waiting impatiently for Avery's signal, then the streets again.

A splat of white powder hit the window like someone had thrown a handful of flour at it. Time to rock 'n' roll. He pressed the button and the window shattered.

A rope unfurled from the top of the frame, just as he'd designed it to. He waited for the majority of falling glass to hit the ground, then rushed forward. He took the rope in hand and tied the end to the nearest parking meter to give it some tension.

Avery appeared in the window, her short-sleeved T-shirt no longer on her body but wrapped around her hands to prevent rope burn. She grabbed hold of the rope with both T-shirt-covered hands and pushed off like a champ. Like she'd done this a hundred times and knew it would work.

He braced for impact and caught her easily. They stumbled back as he set her to her feet. Without taking the time to catch their breaths, they skirted the building back the way Ryan had come until they were out of view should someone look out the ICE office window.

They didn't let up speed until they rounded the corner of the alley and saw the pimpmobile exactly where they'd left it. Avery wilted against the passenger-side door, catching her breath. "You were right. That was fun."

Ryan wished he had time to get lost in her bright, smiling face. Someday, he hoped, he'd have that time. He dropped into the driver's seat and turned the engine over. Avery took the hint and got in.

"What's next?" she said.

"Diego and Alicia are meeting us at my sister's house. Let's jam."

She clicked her seat belt on and settled back. "Sounds good. Just drive safely. If we get pulled over, we're going to jail for sure."

True, that. Still, he covered her knee with his hand and gave it a squeeze. "Probably just you. I've got connections in high places."

She socked him in the shoulder, and he retaliated with a smile he hadn't realized was waiting to get out.

"I liked your escape plan. How long have you had a charge set in the window?"

"Oh, about six months, give or take."

She shook her head. "All this time, right under our noses. Brilliant."

"I don't know if I'd call it brilliant. More like paranoid. I've been in some pretty tight scrapes over the years and developed a bit of a complex about escape options. I didn't like that there was only one way out of the ICE office, so I made myself an alternative."

"Like I said, brilliant. I'll remember that lesson about escape routes, too. Could come in handy."

It was nearing noon. The freeway was more crowded, and though he wouldn't call the pimpmobile inconspicuous, it definitely wasn't the only lowered, tricked-out land whale car on the road. Ryan probably should've taken his hand back from Avery's knee, but he couldn't make himself. He loved touching her.

It was the oddest, most unexpected partnership of his eighteen-year-old career. Someone who matched him in fearlessness, drive and creative problem solving but who he could touch and kiss and find comfort in. What he and Avery were doing didn't make sense in a lot of ways, but for the first time since the breakup of his black ops team, he didn't feel like a lone wolf.

He didn't want to send her away with Diego and Alicia—and more and more, he was sure she wouldn't agree to go.

"You're going to make an incredible agent, or whatever you decide to do next."

"If I don't go to jail."

"You're going to be fine when all the chips fall.

Worst-case scenario, if we're caught, I'm going to tell them I coerced you and you need to say the same." He'd take the fall for her without hesitation.

She smoothed her hand over his, then twined their fingers. "I'd never do that to you."

He shrugged off her concern. "I wasn't kidding about having friends in high places. There's no need to worry about me."

She let out a heavy sigh. "There aren't many black-and-white laws in the secret agent business, are there? It's like one big, huge gray area."

"That was what I always loved about black ops. You do whatever you have to, using whatever methods work, to get the job done—protocol and laws be damned."

"That sounds…freeing."

He huffed. It *did* sound good. Way better than being a desk-bound agent, like he'd thought he might settle for in the next phase of his life. "Yeah. It is."

"Your eyes light up when you talk about your career in black ops. You miss it, don't you?"

He flipped his hand over and curled his fingers through hers, pressing their palms together. "I didn't think I did. I thought I was done."

"What changed?"

If the car had been stopped or they weren't racing to save his family, he would've leaned over the seats and kissed her long and hard. "Let's just say I've had some new life breathed into me and now I don't know which way is up."

Ryan parked around the corner from his sister's house, in a fast-food restaurant's parking lot. The smell of grease and fried chicken made Avery's stomach rumble. They'd nibbled on chocolate bars at the shipyard lair and she'd grabbed a bagel from the breakfast spread that had been set up in the ICE break room, but now she was famished all over again.

She'd have to get something later, though. Rolling in to meet Ryan's black ops teammates with a bucket of fried chicken under her arm might give Alicia and Diego the wrong impression of how dire the situation was.

Stretching her legs while Ryan took stock of their surroundings, she gave the hood of the pimpmobile a pat. "I never thought I'd say this, but I'm going to miss this car."

With a smile, he tipped his head in the direction they needed to walk. Once on the sidewalk, Ryan took her hand. He'd held her hand a lot since they'd escaped the office. She had no idea what he meant by it beyond a need for a connection during this scary, tense time, but she hoped it was also because he enjoyed being close to her as much as she liked being close to him.

"Maybe we should give it a name," Ryan said. "Something more dignified than pimpmobile."

"You're right. He deserves a name."

Ryan's brow shot up. "It's a *he,* is it?"

"I think so. Let's see…it's showy, big and loud. Dependable, because it keeps being where we need it to be."

"That just means it's so ugly no one wants to steal it."

"I've got it. Frank, after the detective in those *Naked Gun* movies."

That earned her a snicker. "Nice. I shame-watch those movies all the time."

They turned the corner onto Ryan's sister's street. "Shame-watch?" Avery asked.

"Yeah, you know. You love watching a movie, but the whole time you're ashamed by how much you love it."

"Kind of like how I felt about my secret agent fantasies until a couple days ago. All that guilt because of how I was raised."

"You're not feeling that way anymore, I hope?"

"No. In fact it finally feels like I'm doing what I was supposed to with my life." There was no doubt in her mind now that this was the life she wanted. She'd been holding herself back, rationalizing that being a support person of an agent was enough, and oftentimes it was. She loved being a secretary, but she loved this fieldwork, too.

"Like I said, you're going to make a hell of a secret agent."

"I hope Diego and Alicia agree." It wasn't every day that she got to meet real-life black ops agents—who also happened to be the closest friends of the man she was falling for.

He brought her hand up and kissed the back of it. "My friends are going to love you. Stop worrying about that."

Fernando and Linda's house came into view. Parked out front was a hulking, blue SUV with a man and woman leaning against the side, chatting.

"Is that them?"

"Yep. Man, it's good to see them, even if I wish it were under better circumstances."

She expected him to release her hand now that his former teammates were in view, but he didn't. With a private, satisfied smile, she gave his hand a squeeze. "I can't wait to meet them."

The first thing that struck Avery once they were close enough to get a good look at Diego and Alicia was that she looked like she belonged in a secret agent movie. One of those femme fatale flicks with the heroine running around in leather boots with four-inch heels and artfully tossing her hair. Already, she exuded sophistication and strength, from her posture and her cherry-red nails, to her long, silky hair and black leather high-heel boots.

Alicia looked at Ryan in a way that spoke of their history, of which Ryan hadn't elaborated on. The small part of Avery's spirit that was petty wondered if she and Ryan had ever gotten friendly the way Ryan and Avery were friendly. It was none of her business, and the past was the past, and all that sage wisdom, but still, she wondered.

Diego was a couple shades shorter than Ryan and slightly scary-looking, with a muscle-heavy build, aviator sunglasses and a natural scowl that gave off a clear don't-mess-with-me vibe.

As Ryan and Avery approached, they pushed away from the car and walked to meet them.

"Thanks for coming," Ryan said, doing the wrestling slap-hug that men did.

"Are you kidding? This is like a summer vacation for me," Diego said. His East Coast accent was a surprise. "Do you have any idea what the temperature is in freakin' Vermont right now? I'm freezing my balls off out there." He nodded at Avery. "No offense."

Avery tried out a smile in his direction, intrigued. So this was Ryan's best friend and the guy who fell in love. His woman must be something else for this sourpuss to quit his career and deal with New England winters. He didn't seem like a man who ever did anything except exactly what he wanted.

She waved off his apology. "None taken. I'd probably freeze my balls off if I lived in Vermont, too."

He smiled and socked Ryan in the arm. Hard. "That's funny. I like this one."

Ryan draped an arm across Avery's shoulders. "This is Avery Meadows, the one I told you about."

Alicia reached her hand out in Avery's direction. "Great to meet you. I'm Alicia."

Avery shook it, her grin still in place, but manufactured now that twinges of insecurity had infiltrated her awareness. Alicia was gorgeous. Beyond gorgeous. Exactly how Avery would picture a real-life femme fatale. Avery bet she didn't need Spanx or high-performance bras, either.

Diego gestured to the house. "There's nobody home, so I'm hoping you know that already and we're not dealing with a missing persons case involving your family."

"No. They're somewhere safe." Ryan nodded toward the garage. "Let's work while we talk. I have a feeling ICE is going to come looking for us here again. Let me open the garage door because we have a car we need to check for a transmitter."

A minute later, they stood around Nikita.

"Nice wheels," Diego said.

"Thank you."

He pivoted to face her, looking stunned. "This is yours? Impressive. What kind of work did you say you do?"

"I'm the ICE office secretary." At his look of disbelief, she added, "But I was born with a need for speed." *Okay, stupid.* Did she really say something that dorky to Ryan's friends? *Unbelievable, Meadows.*

Diego's gaze swung back to Ryan. "Did I mention I like this one?"

Ryan's eyes did their smiley thing. He cupped a possessive hand over the back of her neck. "Me, too."

In no time flat, Nikita's every nook and cranny had been checked. Alicia was the one who found the transmitter on the frame behind the back left tire. Its presence was expected but still made Avery queasy. They continued checking but found nothing else suspicious.

Diego wiped his hands on a rag, then tossed it on a workbench and leveled Ryan with a pointed gaze. "You said your family's in trouble and you need our help to make them disappear for a while, but that you didn't want to explain why over the phone. You ready to tell us yet?"

Ryan rubbed the back of his neck. "I think you're going to need to see it to believe it, so I'll tell you when we get to the safe house my family's staying at."

Chapter 18

Ryan's maddeningly vague riddle about seeing and believing was enough to drive Avery to the brink of sanity. She'd done little else since meeting Ryan at the Mira besides stew on Ryan's secrets and decided it'd be best for the duration of the car ride to find a different topic to concentrate her attention on before her head exploded from anticipation.

"You didn't tell me she was beautiful."

"Who, Alicia?" Ryan shrugged. "She's okay. Why, you didn't like her? I thought you two would have a lot in common."

Avery glanced in Nikita's rearview mirror at Alicia and Diego, who followed in their rental. Before they'd left, Avery almost worked up the nerve to ask if they'd used a pseudonym and fake ID to rent it, but one look at Diego's seemingly permanent scowl and Alicia's perfect designer everything and her intimidation got the better of her.

"No, she's great. I mean, you kept talking about a guy named Diego, that *he* fell in love and all that stuff. You didn't really say much about Alicia except that she'd been injured. She didn't look very injured to me."

"She hides it well. And, yes, Diego did fall in love. He and his fiancée got married a couple months ago in New Jersey." He tugged on a lock of her hair. "You seemed kind of jealous of Alicia. That's cool."

Heck, yeah, she was jealous. "How is that cool? It doesn't feel very cool."

"It's cool because I'm pretty sure no one's felt jealousy over me since my senior prom date, Jen Reichman, got into it with Marie Elena Sanchez after it came out that we'd gone steady in middle school. So I like that you're nervous about it. It turns me on."

She gave an incredulous snort that earned her a sidelong glance from his smiling eyes.

He pried away the hand that had a death grip on the gearshift and cradled it in his. "Just remember, you're the one wearing my gadget watch, not her. That's got to mean something."

"Clever, but I thought the watch gift was because you need my photographic memory."

"That, too. In all seriousness, Alicia and I worked together on the same crew for more than seven years. The first few months, I'll admit, I thought she was hot. At that time, I wasn't around a whole lot of women, with so much training and combat, so all women looked hot to me. But I figured out fast that she wasn't my type."

What is your type? she asked telepathically because she was too chicken to say it aloud. She thought women like Alicia were every man's type.

"What did you think of Diego?" he asked.

Guess her telepathic skills left a lot to be desired. She

exited the freeway and started the slow weave through the streets of the barrio toward the shipyard. "Slightly scary."

He chuckled. "Yes. That's what people say."

"Not you, though."

"That's because we enlisted at the same time, went through the same boot camp and the same SEALs training program. We were bonded for life long before he took a bullet for me."

"He took a bullet for you?"

"Two years into our stint, we were in a firefight in Pakistan and Diego saved my life. He shoved me out of the path of a bullet and it got him in the shoulder."

"Oh, my God. Obviously he was okay."

"The bullet was a clean through-and-through shot and missed everything important, thank goodness. But, you know, when someone saves your life, you can't take that lightly. I mean, I didn't turn myself into a slave for eternity for the guy, but I did pledge my loyalty."

She made a mental note of the affection in Ryan's voice when he talked about his closest friends and family. She wanted to be a part of his world. A part of the people he loved and risked his life to keep safe. It was a pie-in-the-sky hope, but she decided to hold on to it for a while. "You saved my life. And I don't take that lightly, either."

"I don't think that counts since I'm the one who put you in danger in the first place. And, besides, you're the one who saved my bacon in the Mira stairwell and again against Chiara in the ICE parking garage."

She couldn't help a smile. She'd done okay as his partner. Pulled her own weight more than once. "You're right. I did. But I still think you saved me more."

"I'm not keeping track, but if you want to pledge your loyalty to me, I'll take it."

At a stoplight, she smoothed the back of her hand over his cheek. "Done."

He captured her hand and kissed it. "Anyway, after 9/11, when the Department of Homeland Security decided it needed a black ops crew in its ICE division to look out for the country's interests in the global theater, Diego signed on and I followed."

She darted a look at him as she turned onto the shipyard's street. "It wasn't even your idea to join? That's incredible, considering everything you must've sacrificed for your career."

"No, it wasn't my idea originally, but the career change suited me. Even before joining ICE, I lived and breathed combat strategy. I loved it. Going black ops didn't feel like a sacrifice because I didn't have anything to give up. I didn't have a girlfriend or a house, and my family supported me all the way. It felt like the most natural thing in the world. And I was damn good at it."

At the closed shipyard gate, he released her hand and unfolded from the car to open the padlock. After a quick scan of the interior, he pushed the gate open and waved her, then Diego and Alicia, in.

The yard was quiet, with no sign of Ryan's family. Probably they'd heard the two cars' approach and were lying low, as Ryan had instructed them. Once the cars were parked, Diego, Alicia, Avery and Ryan gathered in a circle near the secret lair's door.

Ryan took a deep breath, shifting his hands from his hair to his hips, then crossing his arms, like he couldn't quite decide what to do with himself. "Before we go in and get them, let me tell you what this is all about. Bear with me because I've never said it out loud before."

Everyone nodded, supportive. Avery wanted to hold his hand, but he seemed to need to gather in on himself, getting lost in memory.

"You remember Honduras? The massacre."

Alicia rubbed her arms. "I don't think any of us will ever forget that."

Avery flipped through her mental files and pulled up all she knew about ICE's operation in Honduras. She remembered reading about a massacre in Choluteca involving Vincenzo Chiara and one of his mistresses, though specific ICE agents weren't named. It made sense that the identities of the black ops agents had been protected with anonymity.

"Noemi, Chiara's mistress, had been pregnant, her stomach cut open. The baby dead."

Avery clamped a hand over her mouth. She didn't know that part.

Diego made a growling sound. "Jesus, Ryan, why are you rehashing that? Took me years to scrub that image out of my head."

Ryan looked at each of their faces in turn, sorrow and conviction warring on his features. "Except that wasn't the end of the story. I was the one who checked the mistress's pulse. She wasn't quite dead, but there was nothing we could do for her without risking an international crisis. She was so far gone anyway, it wouldn't have mattered. So everyone else moved on to check the rest of the house, but I stayed.

"I rolled her over, thinking maybe she'd say something or have a note hidden somewhere on her body—something random like that. But I saw a movement and looked more carefully at her stomach. There was a second baby." He rolled his tongue around in his closed mouth. "I took it."

Diego cursed under his breath and stared daggers at the ground. Alicia's eyes were stony, and Avery envied her ability to shut herself off from things she didn't want to feel, because Avery was just the opposite. And as the pieces fell into place in her mind of what Ryan had seen—what he'd done—she was filled with such a sudden, overwhelming flood of anguish and shock that she could barely breathe.

She reached out and pried Ryan's fist open and wedged her hand inside, holding tight to him and letting him know the only way she could that she was right there, supporting him and the choice he'd made. If she could've absorbed his pain through their joined hands, she would've readily shared his burden.

"I held this life in my hands. Chiara's son, except that he was so pure, so innocent, like a message from God, telling me there was still hope left in the world, despite the atrocities that were all around me." He looked at the sky, torment and memory paining his features. "I almost cried, holding that little boy in my hands. What was I supposed to do with it?"

Little boy. Her heart constricted. So her initial thought had been right.

After several long, heavy moments of silence, Avery asked, "How...?"

How had that baby survived? How had Ryan gotten away with smuggling it out of Honduras? How in the world had Chiara not figured it out yet? Then again, maybe he had. Her eyes flickered to Diego and Alicia as she considered the job Ryan was tasking them with.

"I cut the cord and clamped it with a zip tie from my belt, then wrapped him in a towel and held him. He didn't even cry, just whimpered. He was so weak. But he was alive, and that was what mattered. I had to save him, but I knew if Chiara ever found out, he'd kill his son. I knew it as sure as my own name. It was a bitter truth to swallow because my sister had struggled with trying to have a baby for years. And here was a baby boy, and he was a survivor, and I couldn't let him go."

He gathered Avery's hand between both of his, holding on like she was a lifeline, but no one she'd ever known was as strong as him. After the horrors Ryan had seen throughout his career, the pain and evil, how he'd kept his gentle heart was a wonderment, and she was so grateful for it.

She nodded, too stunned to think beyond the weight pressing on her rib cage, and a deep, instinctual desire to wrap her arms around Ryan and tell him everything was going to be okay.

"I paid a villager, Paolo, to take the baby to his house and wait for me. When I got there, his wife had cleaned up the baby and fed him. After that, everything fell into place. A birth certificate was easy to get. I made up a story about my wife having the baby at home and, in Honduras in those days, there wasn't much that some palm greasing couldn't accomplish."

Diego cleared his throat. "After we debriefed in Tegucigalpa, we flew to D.C. to meet with Department of Homeland Security officials about the massacre. You took a different flight." His voice was tight with an emotion that seemed to Avery like love, like he couldn't stand to see Ryan hurting as much as Avery couldn't.

"I brought him here, to San Diego, and gave him to my sister to raise. I'd do it all over again the same way if I had to." He looked at Diego and Alicia, his expression the fiercest she'd ever seen it, as if to challenge either of them to tell him he'd made the wrong choice. Then he turned to look Avery square in the face. "If it takes me the rest of my life or kills me or lands me in prison to make this right for my family and keep them safe—to keep my nephew safe—then that's what I have to do."

Pride and dread warred inside her, along with enough random thoughts to make her dizzy. He was telling her he wasn't free to be with her—and he might never be—because keeping his family safe was his number-one priority. What a good, noble man. He was willing to sacrifice his life. He was going to sacrifice being with her, too.

She couldn't compete with that kind of life mission. She didn't want to. Because she would've done the same exact thing had she been in his position. She'd kill any man who wanted to hurt her family, too. She'd kill that person a hundred times over and, like Ryan, she wouldn't stop until the deed was done.

Then again, what if he did die or go to prison? How would she stand it if she lost him like that? She shoved the thought away before dread could win out over pride. That particular *what-if* was nothing but toxic.

She held his gaze, nodding, letting him know she got what he was telling her in so many words and that she was proud of his choice, even though it was a scary one. All this time, she'd been wondering who the real Ryan was and now she saw, clear as day. Everything he'd done, the choices he'd made, the secrets he'd kept, was because ten years ago he'd made the choice to give a baby—a survivor—a second chance at life. He'd taken in the discarded son of his mortal enemy and loved him for all he had.

Diego started an agitated pacing, his hands on his hips, clearly pissed. If she hadn't sensed his love for Ryan, she would've felt the need to defend Ryan's actions to the other man, but she understood his frustration and helplessness of not being able to ease his best friend's burden.

Ryan sighed. "Out with it, Diego. Let's get this over with."

Diego whirled on him. "You should've told me. Right away. While all that was going on, I was in other parts of the house. I was questioning villagers and tallying the dead, but I should've been helping you, you stubborn SOB."

"This was my cross to bear. There would've been nothing gained in letting it eat away at you the way it's been eating at me. I thought we would've killed all the Chiaras by now. But here I am, ten years later and Chiara's close to finding out, if he hasn't already.

"I got word from Paolo, the man who helped me in Honduras, that Chiara's people were there asking questions, sniffing around the hospital. He and I had a code set up so he could contact me straightaway if Chiara ever returned to his town. I don't know what tipped Chiara's people off that there was anything to sniff around in Honduras, but I'm guessing it's the same ICE agent who's framing me to take the fall for him. Maybe he was looking for dirt on me and found the original flight manifest that showed me flying from Honduras to San Diego. I might never know, and I'm not sure it matters anymore."

Avery gasped, caught off guard again. "You're being framed—by ICE? How? Who?"

"It all came out in the meeting with Dreyer today. He informed me that I was the double agent his people had been investigating and when I demanded proof, he showed me flight manifests that were fakes, including one that said I flew into Honduras the day before you all did."

"That's not how it happened. What other so-called proof did they show you?"

"Photographs of me meeting with Chiara that never happened, clearly doctored by someone who was an expert at it. I don't think the false evidence originated with Dreyer. My instincts are telling me he's on the up-and-up, but he believes whoever presented him the data.

"I thought Chiara was in San Diego to commit a jewel heist, and maybe he still is, but he's got a lead on his son. I can feel it."

A squeak of a door opening had them all turning. Behind a concerned-looking Fernando, a boy jumped up and down. "Uncle Ryan!"

He burst past Fernando, barreling straight at Ryan, all arms and legs and puppy-dog energy. Ryan lowered into a football crouch and snagged the boy around the shoulders before kissing his hair. "This is my nephew, Michael. Michael, these are my friends Diego, Alicia and Avery."

Avery tried on her best, brightest smile in return, so shell-shocked that it was work. She glanced at Diego and Alicia, who seemed to be struggling with their own happy-go-lucky faces. She could almost hear their thoughts because she was sure they mirrored her own. They were looking at Vincenzo Chiara's only known child.

Michael was a scrawny, dark-haired boy with huge brown eyes and an olive complexion that could've spoken to Latino or Italian heritage, a vagueness that allowed him to blend perfectly with Fernando and Linda, thank goodness. No one would ever guess the two weren't his biological parents.

He grinned as he shook each of their hands, revealing a mouth of braces with alternating purple and green rubber bands. Just like that, Avery was smitten with the little man. She understood why Ryan was doing what he was, both the measures he'd taken that fateful day of Michael's birth and the moral shadows he'd slipped into to keep his nephew safe.

Fernando joined the group along with a woman who stood arm in arm with him, worry clouding her pretty features. She was tall like Ryan, with the same dark eyes and high cheekbones, the same calm energy force surrounding her.

"Avery, this is my sister, Linda, and you already know Fernando."

Fernando's frown deepened. "I thought you said her name was Emma."

She couldn't blame him for being suspicious, not with his son's safety in jeopardy. "That was a pseudonym," Avery offered gently. "But I think we're past that now. Thank you for inviting me into your home this morning and storing my car. I'm sorry it turned out the way it did."

Ryan snagged Michael around the neck and the two stumbled back. "Uncle Ryan, you don't have any good video games here and that TV is older than me. No wonder you always come to my house. Your place sucks."

"I know. Sorry about that. I don't get the chance to watch much TV. But I ought to get a gaming system so I can have a chance of beating you at 'Call of Duty' someday. Did you ever pass that level we were stuck on last week?"

"Heck yeah, I did. Next time you come over, I'll show you."

"Deal. Listen, how about you go back inside and let the grown-ups talk for a minute, okay?"

After the door closed and Michael was out of listening range, Ryan turned to Fernando and Linda.

"These are the three people I trust most in this world. You've met Diego a few times at family parties. He's my best friend. My blood brother. And Alicia is my honorary sister. They're the best at what they do, and what they do is keep people safe. You and Michael couldn't be in better hands."

A tingle started in Avery's throat. He made it sound like Avery was going with them. She tried to catch his eye, but he wouldn't look in her direction.

Diego stepped forward. "Here's what we're going to do," he told Fernando and Linda. "We're going to drive through to Las Vegas, get on a plane from there. I'm thinking this is going to go fast, what Ryan has to do to stop Chiara. If that's the case, then Michael doesn't need to know that something is wrong. We go to Disney World and have fun while we're hiding in plain sight with half the other families in the free world. We can decide where to go from there if it looks like Ryan's going to need more time. Sound good?"

Fernando nodded.

Linda fingered the cross hanging around her neck. "Ryan took us there a few years ago. Michael will have a great time. Thank you."

Alicia took Linda's hand, her expression warm and calming. "Computers are my thing. I'll make it look like you've been planning this trip for a while. Plane tickets, internet search history—the works."

"Thank you."

"Why don't you go freshen up, grab some waters and snacks and use the restroom while I have a word with my friends."

Nodding and offering more thanks, they retraced their steps to the safe house.

"Jesus, Ryan. He's the spitting image of his father," Diego said. "Last time I saw Michael was, what, three or four years ago? I guess I didn't really take a good look at him and maybe because I didn't know the story, it would've never occurred to me why he looked familiar, but now…" He shook his head.

"I know. The older he gets, the more obvious the resemblance."

"What about me?" Avery asked. She meant to sound strong and collected, but her words came out like a croak. "Am I going with them?"

Diego muttered something about needing to pee and darted toward the safe house. Alicia followed.

Ryan walked to the chain-link fence that edged the shipyard and kicked it. Avery gave him a few more good kicks before joining him. She hung her hand on the chain link and tried to get him to look at her. No luck.

"Don't send me with them, Ryan. At least give me a say in this. You and I have an understanding. I get you, and I know you get me. That has to count for something."

He pinned her with a hard gaze, his mouth screwed up with emotions bursting to get out. "This wasn't supposed to happen. Not now, with Chiara out there and my family on the run. This—" he gestured his hand back and forth "—you and me, it wasn't supposed to happen. It *can't* happen."

Pushing away from the fence, he prowled to the building, then back again.

His words hurt, but she wasn't paying lip service when she said she understood him. So she knew the torment behind his declaration. "I get it. If Chiara was a threat to my family the way he is to yours, then I'd kill him, too. I'd never stop hunting until I found him and ended his life, consequences to myself be damned. Exactly like you're doing."

Her response must've caught him by surprise because he froze and stared at her with searching eyes.

She squared her chin and looked him straight in the eye. "Your choice makes me proud of the man you are. Proud that I know you. You should be proud of yourself for what you did for Michael."

"I am," he said so quietly she might've imagined it. "If you stayed, then I'd worry about your safety, but I can't afford to split my attention. I have to give everything I have and everything I am to killing Chiara tonight."

"I don't want to be deadweight. I know I don't have the skills to be in the field with you, but I have to do something to help. Use my memory, okay? That was the plan all along. Let me stay here at your secret lair and be your database. We could communicate by phone or email, whatever you need to get this done."

"What if I die? Then what? You're here alone, with Chiara out there."

She couldn't think about that. The possibility was too horrific to imagine. "You know I wouldn't be stranded for long. Diego can give me his cell phone number. I could call him if there's a problem. He'd come get me, you know he would. Alicia, too."

He dropped his hands to his knees, his eyes closed, breathing through flared nostrils, and she knew she'd broken through his defenses. She draped herself over his back, hugging him as tightly as she could. She pushed a hand into his hair and her lips to his temple and breathed with him.

"We're partners," she said, low and quiet. "This is the life I want. I know the risks and I choose this." *I choose you.* But she didn't want to put that pressure on him, not on top of everything else he was going through. There would be time for that later. She refused to contemplate any other outcome.

He stood slowly and set her away from him. The absence of his warmth and strength made her shiver. On his face, he wore the blank mask, the one with a touch of gravitas. His game face. She wrapped her arms around her middle. Maybe she hadn't broken through his defenses after all.

He brushed past her without another word. The door squeaked open. She closed her eyes and gave telepathy one last try. *Come on, Ryan. Do the right thing. Let me stay with you.*

Chapter 19

Ryan paced along the waterfront that bordered the shipyard, watching the boats pass and considering his next move. ICE now suspected him of double-dealing, his family was in hiding and he was running out of time to kill Chiara before the bastard slipped through his fingers again.

With the city crawling with law enforcement and government agencies all on the lookout for Chiara, there was no doubt in Ryan's mind that he'd wait for the cover of night to make his move, whether that meant going after the Jade Rose or hunting Ryan down for details on what happened to his only surviving son.

He hitched his foot on a boat bobbing in the water, one of the half-dozen or so boats dotting the shipyard, both in and out of the water. He couldn't help but look at the horizon, following the line of the Coronado Bridge to the place where Avery had pushed that car over the edge. He'd heard on the police scanner a little while ago that the bridge was closed pending an investigation. That was one brazen move on Avery's part.

She was simply, utterly phenomenal—his only tether to sanity and hope. And what had he done to her in return? He'd corrupted her. Because of him, she'd killed men, maimed others, broken innumerable laws and put her job in jeopardy.

She claimed this was the lifestyle she wanted, and he had no doubt she'd be great at it because she was a natural, but the only reason she'd been dropped in the deep end of secret ops was because of him. Hell, Ryan been a SEAL for three years before he'd killed anyone and a black ops agent for six months before he'd broken his first law of any import.

Yet she'd declared herself his partner and demanded the chance to stay by his side and fight against Chiara for his family's safety. He had no idea what'd he'd done to deserve her loyalty, but he was humbled by it.

With a last look at the bridge, he picked up the police scanner he'd been listening to, as well as the cell phone Diego had texted him on a few minutes earlier to let him know they'd crossed into Nevada with no trouble and returned to the safe house. His secret lair, as Avery called it. He was still smiling, thinking about her using that term, as he worked the security system and pushed through the door. He took one look inside and dropped the scanner and phone.

Avery stood in the middle of the room wearing a red dress and black stilettos. She had to have packed this outfit in her tote bag that morning on purpose. For him. There he was outside beating himself up about the harm he'd done to her and she'd been in here, waiting to seduce him.

"Hi there," she said in a throaty voice that made his blood stir.

He chuffed. It'd been a long time since he'd last felt anything other than ambition and fear. With Avery, just for a little before they'd jumped back into the fray, he wanted to feel with her and show her how very much she'd come to mean to him.

Though their eyes remained locked as he prowled toward her, his peripheral vision took in the aroused flush of her skin, the movement of her breasts above the low-cut dress with every inhale and exhale. She was so intoxicating a force for him that the simple act of walking across the room, letting himself be reeled in by her dark, lusty gaze, felt to him like he was high on the world's best drug.

He was going to make love to her. He was going to have Avery Meadows naked and writhing with pleasure in a matter of minutes, her breast in his mouth, her hair and limbs and scent all around him. He was going to watch her come utterly undone in his arms in a way that neither time nor Chiara nor his corroding sense of self could not touch.

That knowledge was a greater adrenaline rush than the most dangerous black ops mission he'd ever undertaken, more intoxicating than skydiving behind enemy lines to assassinate a warlord or dismantling a live bomb underwater at freezing temps in the dead of night. He looked at Avery in that red dress and heels, her heated gaze, and all he could think was…*hooyah.*

He was halfway across the room when she broke eye contact to tug the dress over her head in one fluid movement. He froze, wholly captivated by the bold move. Her bra was pale pink and sheer, her nipples dark in contrast where they pressed against the fabric, their tips tight like they were aware of the pleasure he was going to elicit from them.

His hands balled into fists, then flexed, anxious to explore the gentle curve of her stomach and ribs, those hips still covered by a satiny half slip, but he forced himself to keep his feet rooted while he shed his own shirt. She wasn't the only one feeling bold.

Her lips fell open as her gaze swept over him, confident and appraising, and he hoped she liked what she saw. His body was his weapon as much as the gun still strapped to his ankle, and he spent every waking moment he wasn't on the job or hunting Chiara keeping his body in top working order.

He stood still, arms at his sides, working through his adrenaline rush while she looked her fill. The next thing he knew, she was shoving her half slip to the floor. She kicked it out of the way.

Now all that was standing between Ryan and an unobstructed view of Avery's body was a matching, see-through bra and pantie set. He would've been fine if she'd been wearing one of those beige bodysuits. Truly, he would have, because either way he was going to have her naked in a matter of seconds. But the image of her standing before him in these black heels and sheer lingerie—those tight nipples, the visible outline of her sex, the darker spot of pink fabric between her thighs that told him exactly how wet and ready her body was for him—was something he was going to carry in his memory for the rest of his life.

She flashed him a saucy look that told him it was his turn for show-and-tell. A flick of his fingers freed the button of his pants, a pull opened his zipper. His arousal surged through the opening with a pulse of relief, pushing against the blue microfiber of his sports briefs.

He dropped his pants and stepped forward, away from them—another step closer to ecstasy in Avery's arms. She studied his goods with dark, dilated eyes, so he palmed himself through his underwear, giving her the show she wanted.

She reached around her back like she was going to unclasp her bra.

"Don't you dare take that off. That's my job." He swallowed, shocked by how low and thick with gravel his voice was, little more than a beastly growl.

She paused with her arms behind her back, her breathing ragged. With a wicked smile, she arched her back, her hands working behind her, and he just knew she was unclasping that bra to find out how he'd react.

No problem. She wanted reaction, he'd give it to her.

Two strides and he was stomach to stomach with her. He seized hold of her elbows, twisting her arms behind her as he muscled her backward two more steps, pinning her arms between her back and the wall.

He took her chin in his hand and brought his mouth down over hers, hard and dirty. With a whimper, she opened for him and gave him her tongue. They kissed like they were starving, and in many ways, Ryan knew he was. He was so wrapped up in the feel of Avery's mouth that he loosened his grip on her elbows. She wormed a hand away from her back and fisted it in his hair hard enough to sting, drawing a grunt from him.

She backed her face up, her swollen, moist lips parted with the effort of breathing, and looked into his eyes. Her whole being radiated greedy desire, and if he hadn't already known she wanted him to take her hard, he would've figured it out when she tugged him back to her mouth by his hair and scraped her teeth over his lower lip with enough pressure to smart, turning him rock-hard and beyond ready to claim her.

He dropped his lips over hers and stroked his tongue into her mouth again. Releasing his hold on her elbow, he clamped his hands around her wrists, slamming them over her head, forcefully, but not enough to do damage. She whimpered softly and did a body roll, like he'd revved her engine with that move. He considered doing it again, but he had no idea how much pain she liked with her pleasure and now was not the time to test limits.

The realization struck him with a pang of longing. Damn it all, he wanted the chance to explore this dynamic with her like a committed couple might. He'd never had that before—a relationship built on implicit trust, one in which he learned through experiences over time exactly what his woman's turn-ons and limits were, and she his.

There were a handful of women in cities around the world with whom he had an understanding and hooked up with when he was nearby and needed to get his rocks off, but those arrangements were about convenience and blowing off steam left over from adrenaline highs, not partnerships built on trust. They were a terrible substitute for what he really wanted in his life.

He dug his fingers into Avery's wrists and ground against her hips as he kissed her. A hundred different sensations crashed over him at the friction of his brief-covered arousal against her pantie-covered flesh, the vibration of her moans against his lips and tongue, her supple breasts crushed to his chest.

He'd wanted to make love to her, but did what they were doing count for that? It had to. A down and dirty screw was still making love when it was with someone you cared about as deeply as Ryan did Avery, right? Because she wanted him like this and he wanted her the same way—and he knew he was falling in love. He knew it as plain as his name, knew exactly what this crazy, fierce desire meant even though he'd never experienced it before.

Was it the same for her? Was it more than lust he sensed pouring out of her? He'd bet his bank account she felt their connection, too. This, with him, had to mean more to her than some secret agent fantasy on her bucket list. They were so far beyond that now it wasn't even worth considering.

Breaking their kiss, he pulled her bra off, then spun her to face the wall and pinned her hands over her head with his left hand. Her supple, rounded backside was even more gorgeous than it'd looked in her party dress. He whapped it with his open palm, gritting his teeth at the perfect sound and satisfying tingle in his palm. She threw her head back against his chest, lost in bliss. That he was the man who put her in that state cranked his arousal up even more. He'd be lucky to last five minutes inside her.

He dragged his lips and nose across her neck, inhaling her sweet, addictive scent. "You're driving me crazy."

She turned her face toward his and gifted him with a dreamy smile and half-lidded eyes. "I drive you crazy with desire?"

How could she question that? He'd never felt so crazed in his life. Not being a man of many words, he thrust deep into the tender skin of her thighs in answer, again and again until they were both panting and desperate. He took her arms from the wall and wrapped her hands around his neck, then closed his hands over her breasts. Her pebbled nipples were as hard and tight as they'd looked. He rolled them between his fingertips, then tugged. Hard, like he was learning she liked it.

She purred in response and pushed her breasts into his hands.

"Time to turn the tables and show you what crazy feels like." He smoothed a hand down her stomach, then lower, to rub his fingers over her wet, clinging panties. "What do you want first?" he growled into her ear. "My tongue, my fingers—" he tucked his hips, rocking into the cleft of her backside "—or this?"

"Only one at a time?"

A rumbling chuckle overtook him. Would she ever stop surprising him? "Avery, baby, I'm going to give you whatever you want."

Avery pressed her face to the wall as she shattered, shamelessly and effortlessly, within minutes of Ryan's talented hands touching her body's center. She purred and arched her hips, wringing a final pulse of sensation from her body.

Now she knew, she thought with another purr. Driving a powerful, dangerous man crazy with desire was even better in reality than it had been in her fantasies. And she'd had her fair share of fantasies.

Rather than being sated, she was still turned on beyond measure and anxious to explore his body. She twisted in his arms to face him, then gripped his cheeks and forced his lips to hers while her hands grazed over his chiseled physique, traveled up the dusting of dark hair on his abs and chest then over his shoulders, coming to land on the biceps she'd been admiring for months. She gave them a squeeze. Oh, yes, this was what she liked. A real man, brawny, with a body as lethal as his skills.

Ryan took Avery's mouth in another wicked, demanding kiss that insisted on her submission to his will. Exactly the kind of hard, rough touch she got off on. Submit, though, she would not. She preferred the push and pull of power, the partnership of pleasure, with the only surrender being to baser instincts. If he wanted her acquiescence, he was going to have to earn it.

She pushed his briefs down, then took him in hand. He groaned into her mouth. She tore her lips from his to look at the prize she'd revealed and exhaled with a hum of admiration. From the top of his head to his feet and every hard inch of flesh in between, he was just about the sexiest naked man she'd ever had the pleasure of exploring.

She stroked him, and he closed his eyes.

"Look at me," she commanded. His eyelids opened to give her a hard stare. This was a new expression of his to add to her mental list, dark and aggressive and lost in lust. She stroked him again, holding his gaze. His eyelid twitched while she worked him, and she could tell he was struggling not to take back control.

Damn, she hoped he made a play for control.

As if reading her thoughts, he twisted a hand around her hair and pulled down, pressing her shoulder, forcing her to her knees. Her body tightened at the wickedly demanding move. With his hand holding tight to her hair, he guided her over him and thrust. She took as much as she could given his size and closed her eyes, drowning in the pleasure of his taste and smell, the way he'd taken control and the way he felt in her mouth.

He jerked on her hair. "Look at me," he ground out. She rolled her gaze up and was rewarded with a lopsided smile that wasn't at all sweet. He touched her cheek. "I love seeing your pretty mouth like that." He pumped into her until she heard his breath grow ragged, then he stopped moving and released her hair, hauling her back to her feet.

She licked her lips, then hooked an arm around his neck and kissed him, telling him the only way she could that she cared about him beyond any man she'd ever known. She felt their hearts coming together, connecting in this primal, authentic way that defied the violence and irrepressible evil swirling around them.

He took her cheeks in his hands and looked her in the eye. "I want you in my life when this is over, Avery. If this mission against Chiara doesn't kill me—"

"It won't." She splayed her hands over his chest. She tried not to be a head-in-the-sand kind of person, but she refused to consider the possibility that she might lose him.

"It might. So I want you to know how I feel. When I'm with you, I see…" His brows knit as though he was searching for the right word.

But she knew what he was getting at, because she felt the same way. "Possibility." The word made her smile.

He returned her smile. "Yes. Endless possibility."

"We're going to be great together."

His hands slid down her back to clutch her butt, pulling her high, forcing her onto her tiptoes as he kissed her again. "We already are. Now get on the bed."

Chapter 20

Without giving Avery time to reply, Ryan pivoted and walked to his discarded pants, pulling out his wallet. She knew what that meant, and she'd never been more ready.

She walked into the messy, ill-furnished bedroom and shoved the bunched-up top sheet and blanket out of the way, then lay down. He appeared by the side of the bed, the condom on and his breathing shallow. He was going to take her so hard and good she was going to dissolve. This was going to be the best ever. The anticipation alone had her feeling like a live wire.

Taking hold of her ankles, he pulled her to the edge of the bed and lined his body up with hers. He set the bottoms of her feet on his chest, gripped her hips and then he took her. She cried out with the bliss of it, and by the time he started to move with deep, soul-jarring thrusts, she lost the ability to make any noise at all.

He took her legs from his chest and turned her to lay on her side before climbing onto the bed himself, behind her. The mattress sagged beneath his weight. He took Avery's top leg and looped it over his hip, then slid into her body once more. She leaned into the heat pouring off his torso as he bathed her arm, shoulder and neck with kisses. Then his thrusts grew slower, more deliberate. He bit down lightly on the base of her neck and reached a hand between her legs.

The build of pleasure was a thing of beauty. He coaxed her body higher and higher, with his hand, mouth and arousal. She didn't stand a chance of lasting much longer, though she wished they could stay locked like that forever. When she sensed herself at the tipping point, she ground back into him. "Hard, for this part," she whimpered.

He moved his hand to her top leg, bracing himself, and slammed into her, hitting her just exactly right. She came apart all around him with a force that felt like levitating, floating weightless in a cloud of rapture. Moments later, he joined her in the clouds with a series of strangled grunts and sharp breaths. It was the sweetest sound she might have ever heard—him losing control like that—because she knew it was from the pleasure he felt with her in his arms. A pleasure she wanted to last a lifetime.

Ryan propped a hand behind his head. They really should get moving, but he needed five more minutes in bed with Avery before he was ready to face the night. "I've been meaning to ask you something."

"Okay, shoot."

"That ex-boyfriend you mentioned, what did he do

that was so terrible? You alluded to it, but you never did say."

She sighed and traced the ridges of his stomach muscles with her finger. "We're lying in bed together. Are you sure you want to talk about my ex-boyfriend?"

"I'd like to know if I need to kick his ass when this Chiara mission is completed."

Her exploring hand went higher, cupping his left pec muscle. "Definitely not. He's not worth either of our time."

"What happened?"

"It was before my best friend Kristen's wedding."

"She's the one who graciously took your two crybabies off our hands."

"Aston and Martin aren't crybabies. They're just above-average communicators for cats. Anyway, I was Kristen's maid of honor and, instead of planning a bridesmaid luncheon, she wanted something more outside the box. Zach had started grousing about how boring I was, so I thought, 'All right, Avery. Here's your chance to show him how not boring you can be.'"

Ryan waved a hand in the air. "Wait a sec—he thought you were…boring? You, Avery Meadows, boring. I've lived a pretty adventurous life, so I think I'm qualified to tell you that you are the least boring person I've ever met. Did this moron meet Nikita? I mean, that right there says it all."

"He thought Nikita was bad for the environment and a symbol of me selling out to corporate American greed."

Avery was right. This guy was not even worth an ass kicking. "How long were you with this guy?"

"Only a year."

"You're going to have to do a lot of living to make up for that wasted year."

"Don't I know it."

"Back to your story. What did you and the bridal party end up doing?"

She tipped her head back and grinned at him. "I signed us up for pole-dancing lessons."

Ryan choked back a sound of surprise. That was not what he'd expected her to say. "Are you serious?"

"Totally. The kicker was that I'd loved pole dancing until stupid Zach ruined it. It was actually pretty challenging and made me feel sexy."

"You've got the sexy part covered, babe. No pole needed."

Against his chest, he felt her cheek move into a smile. "Thank you for saying that. Anyhow, it turned out I was right—a pole dancer really was the kind of woman Zach wanted. After the third class, I caught him in bed with the instructor. And here I was wondering why he insisted on driving me to and from the studio."

"Hold up. Your boyfriend cheated on you with your pole-dancing teacher?"

"Sure did."

He laughed before remembering how much she hated being teased like that. "I'm sorry, I bet that wasn't funny at all to you. It's just…what an idiot."

"I know, I was. I couldn't believe I'd wasted a year of my life on that jerk."

"I was referring to this Zach guy as the idiot. I really am sorry that happened to you."

"Me, too. But he didn't deserve me and I'm just glad I figured out his true colors before I wasted even more time."

"That makes two of us. I have to ask you a very serious question now."

"Okay…"

"Do you own a stripper pole?"

She ran her hand up the center of his chest, tangling her fingers in his hair. "No comment."

So that was a yes.

Her exploring hand dived low, wrapping around him in what was probably an attempt to distract him from the topic at hand.

Having decided that he very much needed to know for sure, he rolled her beneath him and caged her head with his arms. "Avery, do you own a stripper pole?"

"My lips are sealed."

To prove otherwise, he kissed her openmouthed, getting his tongue involved. "Tell me."

"Okay, fine. Yes, I do. But after I caught Zach and Cindy, I'm done with pole dancing. The trouble is I never figured out how to get rid of it. I can't sell it. It won't fit in a trash can. I could haul it to the Dumpster, but what if someone saw me?"

He gathered her in his arms. "How'd you get it to your apartment in the first place?"

"It was delivered in a big, nondescript cardboard box."

"You don't think the delivery guy knew what it was?"

"Maybe, but when I opened the door and saw what it was, I squealed, 'Oh good, my maps are here!'" At least this time, when he laughed, she did, too.

She levered herself up on an elbow and touched his cheek. "I'm not going to strip for you on a pole, Ryan. Never again."

Sensing the lingering pain behind her words, he nodded. Stretching his neck up, he kissed her. "You've got me all wrong. I was thinking of stripping for you."

Smiling anew, she gave him a gentle shove.

"What, you didn't know I pole danced?"

They shared another laugh, then settled into a comfortable silence, his arm around her, her head in the crook of his arm and her fingers moving in lazy patterns through his chest hair. He rubbed his nose in her hair, blissing out on her Avery Meadows scent and the subtle fragrance of her hair care products.

"Pole dancing must've been one of the skills you acquired before we met," she murmured.

Before Avery. What a concept. How had there ever been a *before her?* It seemed impossible that he'd gone so long without her in his life.

He hadn't realized how world-weary he'd been until he'd come under Avery's spell. The job had been like a pot of water, with him the frog. The heat slowly cranked up so he didn't realize he was dying, drowning under the weight of being confronted with the scum of the earth every day, living out of backpacks and hotels without any beauty and light to counterbalance the darkness.

Avery reminded him of how much he loved black ops, how exhilarating it could be—with the right partner at his side. Perhaps he wasn't done with black ops after all.

"We have to get up."

She scooted back to meet his gaze, and he couldn't recall a lovelier sight than Avery naked in his arms, her hair and makeup mussed and a postsex glow on her cheeks. "I hate that you're right. I could lay here happily for the rest of my life, bucket list be damned."

"Me, too, but it's time to gather some intel and get the lay of the land for tonight."

Back in the main area of the apartment, Ryan turned on the five o'clock local news. "Let's see what the media's saying about everything that's going on in the city while I check the scanner to see if it broke when I dropped it."

While he fiddled with the scanner, he saw Avery shake out her dress, then slip it over her head. *Good.* He loved that dress, the way it clung to her curves. Red just might be his new favorite color. Then again, her pink dress had been pretty damn amazing, too. Decisions, decisions…

The news was unremarkable. It recounted the joint ICE–FBI press conference, which revealed nothing that Ryan didn't already know. He tuned out during a commercial to concentrate on the scanner. It looked as though he'd broken it. That was terrible timing.

The news returned, and a female reporter prattled on. Ryan was ready to turn it off when two words had him jumping to his feet. *Jade Rose.*

Avery clearly heard it, too, and came rushing closer to the television.

While the reporter rattled off stats about a cruise ship, the screen flashed onto floor plans detailing each level of the floating hotel's layout before settling on an image of it sitting in San Diego Bay. "Despite the trouble in the city," the reporter's voice-over said, "Azteca Cruises has decided to move ahead with the launch of its latest marvel, the *Jade Rose,* tonight for a week-long cruise to Mexico." The reporter kept talking as the screen image shifted to passengers on an upper deck of the ship, waving to the camera.

Avery's and Ryan's gazes locked. "I thought Jade Rose was the name of the jewels going on display at the Mira tomorrow," she said.

"It is."

"The Lassiter transcript wasn't clear about the Jade Rose being jewels. Do you think it's possible that conversation was actually about this cruise ship? The theory at the office was that Chiara needed money to fund an escape, but what if the *Jade Rose is* his escape?"

He wanted to say no, it was impossible. But was it? "That idea doesn't account for the mention of his cousin Benito in the Lassiter conversation. The jewelry heist makes more sense because that's where his cousin works."

"Forgive me if this is a stupid question, but are you sure you got the right Benito?"

That wasn't a stupid question at all. He'd gotten the information about Chiara's cousin working at the Mira from Director Tau, who'd handed him a list of Mira employees. Ryan hadn't bothered to double-check it. Why would he?

He cursed. Why would he, indeed. What a rookie error. He knew someone at ICE was a double agent. He should've never believed any intel that came out of that office without confirming it himself.

"What time did it say that cruise ship was leaving the dock?"

"Six."

Ryan checked his watch. "That gives me thirty minutes to get across the bay. I want to have a look at the *Jade Rose* passenger manifest."

"Nikita can get us there in time, no problem."

"You're not coming with me. It's too dangerous. Besides, but I've got an even faster idea."

Chapter 21

Ryan revved the motor of the speedboat that had been moored to the shipyard dock. This was going to do nicely. Before he had a chance to get the boat moving, Avery leaped into the boat behind him.

"What are you doing? You know I'd rather you stay here, right?"

She shoved against the dock, pushing the boat farther into the bay. "You need my memory. I was watching the ship's blueprints on the news. How else are you going to know where to go inside the ship? And I can check passenger manifests for inconsistencies or names I've seen before. We don't have time to argue about this."

She was right on both accounts, even if he hated the idea of her in Chiara's sights again. Cranking the wheel, he pushed the throttle and they shot across the bay, toward the setting sun. It'd been a while since Ryan had captained a boat, but like shooting a gun, it was a skill that never went away entirely.

The cruise liner looked like a giant in the water, dwarfing the tall ships docked nearby as well as the downtown office buildings. Ryan ran the speedboat right up next to it, getting a feel for the situation they were going to be walking into.

The passenger ramp had already been closed, the door sealed. The only unsealed opening in the ship looked like the employee entrance and adjacent luggage conveyor. Two bored-looking men hefted suitcases and bags from the terminal onto the ever-revolving belt.

Ryan cranked the wheel and turned around, backtracking to a public dock he'd seen nearby. They sprinted over the Embarcadero, dodging cyclists and pedestrians out for a New Year's Day stroll.

At the employee entrance, Ryan flipped out his badge. "Requesting boarding."

The employee stared at the badge. *"Un momento."*

He dropped the duffel bag he'd been holding and disappeared inside the ship, probably off to find his supervisor.

Patience wasn't Ryan's greatest virtue at the moment. "We don't have time for this," he grumbled.

"They won't leave without the passengers' luggage. We made it in time, and I think this hunch is going to pay off."

No sooner were the words out of her mouth than the sounds of sirens filled the air. A mix of police cruisers and unmarked sedans careened onto the terminal.

Avery grabbed Ryan's arm. "What's happening?"

He had no idea. He searched the tinted windows of the sedans until he saw a familiar face. Agent Mickle. How the hell did ICE find Avery and him so fast?

"Freeze," came a voice over an intercom. "Hands in the air."

"They're talking to us. What do we do?"

They were on the end of a cruise ship terminal, their only escape route blocked by the cars. "I'd say we should run for it, but there's nowhere to go that's not a dead end."

"You think we should just turn ourselves in?"

"No. Give me a sec."

Car doors flew open. Officers poured out, their guns drawn. Ryan looked past Mickle and recognized Tau, Dreyer and the rest of the ICE office. Once again, they were pulling out all the stops for him.

"The deal was that I brought you Chiara alive," he called to Dreyer, staring the other man down. "Is that not the case anymore? I'm trying to do what's right here."

Dreyer lifted the PA microphone to his mouth. "The deal was off when you pulled that stunt with Meadows and went off-grid. We're taking you both into custody. Hands in the air, and we're not going to ask nicely again."

A loud crack sounded from somewhere behind the ICE cars. Gunfire. All the officers and agents ducked for cover. They turned, searching for the gunman. More shots rang out, this time from the agents. Their shots were answered. Ryan scanned the buildings across the road from the terminal. The shooters could be anywhere.

There was a time when Ryan would've stayed and helped defend his fellow agents. But getting framed had a way of minimizing a man's loyalty, and Ryan was no exception.

The remaining cruise employee dropped the suitcase he'd been holding and ran up the ramp into the ship. Great idea. Ryan grabbed Avery's arm and urged her up the ramp, into the ship, as the gun battle raged behind them. He had no idea who was shooting at the agents and didn't care to find out. He was a man on a mission, and nothing was going to hold him back now.

One thing was certain, though. He agreed with Avery—this hunch was about to pay off.

He heard cruise security shouting into walkie-talkies, their keys jangling, before he saw them.

"Where should we hide, Avery?"

"The next door on your left."

Once they were through the door, he pushed her ahead of him. "You lead the way."

"Where to?"

"Somewhere that'll have the passenger manifests."

They ran through the bowels of the ship, past columns of luggage. A deafening roar of an engine built up speed. The ship lurched as if it was getting ready to move.

He didn't blame the captains one bit. There was no need to stay there idly like sitting ducks while a deadly battle was under way on the dock. They sprinted past employee living quarters, then burst through a door labeled Pavilion.

It spit them out in the middle of a huge, ornately furnished lobby with a vaulted ceiling at least seven stories high. Passengers mingled about, chatting and laughing, oblivious to the gunplay happening on the other side of the ship's hull.

Avery tugged his hand. "This is the fastest way to the administrative offices. Let's go."

They skirted the center of the room, then slipped through an unmarked door on the far side of a gift shop.

The office was lit, but empty. "A copy of the passenger manifest will be with the emergency evacuation kit," Ryan said, lugging a canvas tote onto the nearest chair.

They dumped first-aid supplies, walkie-talkies and other equipment from the bag to the floor, uncovering a black three-ring binder. Ryan flipped it open and they got to work scanning names.

"What are we looking for? The name Benito?"

"That's all we have to go on right now."

The passenger names were alphabetized. Benito didn't appear as a first or last name; neither did any of the alternate spellings they scanned for or any of the other names Avery recalled from documents associated with the Chiara investigation.

"I don't know where we go from here," she said. "I'm not seeing anything out of the ordinary."

He closed the binder. Avery smacked her open palm on it. "That's it!"

"What?" All that was on the cover was a copy of the ship's deck plan.

"The Lassiter transcript. We got it wrong."

"I know. There were two Jade Roses in San Diego today. How does that matter now?"

She shook her head and speared a finger at the ship diagram. "Number 337 India. It wasn't referencing a street address. That's a guest suite on the India level of the ship."

To quote Avery—holy smokes. He tapped the gun strapped to his ankle. This was it. "Lead the way. Let's go get Chiara."

He threw the door open. Avery snagged his hand and led them back through the lobby. They were halfway to the elevator nook when Ryan felt something hard poke him in the back. A gun. His insides seized up and his pulse sped.

"We meet again," came Chiara's smooth voice from behind them.

"Funny, we were just coming to visit you," Ryan said, keeping his cool. He chanced a glance at Avery. Panic was written plainly on her face. He twisted, gauging how much backup Chiara had with him and their odds for escape.

Behind Chiara stood two hulking bodyguards with their hands in the pockets of their blazers, most likely gripping guns. How they got guns aboard a cruise ship was anyone's guess. For all Ryan knew, Chiara had cruise security on his payroll.

"This is wonderful because I still have questions for you. We were interrupted this morning. Let's go to my suite, shall we?"

Avery and Ryan were herded into an elevator with Chiara and his bodyguards. As the doors shut, he squeezed Avery's hand, hoping to reassure her. Two against three were not terrible odds, and Ryan had plenty of firepower on him.

"Before we get to your questions, I have some questions of my own," he said.

Chiara seemed nonplussed. "Be my guest."

"Let's start with a basic. How did you manage to get past the ship's security?"

"A friend who has a way with computers owed me a favor, which proved very useful because I'd been looking for a quiet way to return to Italy."

Lassiter. Had to be. "What about your cousin Benito working at the Mira?"

Chiara chuckled behind closed lips. "What do you call that in this country? A misdirect? Cunning of me, no?"

The elevator slowed to a stop, then dinged as the doors slid open onto level twelve—India. Chiara gestured for Ryan and Avery to lead the way. "Suite three-three-seven," he instructed.

When they reached the suite, one of the bodyguards swiped the key fob, then pushed the door open wide enough for Ryan and Avery to pass. It was a large suite by cruise ship standards, with a queen-size bed, a round dining table and lushly appointed plush burgundy drapes and carpet. The drapes flapped in the breeze of the open sliding glass door leading out to a private balcony.

Ryan and Avery were directed to the dining table chairs. Chiara paced in front of them while the bodyguards stood behind. "Enough with your questions, Agent Reitano. My turn." He stopped walking and pivoted forward. "Where is my son?"

That was cutting right to the chase. "You killed him ten years ago in Honduras, remember?"

Chiara smacked his lips. "Nice try. I had an associate of mine look into some old medical records at the hospital in Choluteca after it was brought to my attention that you lingered in Honduras longer than the rest of your team. I wanted to know what you were up to in my territory."

"Who brought that to your attention?"

Chiara gave a sly smile. "Someone who has proved quite useful."

"If you found your son, what would you do—raise him?" Avery asked.

"There you go with your smart mouth again. What I'll do with my son is not the point. The point is that nobody, not even you, Agent Reitano, takes from me and gets away with it. Now I will take from you." He flicked a finger toward one of his guards. The guard stepped forward, drawing his gun, then aiming it at Avery's head.

Without warning, the suite door crashed to the ground, ripped from its hinges. Agent Mickle stood in the threshold. Behind him were Agents Tau, Dreyer and Montgomery.

"The jig is up, gentlemen. I suggest you put your weapons down," Dreyer said.

Ryan couldn't decide if he was glad to see them or not, seeing as how he knew one of them was the double agent. "How did you know to come to the cruise ship?"

"I saw the local news and put it together that we had the wrong Jade Rose," Mickle said. "Imagine our surprise when we showed up and saw you two sneaking inside."

Ryan returned his focus to Avery. The guard's gun had vanished, but he remained hovering over her.

A single shot rang out. The guard nearest Chiara collapsed. Ryan followed the sound to the source. Tau held his rifle aloft, aimed at the second guard who still stood behind Avery. "I'll kill you, too, just as easily."

The breach of protocol stunned Ryan, not that he planned to show it like Mickle and Dreyer, who gaped at Tau like he'd lost his mind.

"Don't aim that rifle in her direction," Ryan warned. One bad shot and she could be killed in an instant.

"You're in no position to make demands, Reitano."

The guard moved from behind Avery and set his rifle on the ground near his felled comrade, then raised his hands in the air. Mickle stepped forward. "Sorry to break up your little meeting, but we have some warrants to serve. Chiara, Reitano, Meadows—get your hands in the air, you're all under arrest."

Ryan and Avery raised their hands. Ryan had no idea what his next move should be. He couldn't let Chiara live, not now that he knew his son was alive and that Ryan had brought him to San Diego.

Chiara raised his arms, but his focus went past Mickle to Tau. "You're outliving your usefulness. This is not at all what we agreed upon."

There it was. The answer to one of Ryan's many questions. Tau was the double agent. It seemed so obvious now. Beside Ryan, Avery gasped under her breath.

Dreyer and Mickle processed the new information at the same time Ryan and Avery did. The next thing Ryan knew, Tau was thrown into the room to stand next to Chiara. "Tell me this isn't true," Dreyer said, more animated than Ryan had ever seen him. "Tell me you're not feeding intel to Chiara."

Tau snickered. "This goes way above your pay grade, Dreyer. I have a deal with the CIA. Chiara, too. Mercenaries like him aren't the worst evil in this world— the people who buy and sell through them are. Enzo and I struck a bargain. I'd help him escape the country in exchange for client lists and proof. This is the break national security needs. The CIA and FBI are preparing to arrest dozens of black-market buyers, thanks to Chiara's help. And my help, too."

"That's quite the B.S. line you're feeding yourself," Mickle said with a sneer. Ryan agreed. He found it really hard to believe the U.S. government would strike a backroom deal with one of the world's most violent men.

Tau's face reddened. "Don't sit there on your high-and-mighty throne and pretend you never blur the ethical lines. We'd never catch the criminals if we weren't willing to play their games. Our careers are played out in the shadows. You know that as well as I do. Laws are for the naive."

"You see?" Chiara said. "I will be exonerated for all this. I'm too valuable an instrument for your government. The secrets I have to share will fell nations. You are wasting your time."

"Be that as it may," Dreyer said. "Get on the ground, down on your stomach, hands behind your head."

"I don't think so." He drew a gun from inside his jacket, then all hell broke loose.

Tau whirled on Mickle, Dreyer and the other agents. Shots rang out. Ryan tackled Avery to the ground, army-crawling her to the bathroom. "Lock the door, get into the shower."

Ryan spun to face the battle, drawing his .45. He couldn't get a clear shot at Chiara, but Tau was right in front of him, exchanging blows with Agent Mickle.

Ryan threw a punch at Tau's kidney. He keeled over. Ryan's and Mickle's eyes met, and a fresh understanding coursed between them. Mickle slugged Tau with an uppercut to his jaw and the other man crumpled to the ground. Ryan rolled him to his stomach and pressed his knee into Tau's back. He took hold of Tau's hair and banged his head on the ground. "You framed me."

Tau spit blood out of his mouth. "You were getting too close to the truth. I needed you out of the way so I could do my job."

Ryan grabbed a zip tie from his pocket and bound Tau's wrists behind his back. "Stay there."

"Ryan!" It was Avery. He lifted his head. Her expression was anxious. She stood in the doorway to the bathroom. "Chiara's escaping. The balcony."

Chiara was already outside, standing on the edge of the balcony rail, his hands braced on the floor of the balcony above it. Against the descending darkness, his white suit glowed and the wind managed to ruffle his slick black hair. The ship was moving slowly and steadily through the calm waters of San Diego Bay only a hundred meters from shore. If Chiara jumped, he'd most likely survive without a scratch.

Ryan couldn't let that happen.

He lunged, but Chiara was fast. He jumped to the next balcony over, then fired shots in Ryan's direction. Ryan ducked inside to avoid getting hit, then returned fire. When he looked again Chiara was nowhere to be seen.

Ryan chanced a step farther out on the balcony, fully aware he'd make an easy target for Chiara's gun. Chiara was climbing, spiderlike, down the column of balconies. There was no way in hell Ryan was going to let him escape this time. He climbed over the edge and dropped into a dangle, hovering a solid twenty meters above the churning wake of the ship.

His feet touched on the lip of the balcony below. He dropped down, then checked again for his target. Enzo was two levels below Ryan and not on a balcony, but a public breezeway. Rather than waste time firing what would most likely be missed shots, risking collateral damage, he continued his climb, touching ground on the breezeway as Chiara disappeared around a corner to the back of the ship.

Ryan gave chase, pushing his legs to their limit. He swiftly bridged the distance to Chiara, propelled along by seemingly superhuman strength or divine grace— or maybe a little of both. There was too much on the line to let his target slip through his fingers yet again.

He slammed into Chiara hard from behind, knocking him into the metal rail. But Chiara wasn't going to give up so easily. His hand lashed out, a knife blade whipping through the air perilously close to Ryan's face. Ryan lurched away as Chiara spun, brandishing the blade.

The two men fell to the ground, rolling. Ryan couldn't get a clear shot off, but he seized hold of Chiara's wrist and pounded it against the floorboards until the knife dropped from his hand and spun over the edge of the rail.

It was all fists now. Chiara's strength and skill surprised Ryan. He wouldn't have thought Chiara knew how to dirty his hands in a brawl. Ryan got several well-placed punches to Chiara's midsection, but Chiara swung back, hitting him hard in the nose. Ryan reeled from the blow and when he opened his eyes, Chiara was shoving off the ground and running at a breakneck speed along the breezeway.

Ryan rocketed to his feet. He squared up, taking aim. This was it.

Then Chiara tripped, seemingly on thin air. He landed face-first on the ground. Avery leaped into view. She spun the wire from the gadget watch around Chiara's neck, choking him.

Ryan ran to support her. He dropped his knee on top of Chiara, securing him first before processing what Avery had done. The end of the wire had been wound around the rail and she held the watch end in her hand. She'd booby-trapped Chiara with a trip wire. Genius.

All the anger and fear Ryan had experienced over the years because of this man came rushing back at him. Without ceremony, he shoved his gun into Chiara's neck. Blinding hate turned the edges of Ryan's vision white and made his gun hand tremble. "I've been waiting a lot of years for this moment, you bastard."

He looked up to see Mickle, Dreyer and Montgomery headed his way. If Ryan killed Chiara now, it would be with law enforcement agents as witnesses to his crime. He had no doubt that Dreyer, who obeyed the letter of the law to a fault, would prosecute him for disobeying a direct order and killing an unarmed man. He'd go to prison, separated permanently from his family and Avery.

He looked over at Avery. All he had to do was choose her. Choose life. Choose not to pull the trigger.

A groan from Chiara caught his attention, but it was too late. In a flash, with one great burst of energy, Chiara knocked Ryan off him and stood, a gun in his hand.

A shot rang out.

Chiara staggered back, then fell to the ground, a bullet wound to his forehead.

Ryan's gaze went to Mickle, who still stood in firing position. He nodded at Ryan as he holstered his gun with a hand that quaked with adrenaline. Ryan knew it was his way of apologizing for the accusations.

Mickle swallowed, studying Chiara's limp and bloody form. "Yeah," he said with a sniff. "That I can live with."

Ryan slid an arm around Avery's waist and held her close. "Are you okay?"

"More than okay. You?"

"For the first time in a lot of years I can honestly say yes, I'm great. Never better."

Dreyer crouched to check Chiara for a pulse then stood, wiping his hand on his pant leg, and regarded Ryan. "It's going to take some paperwork to make it official, but the charges against you will be dropped."

"Thank you, sir." He turned to Mickle. "You really

were worried about Avery this morning. That's why you came to her apartment."

"I was. You're a nice kid and a great secretary, and I didn't want you mixing up with a bad element, like I thought Reitano was," Mickle said with a nod to Avery before returning his focus to Ryan. "I had a hunch there was someone in the office who was dirty, and who else better to suspect than the new guy? So I started looking into your credentials and things weren't adding up. No offense."

"No, you were right," Ryan said. "Thank you for looking out for Avery."

"Like I said, she's a good kid. I still have a lot of questions. Like what did happen in Honduras? No one ever figured it out. With the baby and all?"

Ryan held Mickle's gaze and tried to tell him without words that, partner to partner, he needed him to stand down about that one point. "Nothing," he said. "Absolutely nothing."

Dreyer, Montgomery and Mickle nodded, accepting his answer.

"Amen to that," Avery said.

Ryan and Avery stood on the cruise ship's heliport, waiting for the second ICE helicopter to come get them. The first had transported Dreyer and Chiara's body along with the rest of the agents, including a handcuffed Tau. There hadn't been enough seats available, so Ryan and Avery had happily volunteered to wait.

They watched the passing landscape of San Diego Bay. Though the sun had set, slivers of orange and purple streaked the sky.

Avery snuggled into his arms. "What do we do now?"

"I think we should give some serious thought to each of our bucket lists."

"A week of hedonism with a beautiful woman."

He nuzzled the side of her face. "Babe, I've got some plans for you in the hedonism department that are going to take longer than a week.

"I hope that's not the only item on your list I can help you cross off."

She was right. He did have one more item, and he never, in his wildest dreams, would've guessed that the perfect woman for him to spend the rest of his life with had been sitting across the office from him, waiting for him to get a clue. "I hope you're not trying to propose to me. Because that's my job and I'm only going to get to do that once in my life. It's no fair if you beat me to it."

She squeezed her arms around him. "Take your time. I'm not going anywhere."

"Except with me." He looked into the eyes of the woman who'd stood by his side even when it wasn't in her best interest, even when she was scared and had no good reason to trust him. The strongest, most vivacious person he'd ever met. "I have a new item to put at the top of my list, something that's going to take me the rest of my life to do."

"Sounds intriguing. What is it?"

"Give you everything you've ever wanted and then some."

Her face lit up the night. "Are you going to help me become a secret agent?"

"Absolutely. In fact, I have a business proposition for you. I'm thinking of starting my own company. A secret-agent-for-hire operation. I could use a partner, someone to handle the desk work and join me in the field when she wants."

"I like the sound of that. Where are you thinking of opening this business?"

"I have some ideas. Have you ever been to the south of France?" She shook her head. "They've got this casino in Monte Carlo. Maybe you've heard of it."

She laughed, the sweetest sound he'd ever heard. "I think I might have...."

"That'd be a great place to start scouting locations for our business, don't you agree?"

"Partner, you've got yourself a deal."

Ryan cradled her head in his hands, thrilling to the idea that they were at the beginning of a very big adventure. There was no one he'd rather embark on it with. He brought his smiling lips to hers and with the sea and the heavens as their witnesses, they sealed the deal with a kiss.

* * * * *

Check out John and Alicia's story in the next
ICE: BLACK OPS DEFENDERS *book.*

And don't miss these other stories from
Melissa Cutler:

SEDUCTION UNDER FIRE
TEMPTED INTO DANGER

All available now from
Harlequin Romantic Suspense!

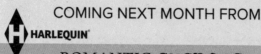

REQUEST YOUR FREE BOOKS!
2 FREE NOVELS PLUS 2 FREE GIFTS!

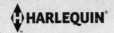

ROMANTIC suspense

Sparked by danger, fueled by passion

YES! Please send me 2 FREE Harlequin® Romantic Suspense novels and my 2 FREE gifts (gifts are worth about $10). After receiving them, if I don't wish to receive any more books, I can return the shipping statement marked "cancel." If I don't cancel, I will receive 4 brand-new novels every month and be billed just $4.74 per book in the U.S. or $5.24 per book in Canada. That's a savings of at least 14% off the cover price! It's quite a bargain! Shipping and handling is just 50¢ per book in the U.S. and 75¢ per book in Canada.* I understand that accepting the 2 free books and gifts places me under no obligation to buy anything. I can always return a shipment and cancel at any time. Even if I never buy another book, the two free books and gifts are mine to keep forever.

240/340 HDN F45N

Name _____ (PLEASE PRINT)

Address _____ Apt. #

City _____ State/Prov. _____ Zip/Postal Code

Signature (if under 18, a parent or guardian must sign)

Mail to the **Harlequin®** Reader Service:
IN U.S.A.: P.O. Box 1867, Buffalo, NY 14240-1867
IN CANADA: P.O. Box 609, Fort Erie, Ontario L2A 5X3

Want to try two free books from another line?
Call 1-800-873-8635 or visit www.ReaderService.com.

* Terms and prices subject to change without notice. Prices do not include applicable taxes. Sales tax applicable in N.Y. Canadian residents will be charged applicable taxes. Offer not valid in Quebec. This offer is limited to one order per household. Not valid for current subscribers to Harlequin Romantic Suspense books. All orders subject to credit approval. Credit or debit balances in a customer's account(s) may be offset by any other outstanding balance owed by or to the customer. Please allow 4 to 6 weeks for delivery. Offer available while quantities last.

Your Privacy—The Harlequin® Reader Service is committed to protecting your privacy. Our Privacy Policy is available online at www.ReaderService.com or upon request from the Harlequin Reader Service.

We make a portion of our mailing list available to reputable third parties that offer products we believe may interest you. If you prefer that we not exchange your name with third parties, or if you wish to clarify or modify your communication preferences, please visit us at www.ReaderService.com/consumerschoice or write to us at Harlequin Reader Service Preference Service, P.O. Box 9062, Buffalo, NY 14269. Include your complete name and address.

HRS13R

Maddie barked and moved closer to Remy, protecting her.
Remy stepped outside and the dog did, too. Remy was tempted
to run.

Wade, appearing at the open door, aiming his gun, stopped
her. Maybe Maddie would go next door, or her barking would
alert Lincoln.

She reentered the house and closed the door before Maddie
could follow. Her heart wrenched with the sound of frantic
barking.

"In the living room," Wade ordered her.

Maddie's barking stopped. She was running next door.

"You've been sneaking around again," Wade said, stepping
close to her with dangerous eyes. "What were you doing at my
store three days ago?"

"What are you talking about?" She played ignorant, the
same as she'd done the last time he'd come accusing her of
spying on him and his friends. That time she'd followed him
when he'd met some men she hadn't recognized. Nothing had

been exchanged, but she suspected he'd gone to discuss one of his illegal gun deals, deals that he expected her to execute for him.

He leaned close, the gun at his side as though he didn't think he needed it to keep her under control. "You know damn well what I'm talking about. You're supposed to be working with me, not against me."

"If working with you means breaking the law, I'll pass."

With a smirk, Wade straightened. "You've already done that. And if you don't start doing what I tell you, the cops are going to find out."

Because he'd tell them. Soon, he wouldn't be able to threaten her like this. Soon, she'd be able to call the cops herself and have *him* arrested. But for now she had to be patient.

Remy spotted Lincoln at the back door. She'd left it unlocked for him, hoping he'd retrace Maddie's path. Sure enough, he had. Wade's back was to him. Careful not to shift her eyes, she used her peripheral vision to watch Lincoln enter.

"I'm only going to ask you once more," Wade said.

Before he could repeat the question, Lincoln put the barrel of his pistol against the back of Wade's neck. "Put the gun down."

**Don't miss
ARMED AND FAMOUS
by Jennifer Morey,
available February 2014 from
Harlequin® Romantic Suspense**

HARLEQUIN®

ROMANTIC suspense

Love leaves no one behind

Black Hawk pilot Sarah Benson was born brave.
A survivor from the start, Sarah is known for her
risky flights to save lives, and
SEAL Ethan Quinn is just one more mission.
But when *she* needs rescuing, it's Ethan who
infiltrates enemy territory—and her heart.

Look for the next title from *New York Times*
bestselling author Lindsay McKenna's
Shadow Warriors series

RISK TAKER

Available next month,
wherever books and ebooks are sold.

Heart-racing romance, high-stakes suspense!

www.Harlequin.com

HRS27857